Delhi Vice

DELHI VICE

BALRAJ JUTTLA

BLOOMSBURY
NEW DELHI • LONDON • OXFORD • NEW YORK • SYDNEY

BLOOMSBURY INDIA
Bloomsbury Publishing India Pvt. Ltd
Second Floor, LSC Building No. 4, DDA Complex, Pocket C – 6 & 7,
Vasant Kunj, New Delhi, 110070

BLOOMSBURY, BLOOMSBURY INDIA and the Diana logo
are trademarks of Bloomsbury Publishing Plc

First published in India 2024
This edition published 2024

ISBN: PB: 978-93-56408-71-5; eBook: 978-93-56407-75-6
2 4 6 8 10 9 7 5 3 1

Typeset in Minion by Manipal Technologies Limited
Printed and bound in India by Replika Press Pvt. Ltd.

MIX
Paper | Supporting responsible forestry
FSC™ C016779
FSC www.fsc.org

To my father,
Jasvinder Singh Juttla (1963–2017)

1

HE SURFACED FROM BENEATH the sacred black waters of the Yamuna. Turning away from the glare of the early morning sun, Lalit surveyed the surroundings with an air of calm he achieved only while bathing in the holy water. The relative quiet and stillness of the river belied the reality that he was, in fact, at the centre of one of the most populous cities in the world. Despite the pleasure he derived from it his wife would protest against his morning ritual, arguing that the waters were unsafe and that the filth and rot of Delhi poured into the river in a never-ending deluge. She would insist he bathe again at the communal tap at the end of their street before she would let him enter their one-room home. All this had little effect on Lalit. He didn't believe that the sacred water could be harmful to him or anyone else, and it was with a wilful disregard that he submerged himself into the river, fully aware it was teeming with industrial chemicals, pesticides and sewage, not to mention the human remains from the Nigambodh Ghat crematorium just a few kilometres to the north.

Nevertheless, in a move to placate his wife, who had vowed to cease cooking his favourite dishes if he didn't give up his daily ablution, Lalit now restricted himself to one visit to the river a week. In a way, he welcomed the change because now he really appreciated the time he spent in the water.

Upriver he could make out the Old Iron Bridge sitting just above the water. Ahead of him, Lalit could see the fields of small holdings from which farmers eked out a living. They stretched as far back as the busy Ring Road that you could follow south into the pulsating heart of the city. The sun still sat low in the sky, and it was pleasantly warm. Once he had recited his morning prayers, he breathed deeply through his nose and spat out sticky, thick phlegm into the river. He blew his nose and then waded back to the riverbank.

As he was negotiating his way through the piles of plastic and rotting vegetables that floated on the surface of the water, something caught his eye. It was much larger than the rest of the trash that lay along the gentle slope of the riverbank. As he waded closer, he could make out amongst the colourful bottles, bags and garlands the unmistakable form of a human body, slumped awkwardly on the bank.

Lalit's initial curiosity now gave way to a deep sense of dread. But unable to look away, he approached the figure. He could now see that it was a woman. Her sky-blue jeans were submerged beneath the knees, and her once-white blouse was ripped and covered in filth. Her hair was caked in mud and hid most of her face, but her eyes were still visible. As he stared back at her empty, wide-eyed glare, Lalit held a hand to his mouth and muttered a prayer. He stood transfixed for a few moments before he could eventually tear himself away, but not before noticing that the woman's neck was a dark mottled purple and that there was bruising on her wrists and forearms that stood out starkly on her pale, pallid skin.

After the magnitude of what he had just discovered dawned on him, Lalit reeled around to find help. Further downriver were two men digging through the rubbish in search of plastic that could be sold and repurposed. 'She's dead, she's dead!' Lalit called out in panic.

The two men looked up and gave Lalit a bemused look as if they had not heard correctly. 'What?' one of them asked.

'There's a girl. She's dead! Come quickly!' Lalit yelled back, pointing in the direction of the body.

The two men now understood. They rushed out of the water and began to run along the riverbank to Lalit, calling out to others in the small field that ran the length of the bank. By the time Lalit had dragged the woman's half-submerged body out of the river and laid her on a clear patch of land, a crowd had formed in the small clearing. As the men jostled with one another to get a good view, Lalit pulled down the woman's blouse that had ridden up to expose her midriff. His eyes began to fill with tears as he reflected on the cruelty of her fate. Not even in death was this woman at peace.

'What happened?' asked one of the men who had come to take in the macabre sight.

Lalit raised his head to look at the crowd. His eyes were red with grief. 'I think the poor girl was murdered,' he said.

2

JASKIRAN SOHAL SAT DOWN on the chair beside Sabeena, the *Delhi Daily*'s deputy editor. 'I want the story on the girl found in the Yamuna,' she insisted. If Sabeena was taken aback by her colleague's sudden appearance, she didn't show it.

'Remind me again?' she replied without taking her eyes off her screen.

'Anjali Mangal,' said Jaskiran. 'They just identified her this morning. She was found in the Yamuna four days ago. The coroner's report confirmed that she was murdered.'

'That makes it a crime story,' Sabeena responded.

'And?' Jaskiran replied bluntly, knowing too well the point her friend was making.

'Jaskiran darling, I love you, but my hands are tied,' said Sabeena, sighing in exasperation. 'You know Vinod has become very particular about the news you cover. Besides, I've given you plenty to work on.'

'Yes, the really hard-hitting stories,' Jaskiran said sarcastically. She looked around the empty newsroom. Despite the fact she came in early every morning in a bid to be assigned the best stories, a strategy that had yet to pay off, it always unnerved her how eerily quiet the place was from its usual hive of activity. The phones sat idle on the cluttered rows of desks; there was no frenetic tapping at keyboards and no continuous hum from the bank of printers along the far wall beneath the grubby windows that looked out onto the shopping promenade below.

Other than Jaskiran and Sabeena, only the assignment editor was stationed at his desk, carefully updating the news diary with the latest leads for the stories that would make tomorrow's paper. Jaskiran looked over at the glass-panelled office of the newspaper's managing editor, Vinod Mukherjee, and felt her frustration grow. 'When is he going to drop this?' she asked. 'I'm a grown woman. He would never have done the same to a male reporter.'

'We've been over this a thousand times,' replied Sabeena. 'I'm on your side in this, but Vinod thinks he's protecting you.'

'Well, I don't need his protection,' protested Jaskiran. 'It was just a bunch of gundas trying to get me to drop a story. I've faced worse harassment on the metro.'

They were talking about the incident three months earlier that had seen Jaskiran removed from her position as the paper's junior crime reporter. Having been sent to cover a violent robbery in Paharganj, Jaskiran had diligently gone about her duties, talking to the victims and any witnesses she could find. But, unbeknownst to her or anyone at the paper, the robbery had been perpetrated by a local gang who wanted to keep their activities out of the media spotlight.

It wasn't long before word reached them that a young, lone female reporter was sniffing around the scene. They had grabbed her as she attempted to flag down a passing autorickshaw to head back to the office. Threatening her with violence if she screamed for help, they took her bag, her notebook and, for good measure, her phone. They warned her that if she wrote anything about them, she would be abducted one day when she left the office.

The ordeal had left her shaken and, to her regret, she had broken down in tears when recalling the events to Vinod and Sabeena when she had returned to the office with no story. Sabeena had been supportive, Vinod overzealous. He had refused to cover the story, bowing to the demands of the thugs. Then, the very next day, he had called Jaskiran into his office and informed her that she would be moved back to general assignment.

'Then who's going to take the Anjali Mangal story?' Jaskiran asked Sabeena.

'Who do you think?'

'Sajid?' Jaskiran sighed. 'How many crimes can one man cover? Can you see him putting in the work, talking to family and friends, building a profile and then following up on all the leads? He'll most likely take the police press releases and whatever is already on the TV bulletins. That is if he even bothers to cover it at all.'

Sabeena was unmoved by Jaskiran's protests and continued working at her computer. When it was clear that Jaskiran had finished complaining, she glanced sideways at her forlorn friend and took pity on her. 'Don't get yourself so worked up about one story,' said Sabeena. 'Why do you even want it?'

'Because you know how things will go now,' Jaskiran replied. 'It won't be long before the TV news will run stories about her personal life and commentators will question her morals. Eventually, it will be framed as her own fault that she got murdered regardless of whether the police find the culprits.' Jaskiran took a breath and sighed before adding, 'I feel that it shouldn't be relegated to a few column inches in the middle of the paper just because we couldn't be bothered to follow up on it. A girl died, Sabeena. She deserves attention, and she deserves justice.'

Sabeena now turned to face her dejected colleague. It was Jaskiran's passion that made her stand out from the other young reporters at the paper and it was what had first caught Sabeena's eye. 'Look,' began Sabeena, 'because I don't want you sulking all day, I'll assign you another first merit story. And while you do that, I'll try and speak to Vinod again, but I can't make any promises.'

'Thank you,' said Jaskiran, her eyes flashing with gratitude. 'So, what's the story?'

'A political rally. Ashok Chopra, the new star of the Indian Workers' Party. He's holding a rally this afternoon at the Ramlila Ground. Usually, Mohan would be all over it, but he has to go cover today's session at the Lok Sabha. Does that make you feel better?'

Jaskiran's initial enthusiasm at getting a better story had been dampened. Covering a rally in the searing afternoon heat wasn't exactly what she had envisioned. She didn't believe the latest crop of politicians, with their stage-managed image and bombastic rhetoric, were any different from the politicians who had come before them. 'Great, a sweaty afternoon surrounded by supporters-for-hire, sycophants and anybody with nothing better to do than watch a politician promise to fix all their problems and cure all diseases with cow dung,' Jaskiran ranted as she made her way back to her desk at the far end of the room.

'Well, my dear,' Sabeena called out teasingly, looking over the top of her Prada glasses. 'Do you want the story or not? I can give it to someone else if it's beneath you.'

'No, I'll take it,' Jaskiran responded with as much enthusiasm as she could muster. It might not be the crime beat, but at least it was a story.

3

RAJESH GUPTA GLANCED AT his watch. 'Shit,' he sighed. At this rate, he would be late for work again. Shielding his eyes from the early morning sun to get a better view of the sidewalk ahead, there was still no sign of Karishma. At first, his girlfriend's insistence on seeing him every morning had been endearing, but four months on, Rajesh wasn't so sure. Racing perilously through Delhi's morning traffic on his scooter to pick her up for their shared daily commute to work quickly became a chore he could do without.

His employers were also beginning to notice. Rajesh often showed up later than many of his colleagues at the *Delhi Daily*. He had been reprimanded by his manager, Sabeena, who reminded him that junior reporters didn't have the luxury of choosing their own hours. He looked at his watch again. It had once belonged to his father. The black leather strap was frayed from years of daily use and the glass face was ever so slightly cracked – but the stubborn hands still turned, telling Rajesh that it was almost half past eight. Soon, no matter how much he dodged and weaved through traffic, there was no way he could get Karishma to her design studio in Chanakyapuri and still make it to the newsroom before 9 a.m.

At last Karishma turned the corner, walking rather slowly Rajesh noted with some irritation.

'Sorry,' she said before planting a kiss on his lips. 'Big lecture from Mom.'

'About?'

'The usual. Don't go out late at night. Be careful around boys. It's all because of this girl whose body they found in the river. It has Mom in a state of panic.'

'Maybe she'd feel better if she met me?' Rajesh asked casually.

Karishma sat behind Rajesh on the scooter. 'We've had this conversation before, Rajesh,' she said. 'It's not the right time to tell my parents yet. They'll freak out.'

'Why? Your sister has a boyfriend already. Your parents don't seem to mind him coming by the house.'

'That's different,' Karishma responded.

'How?'

There was no answer from Karishma, but Rajesh felt he knew the difference. Karishma's sister was dating a high-flying real estate executive from a prosperous family. Karishma's parents couldn't wait for her sister to marry him and receive the social cachet from such a fortuitous match.

He glanced over his shoulder and saw that Karishma was pouting and looked disinterested in the conversation. It was a topic she didn't want to discuss any further, and as was her way, she simply wouldn't engage with him until the subject was changed. He sighed in resignation before firing up the scooter's engine.

The journey continued in silence until they came to a stop at a red light. Rajesh, noting Karishma still looking sullen, pulled out a copy of that day's newspaper from his bag. Unfolding it carefully, he looked down with immense pride at the front page before handing it to Karishma.

'Look who made the front page,' Rajesh said, attempting to sound nonchalant.

It had the desired effect. 'You're kidding? *You*?' Karishma's morose mood evaporated and was replaced with excitement. 'This is amazing!' she cried, squeezing him tightly.

'And it's an exclusive,' Rajesh declared, beaming.

The story in question had come to Rajesh's attention the previous day while he had been out to lunch. Standing in line for his omelette from the street vendor, Rajesh had heard of an accident and a police cordon a few streets away. With a stack of press releases on his desk to filter through, the thought of covering something live, even if it was as mundane as a car accident, was too much to ignore. Arriving at the scene, he found the usual crowd of spectators but there seemed to be no other journalists. The police, who initially believed it to be nothing more than a road accident, had woefully misjudged the situation and had been unable to cordon off the crash site effectively. Rajesh quickly realised there was more to the story than he had originally thought.

The crash had involved a hotel bus on its way back from Indira Gandhi International Airport, having picked up a group of foreign holidaymakers. Barely in the country an hour, the tourists were still acclimatising to the sights, smells and sounds of Delhi when their bus collided with a lorry that had failed to stop at a junction. It resulted in a few nasty bumps and a number of broken bones, but luckily no one was killed. Unfortunately for the tourists, that was not the end of the ordeal.

The crash had also caused their luggage, which had been strapped to the roof of the bus, to spill out across the busy junction. What began as an opportunistic thief making off with a small duffle bag filled with an American tourist's pyjamas soon descended into a massive free-for-all as scores of passers-by and motorists grabbed what they could from the horde of plastic, leather and polyester treasure chests. With the crowd's thirst whetted, and when there was nothing left of the luggage, some of the more brazen thieves turned to the crash victims themselves. Wallets were lifted, purses went missing and one scoundrel even took the driver's wristwatch while he lay unconscious at the wheel.

Due to the lack of a proper police cordon, Rajesh had been able to move freely around the site and talk to the victims. Their moods ranged from abject despair to vitriolic rage. He had also spoken to many eyewitnesses who claimed to have seen the whole thing. He then returned to the office and wrote up the report that would become his first big break. 'A New Low?' read the headline above a picture of a German tourist with a blood-soaked rag tied to his head, wrestling with two thieves over an iPad. The story had received international attention. Overnight, news stations across the world featured the story and in the morning it had become the talk of the city.

The lights changed to green, and they set off once again, this time with Karishma ceaselessly talking in his ear about how jealous her friends would be and how she couldn't wait to see the look on their faces. At first, Rajesh was delighted with Karishma's reaction, but as she went on talking, he began to feel uneasy about the idea that until now she and her friends had constantly compared him to those with more successful careers. *How little Karishma has had to feel proud of me until now*, thought Rajesh.

When they arrived at her studio, he tried to put such thoughts aside. Karishma hopped off the scooter. 'Don't forget,' she said. 'I told my friends we'd meet them all at Bar Rouge this weekend. Dress smart.' She wagged her finger at him while smiling.

'Again? We went out with them last weekend, and I don't get paid for another two weeks.'

'Relax,' Karishma said in a placating tone. 'I'm sure it won't be a crazy one. It's a really chill place.' She leaned forward and kissed him before strolling to the studio entrance. Rajesh didn't hang around to watch her walk away. He was late enough already.

4

Across town, at the offices of Delhi Financial Corporation, Rahul Yadav stood staring out of the floor-to-ceiling windows of his large corner office. A haze hung like a veil over the city, impenetrable to any breeze and offering no relief to its inhabitants, their lungs filled with its toxic air. *It corrodes them all from within*, he thought to himself as he looked down on the city and contemplated how hard he had fought to elevate himself from the masses. His continued progress was now in serious jeopardy.

The sound of the news bulletin from the TV on the wall made him turn around. He limped across the carpeted floor with the aid of a cane to his oversized desk. Picking up the remote, he turned the volume up further. The news station's graphics flashed across the screen to a crescendo of dramatic music before cutting away to a bespectacled middle-aged reporter standing amidst a protest somewhere in the city. 'Police hunt killer of Anjali Mangal,' the reporter announced. It was the news that Rahul had both expected and dreaded.

His body tensed as he watched the reporter on the screen speak to a group of protesting women. The leader of the group was Ayesha Begum, an outspoken member of the Delhi Legislative Assembly. 'What we see today is the result of the Delhi government failing to address the ongoing pandemic of violence toward women,' said Ayesha. As always, she looked elegant dressed in a salwar kameez and spoke with perfect poise directly to the camera. 'There are cases like this occurring every day all over India, and each time the police, local politicians and national agencies do too little or nothing at all. But in my city, in Delhi, we will not stand for this anymore. We will not have more cases like Anjali's, who was brutally murdered and her body thrown into the Yamuna to be forgotten.'

Ayesha went on to claim that the police declared it a suicide even before the autopsy had been conducted. 'It was only because of pressure from myself, the Democratic Union Party and the Women's Voice group here today that the autopsy was carried out correctly, and it was found that the injuries on her body confirm conclusively that Anjali was murdered,' said the politician. 'The police are finally treating this as a crime but have lost vital time. It's a disgrace. The so-called Indian Workers' Party has the majority in the Delhi assembly but has done nothing for a decade. People are waking up to this fact, and I am confident that the Democratic Union Party will take back the assembly later this year and clean up this city.'

Ayesha continued to passionately rally against her political foes, but Rahul had heard enough. He closed his eyes for a few moments of quiet contemplation before accepting that the situation was now escalating quickly. It had become a media circus and a political talking point, and things were likely to get worse. He could feel his ulcers burn within him. He knew he had been careless, but what else could he have done? She would have ruined everything.

Just then, there was a light tapping at the door. Rahul's secretary, Prashant, walked in carrying his morning cup of tea. The sight of his secretary's smiling, dim-witted face offended Rahul, and he felt the urge to throw the TV remote at the oaf. But instead, he restrained himself and watched Prashant approach the desk. It was only because his anger needed to be channelled somewhere that Rahul felt such an urge. He knew that this was how the public and media felt now about Anjali's murder. He sighed as he dismissed Prashant with a wave of his hand; the secretary left without a word. If the public wanted someone to blame, Rahul would give them what they wanted.

5

AT THE *DELHI DAILY* the newsroom had come alive with the arrival of the many editors, feature writers, ad executives, designers, photographers and reporters who made up the staff. Among them all, Jaskiran was trying to fathom enough enthusiasm to begin writing yet another 'soft-news' story. This one was about a local school's fundraising drive to buy new textbooks to replace the outdated and inaccurate editions they had possessed for over thirty years. She sighed heavily, almost in defeat, when a burst of laughter behind her provided a welcome distraction.

Turning around, she found the source of the laughter to be a small gathering of her colleagues. In the centre of the huddle was Rajesh, one of the junior reporters. He was triumphantly holding up the day's paper that displayed his name in bold type on the main story's byline. His tall, athletic frame made him stand out in the crowd. He was animatedly regaling them with the story of how he landed the scoop.

A swell of anger rose within Jaskiran before simmering into resentment. *Of course Rajesh makes the cover before me*, Jaskiran thought to herself. Rajesh was barely out of university, but his easy charm and confidence made him popular in the office. Jaskiran sighed again. *Why do I have to work twice as hard for what others are simply handed?* she thought bitterly.

Jaskiran was not the only one unhappy with her current situation. On the other side of the newsroom, the paper's editor, Vinod Mukherjee, sat in his glass-panelled office cursing the faltering air-conditioning as he wiped his sweaty brow. Across from him sat Sabeena and the paper's chief crime reporter, Sajid Chaudhury.

'Come, come, just tell me what it is you want?' said Vinod, visibly annoyed.

'What I want?' Sajid said as if the answer was obvious. 'I need a crime reporter, Vinod. I can't be everywhere at once.'

'You spend most of your time in back-alley bars. Why don't you try and do some actual work? You could cover twice as many stories.'

'You mean publish twice as much spin!' Sajid hit back, offended. 'That's not real journalism. I need to go where the real stories are, not just repeat the PR that the police put out. You used to know this.'

Sajid's words cut deep. Vinod silently looked out across the newsroom. He had once been an accomplished reporter and had worked his way up to the position of managing editor. That was over ten years ago. The move to a permanent desk job and away from the excitement of the field had softened him in more ways than one. During his time as a reporter, he had thrived on chasing down leads and shining a light in the darkest recesses of society. It had filled him with a drive and excitement he had failed to find anywhere else.

Now, accountable to a board of trustees and with his staff's welfare and job security weighing heavy on his shoulders, the constraints of responsibility had slowly worn him down. With the passing years his appetite for inquisitive journalism and exclusives dampened, replaced by a need to meet quarterly targets, to not upset advertisers and to give the readers the sensationalist headlines they craved, which were often steeped in insinuation and hearsay and short on genuine investigation.

Almost as a direct result of his dwindling appetite for news, his waistline expanded as he searched to fill the void within him, consuming everything from the daily tiffin prepared by his wife to the gulab jamun, aloo tikki and other fried snacks from Delhi's street stalls and, coveted most of all, the mutton shami kebabs from his favourite vendor in Chawri Bazaar. Wiping the last of the sweat from his brow, he looked at Sabeena. Young, ambitious and with a steely determination, Sabeena was a natural leader, and Vinod often found himself turning to her for advice. It was clear to anyone at the paper that she was destined for his chair, and in his most candid of moments, usually after downing a few pegs of whisky, he would admit to himself that she would probably run the paper better than he ever could.

'What do you think?' Vinod asked her. 'Can you get someone from another paper?'

'I can get in touch with my people at the *Times*,' Sabeena replied. 'There might be a junior crime reporter we could poach with an offer of a more senior position. I've also heard that Dilpesh Kulkarni at the *Star* no longer gets along with his editor, so he might be interested … but …'

Sabeena trailed off, prompting Vinod to ask, 'What?'

'That could take weeks and won't help us now,' she continued. 'Also, it would lower morale among our reporters if we brought in someone new for a role that they are capable of filling.'

Vinod was sceptical. The crime rotation was a demanding role. Crime reporters were disliked not only by many in the police but also by the city's criminals. He knew from experience that it required mental strength, self-belief and confidence to do the job. These were not qualities Vinod saw in his young staff, many of whom were fresh out of university.

Sabeena exhaled loudly, 'Jaskiran should be reinstated.'

'Absolutely not,' Vinod cut her off before she could continue. 'We have had this discussion. You were in this very office when she broke down in tears. How can I put her back into harm's way?'

'That was an unfortunate incident, but it hasn't frightened her away. She wants to be working crime, and she deserves it. She's hard-working and a great reporter. She's been with us nearly five years, and I'm telling you, if we don't show here some appreciation, another paper will gladly take her.'

'Sabeena, please,' said Vinod, holding out a hand to request her to stop. 'I know all this, but I can't. Her family came to see me, and I promised them that I wouldn't put her in jeopardy again.'

'Her family doesn't get to control her life; she is an adult,' Sabeena said, dismayed at what she was hearing.

'That may be true, but she is also my employee – and I decide the stories she works on,' said Vinod, in a manner that underlined the finality of his decision. Sabeena sat back with her arms folded, clearly angered.

Sajid, having no interest in office politics, decided to break the silence. 'What about him?' He gestured across the newsroom to Rajesh, who was busy reenacting the events of yesterday's accident to a group of amused colleagues, oblivious to the attention he was now receiving. 'He made today's front page, right?'

'He got lucky,' Sabeena retorted, still annoyed.

'Lucky is good,' said Sajid. 'We need lucky reporters.'

'Rajesh is junior to Jaskiran,' said Sabeena. 'He's only been here a couple of years. Do you really want to elevate him to the crime rotation when he is so inexperienced? It will ruffle feathers among our other reporters who have been here longer,' Sabeena rebutted, looking at Vinod.

'Yes, but he is very confident and likeable,' said Vinod quickly. He was eager to shift the focus of the discussion away from Jaskiran. 'He will be able to win people's trust. What do you think, Sajid?'

'I'm willing to give him a chance,' said Sajid with a shrug.

'Right, that's settled then,' Vinod said with a smile. He was happy that the matter was resolved so quickly. 'Rajesh will help you with the crime beat.'

'And Jaskiran?' Sabeena asked, arching an eyebrow.

'We will find something for her, I promise, but not crime, please,' said Vinod. 'It's been said, and I have to agree, that the crime beat is not a place for a young woman.'

Sabeena bristled at the remark and stood to leave. 'I disagree,' she said. 'There's no position in this company a woman couldn't fill.' She gave him a piercing look before heading back to her desk. Sajid stifled a grin as he followed her, leaving Vinod awestruck and reaching for the jalebis.

6

SO IT CAME TO be that later that day, Rajesh found himself outside the three-storey apartment block in the North West Delhi neighbourhood of Rohini where Anjali Mangal had lived with her parents. The relatively clean street was bordered by identical-looking apartment buildings built in the late 1990s to house Delhi's burgeoning middle classes. The upper-level apartments had balconies adorned with tables, chairs and small plants; many were also being used for drying clothes. The entire complex was closed off from the road by a six-foot perimeter wall, with an iron gate at the entrance.

Rajesh noted that the area was remarkably quiet. The usual din of Delhi's traffic was reduced to a distant hum punctuated by the sounds of unseen children at play and the occasional shrill cry of a black ibis perched on a nearby telephone line. Rajesh thought of the crowds and noise of his own neighbourhood, where he shared a cramped apartment with his mother and two younger siblings. He couldn't help but wonder if he would ever be able to provide a better life for his family. It was a thought that momentarily spoiled his good mood.

Despite the sober nature of his assignment, Rajesh had been elated to have an opportunity to leave the confines of the office and he tried to think back to when the sun had felt so good on his face.

While he was basking in its warmth, relishing the slight breeze in the air as he walked to the gated entrance, he thought back to what Sabeena had told him before he had left the newsroom. She had given him instructions to build a profile of Anjali and her family. He recalled the look of disbelief on Jaskiran's face when she heard about his new assignment. Rajesh had savoured the moment because he had always felt Jaskiran looked down her nose at him as if he didn't belong at the paper. Perhaps it was because he hadn't graduated from a prestigious university like she had or, as Rajesh often suspected, for more personal reasons. It was well known she came from a wealthy family, while Rajesh had little more than what he made from the paper. It was conceivable that Jaskiran simply thought herself a social class higher than Rajesh. He had met women like her many times at clubs and bars all over Delhi. They wouldn't even look at him, thinking themselves too precious, while others treated him like a strange circus attraction to be experienced and forgotten. Jaskiran was clearly the former. *But is the difference in our social class really that obvious?* he wondered, assessing his outfit self-consciously. He now noticed a hole in his corduroy trousers below the belt buckle and saw that his shoes were scuffed and in danger of losing a sole.

His silent examination was disturbed when he noticed he was being watched. Across the road from Anjali's apartment, sitting on a charpoy stationed on her apartment's first-floor balcony, an elderly woman watched him with keen interest. Staring up at her, Rajesh smiled and waved awkwardly; the woman smiled and waved back in kind.

Putting thoughts of Jaskiran aside and vowing to buy some new shoes, Rajesh turned his attention back to the assignment at hand. Passing through the gates of the apartment complex, Rajesh strode toward the watchman's hut, the peeling white paint in bleak contrast to the well-kept apartments it guarded. Peering inside, Rajesh found a small transistor radio perched on a shelf, a wooden stool and little else. Rajesh looked around but didn't see the guard anywhere. The children he had heard from the road were playing together, while by the narrow flowerbed that ran parallel to the perimeter wall, a young girl was cradling a doll in one arm while pulling the petals off flowers with her free hand. Closest to Rajesh, a young boy sat atop the low walls that formed the veranda of the ground-floor apartments. The boy looked glum as he stared at his shoes and kicked his heels against the concrete wall beneath him.

'Hey,' Rajesh called out, and the young boy looked up at him with bloodshot eyes. 'I am looking for the Mangal family. Do you know where they live?'

The boy seemed to study him for an eternity. 'Number 16,' he finally said, pointing to the far side of the complex. He turned away to watch the other children play.

Rajesh made his way across the complex to the ground-floor veranda of number 16, which could be accessed directly from the communal gardens that circled the buildings. He could see that the windows were closed and the curtains were drawn. He knocked on the door and wasn't surprised when no one answered. Rajesh tried the neighbours too, but even though he could hear the shuffle of feet inside – and even saw a twitch of the curtains – no one opened their door. He knew he couldn't give up that easily and returned once again to Anjali's apartment. He knocked again and waited.

'They've gone,' said a voice behind him. Rajesh turned to see the boy once again. He was chubby, and his cheeks were red from the day's heat. His hair was parted in the middle and fell down to his eyebrows.

'Gone where?' Rajesh asked, stepping away from the door.

The boy merely shrugged. Rajesh thought he was perhaps wary of speaking to a stranger.

'My name's Rajesh. I'm a reporter with the *Delhi Daily*. I wanted to speak to the family about what happened to Anjali.'

The boy seemed to be deliberating on whether Rajesh was telling the truth.

'You don't look like a reporter,' said the boy.

'What do reporters look like?'

The boy pondered the question. 'Older,' he said. 'You don't even have a moustache.'

Rajesh laughed, and the boy smiled.

'What's your name, kid?'

'Roshan.'

'It's nice to meet you, Roshan. I saw you by the front gates. You seemed upset. Is it because of Anjali?'

The boy looked at the ground, saying nothing. 'Did you know Anjali well?' Rajesh continued.

'She was my friend,' the boy muttered.

'She was nice to you?' Rajesh asked gently.

Roshan shrugged again. 'I guess so. She would let me practise my card tricks with her. I want to be a magician.' Roshan now looked up to read Rajesh's reaction. Satisfied that Rajesh didn't find the revelation comical, he continued, 'She would also let me play games on her phone and take pictures with the filters that make you look like an alien.' Roshan seemed to brighten at the recollection. 'She wasn't like the others,' he continued. 'The older ones here don't like to play with us kids. They think they are too cool to be seen with us.'

'But not Anjali,' Rajesh said reassuringly, and Roshan nodded.

'She would read to me. The Ramayana and other books, too. She would play all the characters.' He smiled again. 'I would sit on the steps here, and she would sit there.' Roshan now pointed to the chairs beneath the window.

'You were close to Anjali,' Rajesh said as more a statement of fact than a question. 'Did you see her the night she …' Rajesh trailed off, unable to say the word.

'Died?' Roshan ventured.

'Yes, the night she died,' replied Rajesh, slightly embarrassed by his own reticence.

Roshan nodded. 'I saw them leave,' he said.

'What do you mean, "them"? She left with someone?'

'Yes, I walked her to the main gate. I had lost my old set of cards at school, so she promised to go to Toy Kingdom and buy me a new set so that I could keep practising my tricks. Then she said that she would be back late and told me to go home. I said that I wanted to go with her, but she said no. I saw her get into a car.' Tears began to fill the boy's eyes.

Rajesh placed a hand on Roshan's shoulder. 'Who did she leave with?' he asked.

The boy was crying now, the tears flowing down his soft cheeks. He shook his head. 'I don't know.'

'Do you think it was a taxi, maybe?' Rajesh prodded.

'No, I mean, it didn't look like one. It was a nice car. Silver and it only had two doors. Like a sports car.'

Before Rajesh could respond, a voice called out behind him: 'Who are you?'

He turned to see a security guard approaching him, flanked by the children who had been playing by the front gate. They parroted the guard's question. Embarrassed by his tears, Roshan quickly turned his face and wiped his eyes with the back of his hand.

'I'm a reporter with the *Delhi Daily*, and I'm here to talk to the Mangal family,' Rajesh responded confidently.

The answer didn't seem to impress the guard, and he now grabbed the much taller Rajesh and attempted to pull him back towards the gate. 'And who am I?' he asked Rajesh, his head cocked to one side insolently as he looked up at the younger man. 'I'm the one who keeps uninvited guests out.'

'But I *am* invited!' Rajesh lied, trying to squirm out of the guard's grip. 'The family have invited me to speak to them.' He was surprised at the strength the feeble-looking guard possessed as he was dragged along to the gate. *He must be in his fifties*, thought Rajesh. His dark skin pulled taut against his lean face, a well-trimmed moustache and a spotless uniform, complete with a red-trimmed cap, alluded to a man who took his appearance seriously.

Rajesh felt the guard's grip slacken as he turned and laughed in the direction of the children. 'This boy thinks I'm stupid,' he exclaimed loudly before turning back to Rajesh. 'The family hasn't invited you; they are not even here. They left to avoid all you reporters. You've been coming non-stop ever since,' the guard hesitated, turning slightly to acknowledge the presence of the children. 'Anyway, I'm under orders to not let any reporters in.'

'Who gave the order?' Rajesh asked.

'The residents' welfare association. They don't want to be bothered.'

Rajesh was momentarily stumped. 'What about you?' he asked. 'You must have known Anjali?'

The guard, letting go of Rajesh now that he was back at the gate, waved his hands in front of him as if to dispel the question from the air like a bad smell. 'I'm just the guard. Don't get me involved. I am saying nothing.'

'But you must have been here on Friday night? Did you see her leave?' Rajesh was beginning to sound desperate, his earlier confidence quickly evaporating.

'I'm saying nothing,' the guard said again abruptly.

Some of the younger children immediately mimicked the guard's haughty tone. 'I'm saying nothing. I'm. Saying. Nothing,' came the chorus. This was not how Rajesh envisaged things to go, and he was momentarily stumped.

The guard, now slightly alarmed by how well his hostile behaviour had dismayed the reporter, gestured for the children to go back to playing and away from the entrance.

Many of them obliged, but Roshan only retreated a few steps before turning back again. By now, the guard was once again facing Rajesh but spoke with a far more conciliatory tone. 'Look, my young friend, what is your name?' the guard asked.

'Rajesh.'

'Rajesh, I am Iqbal.' The guard placed a hand over his heart in greeting. 'I know you are just trying to do your job. But I need to do mine too. If I help you, I am risking much but gaining nothing.' Iqbal stressed the last two words. After a brief pause, Rajesh understood what Iqbal meant. He sighed and pulled out his wallet. *You should have expected this*, he chided himself. *Nothing in this city comes for free, especially information.*

'I do not have much,' Rajesh said, showing the guard the few sorry-looking notes in his wallet. As his family's primary provider, he couldn't afford any extra expenses. But he told himself that if it helped make the story a success, it would be money well spent. He reluctantly handed over two hundred-rupee notes.

Iqbal placed the notes in his shirt pocket with no more than a cursory glance. 'That will not get you much,' he said. 'Another reporter gave me five times as much just to take a picture of her apartment.'

'But that's all I can afford,' Rajesh replied plainly.

Iqbal frowned. 'What do you want to know?' he asked. His tone was brusque now that he understood that there was nothing more he could get for his cooperation.

'Did you see Anjali leave the night she died?'

'No, she must have left when I was on my rounds. There are three blocks in the compound, and I have to secure them all. We've had beggars jumping the wall at night to sleep behind the bins.'

'Did you know her well?'

'Yes, very well,' said Iqbal. 'Anjali was a lovely girl, very pretty.' Iqbal paused as if recalling her in a way that made

Rajesh uncomfortable. 'She would always say hello and talk if she had some time.'

'What did she talk to you about?'

Iqbal hesitated, not expecting to be asked to divulge so much about his personal relationship with Anjali.

'We ... would talk about my family,' he said hesitatingly. 'I would ask her about her studies.'

'That's a lie!'

They turned to see Roshan emerge from behind the hut. 'Anjali never spoke to you about anything!' Roshan cried out. 'She didn't even like you. She said you always stared at her whenever she walked past.' He looked close to tears.

Iqbal's face clouded over in barely contained rage, and he swiftly approached the boy. 'Go,' he said, pointing back towards the other children. 'Before you get into trouble for talking too much.'

The threat seemed to have the desired effect, and Roshan's defiance melted away into a look of real fear. He shifted back in the direction of the other children, who had now stopped to watch what was unfolding.

'Is he telling the truth?' Rajesh asked, irritated. 'Have you been lying to me?'

Iqbal turned and looked at Rajesh as if he were a nuisance.

'No, he's just making trouble,' he said. 'Now you have to go. I shouldn't be seen talking to you.'

'But the money I gave you?' Rajesh protested as Iqbal began closing the gate once Rajesh was on the street.

'What more do you want from me? I am just the guard. How much can I know?'

'But you haven't told me anything!'

'Look, consider it a down payment for when the family returns. I'll let you in to ask them all the questions you want.'

'And when will that be?'

'How should I know?' Iqbal shrugged.

'You're just the guard,' Rajesh chimed in sarcastically, which brought a gap-riddled grin to Iqbal's lips.

Rajesh was about to protest further when his phone buzzed. Opening the message, he saw it was from Sabeena and marked in all caps – 'URGENT: Get to Gandhi Nagar police station. They've got Anjali's killer. Press conference is in one hour. Hurry!'

7

ASHOK CHOPRA'S RALLY WAS being held late in the afternoon to avoid the heat of the day. Jaskiran, deflated on learning that Rajesh was being assigned to the crime beat, was eager to get started on a real news story of her own. She had arrived a little early yet was surprised to find the maidan was almost at capacity already. The sand-covered expanse of the Ramlila Maidan, which usually played host to the cricket games of local children, was now awash with thousands of people, all enthusiastically hemmed in, ready to get a glimpse of the latest young upstart in the convoluted world of Indian politics.

Jaskiran knew a little about Ashok Chopra before she had been assigned to cover the rally. He was an outspoken member of the Delhi Legislative Assembly for the Indian Workers' Party, the largest party in the Delhi government, and had often been heralded as its new rising star. Although Jaskiran had always assumed that his rise had been built on the foundations of a political dynasty or paved with the influence of rich benefactors, she was happy to concede it didn't seem to be the case. A relatively private man, there wasn't a lot of information freely available on his early life, only that Ashok had grown up the only child of middle-class parents; his father had been a local politician in Uttar Pradesh. Both parents tragically died in a road accident when Ashok was just a young boy. Ashok had survived relatively unscathed. Picking up the pieces of his life, he quietly put himself through school and worked in the private sector ever since. That was up until five years ago when out of obscurity, he ran and was elected to the Delhi Legislative Assembly.

Jaskiran presented her press badge to one of the rally organisers, who handed her a lanyard to wear and directed her to the press section close to the front of the rally. From there she could get an unimpeded view of the pavilion from where Ashok would make his address. The pavilion had originally been built in the early 1960s to host Queen Elizabeth II. Since its construction, some of the biggest names in politics had delivered speeches from that stage. Jaskiran realised that by holding the rally on this ground, Ashok Chopra was staking his claim as a major player in Indian politics.

With her interest piqued, Jaskiran spent the next half an hour speaking to some of the eager spectators close to the press section. It was a diverse crowd, with many families and their young children in attendance, hordes of university students chanting slogans in chorus, and old men claiming with certainty he was the modern reincarnation of Nehru. His supporters seemed to possess a genuine affection for Ashok and were optimistic about the changes he would bring to their lives and to the city and, by extension, the country, which they felt had lost its way. So by the time Ashok finally ascended the steps to the pavilion amid rapturous applause, Jaskiran sensed a feeling of joy washing over the crowd like a breaking tide. Despite herself, Jaskiran felt a tinge of excitement too.

Ashok savoured the applause and jubilation. He half-heartedly tried to bring the crowd under control by thanking them for their support, which only set them off again even louder than before. His delight grew every time the crowd roared back after each gesture of appreciation. From where Jaskiran stood, she could see him perfectly.

He didn't look like any Indian politician she had ever seen before.

He was perhaps in his mid-thirties, but his clean-shaven face made him look almost adolescent. He opted for Western clothes rather than the traditional Indian attire that many in his party favoured. His tight-fitting outfit made it clear that he kept in shape. He spoke perfect English but switched freely to Hindi as he continued to try and bring the crowd under control.

Once the crowd had settled suitably enough for him to be heard over the speakers, Ashok began his career-defining rally in earnest. He presented himself as a poor orphan who was proof that India was a land of opportunity. As the applause erupted yet again, Jaskiran looked around at the jubilation on the faces of the spectators. He had them eating out of the palm of his hand.

For almost two hours Ashok spoke on topics that – judging from the response he received – were close to the hearts of his listeners. He spoke passionately about the need to stamp out corruption across all government departments and the police. He lamented the recurrence of preventable diseases in the suburbs and the lack of basic sanitation services to serve them. He spoke of the importance of adequate education programmes for those in poorer areas of the city and new legislation to support Delhi businesses. He also talked about the need for improved safety for women in the city to curb the horrendous crimes that had maligned the image of Delhi and Indian society and proposed harsher punishments for crimes perpetrated on women and a zero-tolerance crackdown on eve-teasing.

Finally, he spoke about turning Delhi into a truly 21st-century city with the development bill he had spearheaded that was set to be passed into law in the coming days. He claimed it would herald a new beginning for Delhi, a city that had been rebuilt time and time again for a millennium, and now would be rebuilt anew for the first time in the modern age.

As the rally began drawing to a close, Jaskiran decided that she wanted to speak to Ashok in person. A number of other reporters had the same idea, and she took her place amongst them by the stone steps that led up to the pavilion. A line of security guards and party volunteers kept anyone from getting too close, and she resigned herself to try and grab his attention as best she could when he passed by to his waiting car.

She looked up at the side-long view she now had of Ashok as he said his farewell to a crowd that had lost none of its fervour.

'And here, between the edifices of the old city and the new,' he said, gesturing first towards the white-marbled Faiz Ilah Masjid, visible beyond the far corner of the maiden and then to the shiny, towering Civic Centre building behind him, 'we, the people of Delhi, will soon emerge from the old ways of corruption, poverty and ignorance to a truly new Delhi, a Delhi of change, of optimism and of prosperity.' He waved both hands in the air in farewell as the crowd burst into deafening applause. The cheering and hollering were so loud that Jaskiran feared Ashok wouldn't even hear her when he passed by to his waiting car. She found herself being pushed by the surging crowd behind her into the tightening cordon of guards.

A few of the more experienced journalists were already firing questions at the politician.

'Ashok sir, what do you say to your detractors who claim you are simply a social climber? They say if you attained any real power, you would do everything to keep the status quo intact?'

'I'd tell them to be ready to eat their words,' Ashok deftly responded to the now dejected-looking reporter who had hoped for a more emotional response to his provocative question.

As Ashok approached closer still, the crowd surged forward once more. Thrust again towards the line of security guards, Jaskiran lost her footing and tumbled to the ground. As she tried to get to her feet, another wave of eager spectators pushed forward. 'Can't you see that I'm down here?' she shouted. 'Stop acting like a bunch of bandars!' But it was to no avail. The crowd continued to step all around her, kicking sand in her face as they did.

As she began to crawl towards the safety of the security cordon, Jaskiran felt a hand grab her below the arm and ease her up. Assuming it was a policeman who had helped her, she turned to thank them but instead found herself facing a concerned-looking Ashok Chopra.

'Are you okay?' he asked.

'Yes, thank you,' she replied, surprised. He took her by the elbow and ushered her through the security line, which closed ranks again as they passed. When they reached his waiting car, Ashok gestured for her to get in. Jaskiran did so without question, seating herself on the comfortable cream-coloured leather before brushing the dirt off her jeans.

Ashok told his driver to get going before turning back to Jaskiran. 'I'm sorry about that,' he said. 'People get so charged with emotion at these events that they have a hard time controlling themselves.'

'It's fine,' Jaskiran replied. 'I'm okay.' She was a little amused at her own serendipity. Moments ago, she would have been happy with a throwaway comment from the politician, and now here she was talking to the man privately in his luxurious, chauffeur-driven car.

'What's your name?'

'Jaskiran Sohal. I'm a reporter with the *Delhi Daily*.'

Ashok now noticed the lanyard around her neck and the press badge it contained. 'A journalist!' he exclaimed, sounding delighted. 'Tell me, what did you think of my speech?'

'I thought you were very good,' Jaskiran replied kindly. 'A natural.'

Ashok looked pleased. 'Thank you very much. I hope you don't mind me saying, but I noticed you as I was coming down the steps. You're a lot younger than the other reporters, easier on the eye too. Many of the usual reporters I see at my events were likely around when the first Parliament was formed.'

His comment about her appearance didn't go unnoticed, and Jaskiran couldn't help but fire back. 'Did you mean any of what you said out there?' she asked, in an attempt to give him a reason not to like her.

It almost worked; he looked at her with an expression of discomfort. After a few moments, he began to smile again.

'I like your style, Jaskiran, straight to the point,' he said. 'And I'm sorry, I meant no offence. It was an inappropriate thing to say. I want you to know I feel very strongly about the welfare and security of the people of this city, especially our women. I want to change the city for the better, and yes, I meant every word of what I said.' His demeanour was now all business.

Jaskiran believed him but didn't feel like letting him off the hook just yet. 'But the things you say about anti-corruption, having zero tolerance on crime and being pro-small business,' she continued, 'it's hard to believe at least some of it isn't pandering. There's a perception that most politicians are so caught up in getting what they can for themselves that they often forget whom they should be serving.'

'I didn't get into politics to increase my own net worth,' Ashok said sharply. The topic seemed to have touched a nerve. 'I already run a successful business. If I wanted to get richer, I could do that without politics. It's a particular kind of grifter, one with no perceivable real-world skills or talent that turns to politics to enrich themselves. It is their lack of integrity and morals – characteristics that would make them pariahs in the real world – that allows them to flourish in politics. That is not who I am.'

Jaskiran looked at him and almost nodded in agreement. 'But you do want to be more than an MLA, right?' she asked with a wry smile.

Ashok smirked to confirm that Jaskiran was not wrong.

'A cabinet position, perhaps?'

'For a start,' he answered.

Jaskiran was about to ask another question when they arrived at the maidan gates.

'I hope you don't mind, but I'll have to let you out here,' said Ashok. 'I've got to go visit my team and debrief. You understand; work out our next moves.' Ashok let out a mock sigh at the mechanics of political life. 'But I'll tell you what, perhaps we can schedule an interview and you can ask me all the questions you want. Something tells me that if I can convince you that I'm for real, you'll have no trouble convincing your readers. How does that sound?'

Jaskiran knew that there was more to the offer than just the interview, but it was too good to turn down. 'That sounds great,' she said. 'Here's my card. Maybe we could arrange something this week while the rally is still news.'

The car came to a stop just outside the gate and Jaskiran climbed out.

'Until we meet again, Ms Sohal,' said Ashok, smiling at her through the open window.

'Yes, Mr Chopra, until we meet again.'

8

WHEN RAJESH ARRIVED AT the police station for the press briefing, he was ushered into a small room in the interior of the building. The windows looked out onto a bare courtyard and the air smelled old and musty. One of the fluorescent lights above flickered continuously. There were a dozen chairs lined up in three rows in front of a small table. The first row was already occupied by reporters busy writing notes or tapping on their phones. Rajesh took a seat in the second row. As the minutes passed, more reporters entered, each looking more flustered than the last.

When the room was three-quarters full, three police officers entered and seated themselves at the table. A chorus of protests erupted in both Hindi and English from the reporters.

'What's the meaning of this?' shouted one reporter. 'Why have you called the briefing so suddenly?'

'I've had to cancel other meetings to be here,' complained another. 'A little more warning would have been helpful.'

The station house officer held up his hands to placate the reporters. 'I understand that it was very short notice,' he said, 'but please, Deputy Commissioner Arvind Sagar has some important updates on the case of the murder of Anjali Mangal. Now quieten down.' After a few more grumbles, the reporters eventually fell silent.

The deputy commissioner, a large, overweight man with a thick moustache, now addressed the room. 'I am very pleased to announce that last night we arrested the victim's boyfriend, Vivek Trivedi, at his parents' address in Tilak Nagar,' said Sagar, sweat glistening across his brow and bloated cheeks. 'We had it on good authority that he was out with Anjali the night she went missing. In searching his home, we located a necklace and bracelet, which the deceased's parents have confirmed belonged to Anjali. Faced with these facts and some excellent interrogation work, we retrieved a signed confession from Mr Trivedi just a few hours ago.'

The deputy commissioner paused and stroked one edge of his moustache as the assembled reporters typed furiously on their phones and laptops, eager to get the breaking news to their editors as soon as possible. He then continued, 'I would like to give special mention to Inspector Shah here,' he indicated to the man on his right who had not yet spoken, 'who was the primary IO and arresting officer. His swift action and interrogation skills enabled us to bring this case to a speedy resolution.'

There were a few sniggers from some of the more senior reporters who understood that 'interrogation skills' often meant that the officer was particularly good at inflicting pain on suspects during interrogations while leaving no visible evidence. However, Inspector Shah did not smile. *He almost looks nervous*, thought Rajesh.

'Now,' said Sagar, 'I only have time for a few questions, so please ask what you want to know.'

All the seated reporters except for Rajesh raised their hands almost at once. The station house officer pointed at a reporter in the front row.

'Can you tell us what the motive for the murder was?' asked the reporter.

'Yes,' said the deputy commissioner. 'It seems that the deceased had met with Mr Trivedi to end their relationship. She had told him that her family would not approve and that she could not see any future for them. Mr Trivedi had not been able to accept her decision. They had fought, and in the struggle, Mr Trivedi had killed Ms Mangal.'

The station house officer now pointed to another reporter.

'Sir, could you give us more details on the events leading up to the murder and the murder itself? You have not told us the particulars surrounding the murder, where did it take place, how was it committed?' asked a spectacled man sitting beside Rajesh.

Sagar seemed annoyed at the question but quickly flashed a jovial smile. 'Well, I didn't want to just give that up,' he said. 'You need to work for the first-class information.' There was a smattering of polite laughter before he continued, 'Anjali left her house at approximately 9 p.m. without her parents' knowledge. She met with Vivek, and the two of them took a bus to Golden Jubilee Park.'

As the deputy commissioner continued, Rajesh stopped taking notes, aware the account didn't match Roshan's version of events. He instinctively raised his hand so abruptly that it caused Sagar to falter in his reply. Distracted, he gestured in Rajesh's direction. 'Yes, you in the second row,' he said irritably. 'Couldn't you have waited for me to finish?'

Rajesh hesitated, as he realised that he had become the focus of attention in the room. Sagar was glaring at him. 'I'm sorry,' he finally managed. 'But I have it on eyewitness account that Anjali left in a car the night she was killed. I'm just wondering why Vivek would want to keep that detail from you and say they took a bus?'

The attention now turned away from Rajesh and back to the front of the room. It was the deputy commissioner's turn to hesitate. Rajesh noticed the slightest change in Inspector Shah's expression too. For the first time since the briefing began, he relaxed his jaw muscles, and his lips were now parted. Rajesh presumed that it was as close to an expression of surprise that the man would show. The inspector shifted his gaze from the reporters to Sagar, who was now leaning against the table as if to get a better look at Rajesh.

'Who are you?' asked the deputy commissioner.

'Rajesh Gupta from the *Delhi Daily*.'

'Well, Rajesh Gupta from the *Delhi Daily*, you are living in a fantasy world,' retorted Sagar. 'Now, who is this supposed witness?'

'Well, they are a neighbour living in the same complex as the Mangal family,' Rajesh replied hesitantly.

Sagar now looked triumphant. 'That's not possible,' he said. 'My officers have interviewed every one of her neighbours. No one saw her leave. She even slipped past the night watchman. So, if you really have a source, give us their name.'

Rajesh felt the silent anticipation in the room. This was new territory for him, and he wasn't sure how much information he was supposed to divulge even to a senior-ranking police officer. Besides, something about the way the deputy commissioner had asked the question made him uneasy.

'I can't reveal the identity of my source,' Rajesh replied slowly, as if unsure it was the correct answer.

The deputy commissioner turned away muttering inaudible expletives before turning back towards Rajesh. 'Well, then you're either lying or have been lied to,' said Sagar disdainfully. 'The truth is that Mr Trivedi's family does not own a car. They have a scooter, but it was with his father that night. Now, is this good enough for you?'

Rajesh felt that the senior police officer was trying to embarrass him into submission. He conceded, nodding to indicate that he had no further questions.

'Good, I'm happy we can accommodate you and your illustrious paper,' said Sagar, before turning to the station house officer and saying loudly enough for the room to hear, 'Didn't the *Delhi Daily* have any other reporters they could have sent other than this boy?' The insult sparked a chorus of scornful laughter from the rest of the room. Rajesh was stung by the officer's barb and the condescending behaviour of the other journalists. They were supposed to be his peers, but perhaps they didn't think so.

The feeling took him back to his childhood and the countless times his classmates had singled him out for ridicule. There he was again in his school's playground, taunted by the other children because he was the only one who played sports barefoot while the rest wore new boots, his smart school shoes too expensive to risk damaging. He would hobble home, his feet often bleeding, and plead with his parents not to send him back. He couldn't take the humiliation any longer, but they would simply tell him that he couldn't give up because they were spending all the money they had to send him to a good school in the hope that he would build a better life for them all. So there was nothing he could do but grin and bear it, a thousand indignations throughout the years that fostered within Rajesh, like many who come from little and find themselves elevated to a world beyond their upbringing and social circle, feeling like an imposter, and worst of all, they feel the rest of the world believes they are too.

'It was in a secluded area of the park,' the deputy commissioner continued, snapping Rajesh away from his recollections and into the present, his humiliation turning to anger, 'where Anjali told Vivek that she wanted to end their relationship. This sent Vivek into a rage, and he attacked Anjali, strangling her to death. He then left her body in the river and fled. Her body was discovered the next morning further downstream by locals bathing in the river.'

Rajesh watched as the other reporters steadily took down notes and typed on their laptops. *They hadn't been there with Roshan*, he thought. That boy had been clear about what he had seen, and there was no reason to doubt him. Rajesh wanted to press the issue further and raised his hand once more.

'I see our young reporter needs some more help,' said Sagar wearily. 'What can we clear up for you now?'

'Have you had the suspect's story confirmed? I mean, have you located the bus driver to back up what he said?'

A shadow seemed to pass over the deputy commissioner, his mood darkening.

'Still with this?' he bellowed. 'Do you think we are amateurs? Of course we have the bus driver's account, and he can confirm everything. Anjali and Vivek boarded the 167 bus around 9.20 p.m. and were dropped off close to the entrance of Golden Jubilee Park.'

'What is the bus driver's name?' Rajesh asked defiantly.

'Listen!' the senior officer erupted. 'We have a confession from the number one and only suspect in this case. Her possessions were found at his home. He has fully cooperated with us, and there is no reason whatsoever to doubt his version of events. Your cheap tricks to create a scandal and sell more copies of your third-rate paper will not work here.'

Sagar suddenly stood up, pushing his chair back with such force that it almost toppled over. Inspector Shah and the station house officer also rose. 'That's all the questions we have time for. You can thank our young friend,' the deputy commissioner said curtly and left, followed by the other officers.

When they had left the room, the assembled reporters stood to leave. 'Thanks kid, what a waste of a trip. Next time let those with a little more experience show you how it's done,' one of the older reporters moaned to Rajesh as he slung a bag over his shoulder.

'They were valid questions,' Rajesh said defensively as the reporter walked out, grumbling to himself.

Standing outside the police station, questions raced through Rajesh's mind. If Vivek Trivedi did pick Anjali up in a car, why would they take a bus after that? And if Vivek didn't own a car, whose car were they in? It didn't make sense. Someone wasn't telling the truth. Rajesh pondered his next move as the daily kinetic life of his fellow Delhiites continued around him. At times like these, when deep in thought, he often imagined he was encased in a bubble that shielded him from the rest of the world. The energy of the city deflected around him, stretching and pulling in a million different directions while he stood untouched by its meandering chaos, trying to make sense of it all.

A car horn beeped beside him, and his thoughts were shattered; the bubble burst.

9

'HOW IS IT THAT you manage to completely mess up a straightforward assignment?' Vinod asked Rajesh as he sat behind his desk, looking up at the young reporter as if he had carried in a bad smell. Rajesh's expression was one of complete confusion. He had only moments ago returned from the press briefing. Heading straight to Vinod's office to tell him what had unfolded, he had barely opened his mouth before Vinod began berating him.

'What do you mean, sir?' Rajesh responded, letting the office door close behind him.

'I mean, why am I getting an angry phone call stating that you were a disruptive influence during the briefing and that you would not cease questioning the validity of the deputy commissioner's account? Which, by the way, came directly from the man who has confessed to the crime!'

A feeling of embarrassment washed over Rajesh. He had hoped to give Vinod his version of events, which would have omitted the part where his questions had led to the deputy commissioner storming out. 'Actually, I was about to come and talk to you about that,' he said. 'I may have picked up on something the police have overlooked.'

'Like what exactly?' asked Vinod. 'What was so important that you felt the need to embarrass the deputy commissioner in front of a room full of journalists? Journalists you shouldn't be giving away your exclusive information to, I should add.' Vinod was now wagging his finger as if speaking to a particularly naughty puppy.

'Well,' Rajesh said, 'the deputy commissioner claims that Anjali's boyfriend, Vivek, did not own a car. Yet when I spoke to Anjali's neighbours, one said that they saw Anjali getting into a vehicle the night she was murdered. I tried to speak out about this but was told I had my facts wrong. I want to go back and see if the eyewitness will go on the record. Perhaps they know someone else who can corroborate the story.'

Vinod took a moment to consider Rajesh's remark. 'Okay, so who is your witness?' he asked.

Rajesh hesitated. 'Anjali's neighbour,' he replied eventually. 'They were with Anjali when she left that night.'

'Then why have they not come forward and spoken to the police?'

'I don't think the police would have considered listening to them even if they had come forward.'

When Vinod looked confused, it was clear to Rajesh that he would have to come clean. 'He's a young boy who lives next door to Anjali. He followed her to the gate.' Rajesh closed his eyes as he said it, aware of what would come next.

As if on cue, Vinod began laughing. 'You almost had me there.' He slapped his palm against the desk to convey his amusement. 'But you don't honestly expect me to risk the ire of the police on the account of a child. He will probably change his story in a week anyway, leaving us looking like gullible fools.'

'But sir, the fact they rang you so soon after the press conference must tell you they are worried I am onto something?'

'No, it just tells me they are angry, and angry police officers are to be feared more than angry crooks. If they see you hanging around the family's apartment, they may take the lathi to you – or worse, they will come here and give it to me! No, this won't do. The police have incriminating evidence, and they have a confession. While they have these two elements, we are not to challenge the narrative. Do I make myself clear?'

'But sir!' Rajesh tried one last time. 'This could be a real scoop for the paper. Surely you can see that?'

Vinod sighed with disappointment. 'You know, Rajesh, I was hoping you'd be a little more pragmatic. Anyway, the deputy commissioner will expect me to discipline you in some way to show that I have taken him seriously. As much as I hate to do it, perhaps it's for your own good – you're off the story. Send your notes to Sabeena and she'll reassign you. I don't want you near this until the police have forgotten about you.'

Rajesh was shocked. 'You can't do that!' he cried. 'It's my story!'

Vinod was affronted at Rajesh's tone. 'Maybe you've forgotten who you're speaking to,' he said. 'But let me remind you that just because we speak frankly to each other does not make this a conversation among equals. I decide who covers what. Now get out before I have you thrown off crime rotation altogether!'

Chastened, Rajesh held his tongue and sulked out into the newsroom.

Jaskiran, who had been keenly watching the animated scenes coming from Vinod's office with some delight, now appeared the face of ignorance as Rajesh sat down heavily at his desk beside her.

'Why so glum?' she asked, trying to sound casual.

Rajesh sat brooding, unsure if he wanted to divulge both the events of the press briefing and his humiliation to someone who had never taken an interest in him before. Eventually, the need to unburden himself was too much to resist. 'He's scared,' Rajesh muttered.

'What?'

‘I said he’s scared,’ Rajesh responded again, sounding angry. ‘I found something about the Anjali murder, Jaskiran.’ He wheeled his chair over to Jaskiran’s desk. ‘But Vinod won’t let me investigate. He’s been scared away by the police.’

‘What do you mean? What did you find out?’

Rajesh told Jaskiran everything that had happened that day, starting from his visit to Anjali’s apartment and his talk with Roshan to the press conference and the police’s call to Vinod.

‘What are you going to do?’ Jaskiran asked.

Rajesh shrugged. ‘What can I do? Vinod has already thrown me off the story. Tells me it’s for my own good.’

Jaskiran had heard something similar herself once before and understood how powerless Rajesh must have felt. *But if there is even a small chance that Rajesh is right and the police had not investigated Anjali’s murder correctly, it deserves to be followed up*, she thought.

‘I can help,’ she said resolutely.

‘How?’ Rajesh asked, confused.

‘You said that you’ve been taken off the story because the police don’t want you poking around. But they don’t know anything about me. I can start investigating.’

Rajesh felt slightly uneasy about the proposition. ‘And if you help me,’ he asked, ‘what do you want in return?’

‘If I find something new, I want to share the byline if there’s a story worth printing,’ replied Jaskiran. Her eyes were wide with excitement. She hadn’t felt a thrill like this since before she’d been kicked off the crime rotation. She realised now how much she missed it.

Rajesh contemplated the offer for a moment. Despite their differences, he had to admit that Jaskiran was a great reporter, and he could certainly use her help.

‘Okay,’ he said with a nod. ‘Will you talk to Roshan and see if he’ll go on the record?’

Jaskiran shook her head. 'No, Vinod is right about that,' she said. 'A child is an unreliable witness without corroborating evidence. I'll visit Delhi University tomorrow and speak to Anjali's friends and teachers. If you're right, it's where we'll find out who she socialised with – who Vivek might have come with that night.'

Rajesh couldn't help but be impressed as she went straight to work, calling the university to arrange meetings with Anjali's professors. As he watched her speak on the phone, Rajesh felt a tightness in his chest. A vague apprehension seized him and dented his confidence. He began to question whether he had made the right choice. If he got caught chasing this story, it would surely cost him his job. Perhaps the best thing to do was follow Vinod's advice and fall in line. He could wait for another story because there would always be another story.

No, he rebuked himself. He was a journalist, and this was all part of the job. Besides, if he could prove there was another accomplice, it was the type of exclusive that would have every paper in the city fighting over him. Rajesh decided to put any doubt to the back of his mind, but the tightness in his chest persisted. He realised now the feeling growing inside him was fear.

10

Ayesha Begum descended the steps of the women's shelter in Jahangirpuri followed by a group of smiling nurses. At the bottom of the steps, she offered them a namaste before shaking hands with the head caretaker and posing for a picture taken by the only photographer to have shown up. Ayesha smiled warmly one last time and waved as she entered through the open door of her SUV.

As soon as the driver closed the door behind her, and she was confident she couldn't be seen through the tinted glass, Ayesha's smile melted away.

'What a fucking disaster,' she said. 'There was hardly any press there. What happened?'

Ayesha's assistant, Shriva, looked up. 'I tried, ma'am,' she said, 'but journalists don't seem interested in these types of initiatives for women.'

'Unless one of them ends up murdered by her alcoholic husband, right?' Ayesha spoke to no one in particular. 'Fucking vultures.'

She looked out of the window and saw a few of the children from the shelter playing on the side of the road. A small girl no more than five or six years old was stroking a stray dog behind the ears. She wore filthy clothes most likely scavenged from bins and her bare feet and legs were stained with dirt. Ayesha thought of the child's young mother inside, who had been advised by the staff at the shelter to give up her four children to a home. They had told her it would be the best thing for her children and give the mother a fresh start.

The woman had cried in front of Ayesha, pleading for guidance. She couldn't imagine a life without her children but despaired at the one she could provide for them. What should she do? the woman had implored.

What should she do? Ayesha thought. Looking at the girl again, she couldn't help but see a never-ending cycle play out right before her. *They don't stand a chance*, she thought. Ayesha felt a pang of sorrow penetrate her armour of anger. So unexpected was it that it took her away from her thoughts.

Ayesha steeled her heart against the feeling to ensure that her faltering resolve didn't show on her face. 'Why these women have so many children is beyond me. They need to take responsibility for their own bodies before they can do anything else. Look at this little girl here, playing with the flea-infested dog.' She gestured toward the driver, who watched her from the rear-view mirror, 'Go, get me away from here.'

Shriva felt troubled. For a brief moment Ayesha had seemed almost frightened by something she had seen out the window. But the thought was almost absurd to Shriva. The Ayesha Begum she knew was scared of nothing. She adjusted her glasses and looked at Ayesha, who seemed tired and deflated. Shriva thought she could do with some cheering up. She opened her notebook and flicked through the pages until she found the highlighted notes she had made earlier that day.

'I have some good news,' Shriva announced with a smile. 'We have found the Mangal family. They are staying at the Grand Bharat in Gurugram.'

Ayesha looked to her assistant, her instant elation quickly giving way to bewilderment. 'A hotel?'

'Yes,' replied Shriva. 'I asked my contact, and they said it was because the family wanted to escape the media attention.'

'Are they stupid? Here I am fighting to get justice for their daughter, and they are having a holiday? The press wants to speak to them. They want the grieving mother on film, the angry father vowing vengeance. Amateurs! They are starving the story of the oxygen it needs.' She stopped herself and pondered her own point.

'Now that the police have charged the boyfriend,' said Shriva, 'the family will return in a few days and release a statement. But nothing more.'

Ayesha was barely listening, her own line of thought fuelling a growing suspicion.

'The Grand Bharat … that's a luxury hotel, correct?'

Shriva scanned her notes before answering, 'Yes ma'am, a five-star resort.'

'Your contact has access to the hotel's records?'

'Yes ma'am, they are close to one of the front desk staff.'

'Find out who is paying for their stay.'

Shriva nodded and took out her phone immediately.

Something didn't add up, but perhaps the family was right; now that the suspect had confessed, how much more could Ayesha squeeze from this story? Maybe she needed to find a new cause to champion. Standing up for women's rights and highlighting the violence they endured in the city resonated with specific demographics, but the media and large swathes of the public, both rich and poor alike, saw it as an endemic issue. It was of this place and would forever remain, its root causes too numerous and deeply entrenched that no government policy could ever hope to displace it. To them, standing up to violence against women was like opposing the monsoon rains.

In a city like Delhi, she knew she wouldn't have to wait long for the next story to hit the headlines, and she would be ready to face the cameras again and play her part. But it wouldn't be enough to win the upcoming election for the Democratic Union Party. She knew that she had to do more than just appeal to the public for votes; she had to smother her rivals and starve them of votes. Her political career depended on it.

To her rivals, the media and even some in her own party, Ayesha was an aberration: a young, educated Muslim woman making great strides in Indian politics. They had unkindly compared her to a marauding shark, a creature that had to keep moving to survive. Being motionless meant death. Ayesha always disagreed with the analogy and found it disingenuous. It proposed her survival was firmly in her own hands. That she could simply continue surviving in the cut-throat world of politics of her own volition. When in truth, life, just like politics, doesn't exist in a vacuum. For her to succeed meant countless others must perish. And that's how she saw things; failure was the gaping jaws of a relentless beast pursuing her. She couldn't outrun it forever, that was folly, but she didn't have to. All she needed to do was to keep feeding the ravenous beast those who stood in her way. That was the trick.

11

JASKIRAN'S SHIN CRASHED AGAINST the pad with a satisfying impact. She planted her foot back on the mat and repeated the sequence. Right and left jabs followed by another low kick.

'Good, Jaskiran!' her instructor Akash yelled from the front of the studio. 'Again!'

Jaskiran's partner, Geeta, steadied herself against the pads for the impending attack. Jaskiran took a deep breath before continuing with the combinations, burning them into her muscle memory until they felt fluid.

'Now switch,' shouted the instructor. The dozen women in the studio traded places with their partners. Jaskiran now held the pads as Geeta prepared to attack.

She watched Geeta repeat the same sequence, feeling the force behind each strike. She looked at her partner closely and saw that her body was taut and sweat glistened on her forearms and shoulders. There was a look of focus and steely determination across her face.

Jaskiran had never asked Geeta what made her want to take self-defence classes, but something told her it was more than just a precaution. Something traumatic had happened to her; looking around the studio, Jaskiran was sure the same was true for many of the other women in the room. For some, these classes were the only option they had left.

It was no secret that most cases of violence toward women in Delhi were perpetrated by their own husbands or boyfriends. Many women felt too ashamed to take such accusations to the police or were prevented from doing so by their families. Even if they broke free of an abusive partner, they would live in fear of reprisal attacks. Jaskiran thought of Anjali Mangal again and how her death was almost a textbook example of the crisis plaguing the city.

Jaskiran thought back to her run-in with the young thugs and then focused on what she would do if they were there now. She gripped the pads tighter, pushing against the force of Geeta's strikes. She saw their laughing faces again. They looked little more than a bunch of kids. Teenage boys with tattered clothes, foul mouths and no futures. But she knew there was more to them than that. There was an easy violence to them.

Their haunting black eyes, chasms to a world of misery that she knew little about, had looked at her as if she were some creature in a zoo, something from another world that they had seen from afar but never up close. There had been groping hands that had pinched and grabbed at her. She had left that part out when retelling the ordeal later to Sabeena, Vinod and even her family.

Those boys, not yet men, had so easily ignored her pleas. Her fear had only seemed to encourage them. She shuddered to think of what they would grow up to become. What horrors would they unleash on those unfortunate enough to cross their path?

'Time!' called the instructor. 'Great work today, ladies.'

Jaskiran's shoulders slumped, and she dropped the pads to the mat. She breathed deeply, a chill ran down her spine, and she noticed her heart beating hard against her chest. She instinctively turned to the large floor-to-ceiling windows that looked out at the city. But, beyond her own reflection and those of the studio lights, the city was dark, and a sense of trepidation filled her for what lay waiting in the shadows.

12

RAJESH CLIMBED THE STEPS to a first-floor walkway that overlooked the dimly lit backstreet below. He could hear music emanating from the black door ahead of him. As he made his way toward it, he passed a man unsteady on his feet and noticed that he was urinating against the wall. The man looked at Rajesh, staring impassively at him with dark and bloodshot eyes. Rajesh tried to avoid the man's gaze as he shuffled past. Arriving at the entrance to the bar, Rajesh peered through a metal grill cut into the wooden door. There was a man sitting on the other side. Rajesh flashed him an uneasy smile. The man opened the door and let him in without a word.

Inside, a narrow, dimly lit hallway led to a drinking den. A makeshift bar ran the length of one wall, its shelves empty but for a few bottles devoid of any labels. Rickety wooden tables were placed in no particular order around the remaining space in the room. Most of the tables were empty, but a few were occupied by men sitting on chairs or upturned crates, taking little notice of Rajesh. The retro Bollywood dance music did little to brighten the scene.

Rajesh scanned the room until he saw Sajid sitting in the corner by a window. He raised a finger to acknowledge Rajesh. Taking a seat opposite Sajid, Rajesh looked down at the street, which was illuminated by neon shop signs and the headlights of passing vehicles. Everything seemed to be cloaked in creeping shadow, a hidden story of misery.

'Does this place make you uneasy?' Sajid asked, almost smirking. The veteran reporter's eyes looked magnified behind the oversized glasses he wore. His hair was dishevelled and peppered with grey, as was the stubble on his face.

Rajesh recognised the question as a test and straightened himself. 'No, it's just a little difficult to find, that's all.'

'I'm meeting a source here later. Believe it or not, some people feel more comfortable in this setting than in a trendy restaurant.'

Rajesh looked down at the small glass of brown liquid cupped in Sajid's hand. 'I didn't realise you drank,' he said.

'Does it surprise you?'

'I thought you were a practising Muslim.'

'I used to be,' Sajid said, before taking a sip from the homemade liquor. 'But over the years, the things I've witnessed doing this job … it changes you.' He shook his head.

'Made you question if there is a God?'

'No, I still believe in God. I just don't like him very much.'

Both men laughed, although Sajid's laughter was tinged with regret. 'So,' Sajid changed the subject, 'let me see if I have the facts as Vinod relayed them. You have come across some evidence that directly contradicts the official police account and the suspect's supposedly genuine confession. Is that correct?'

'Yes, that about sums it up,' agreed Rajesh. 'But Vinod has taken me off the story. He's scared of what the deputy commissioner might do if he didn't.'

'Who is the deputy commissioner?'

'Arvind Sagar. Do you know him?'

'Yes, by reputation mostly,' Sajid replied, trying to remember the senior officer's face. 'Nasty piece of work.

Gets results, but to hell with ethics. Vinod was right to be cautious. He's not the kind of man someone like Vinod would want on his case. But what will you do?'

Rajesh hesitated for a second before answering, 'Actually, I'm going to keep working on the story. In secret.'

'Good,' said Sajid, pleased with Rajesh's determination. 'Because it sounds like you might have something here. The fact that the deputy commissioner went so far as to try and scare you off the story tells me their confession might not be as watertight as they want everyone to believe.'

Sajid indicated to the bartender to bring Rajesh a glass of whisky. The bartender sauntered over with a glass and the bottle. He poured Rajesh's drink at the table before topping up Sajid's glass too. Sajid slipped the bartender a few rupees and then held up his glass. 'When you get a sniff of a real story,' he declared, 'you have to keep going even when it's the hardest thing to do. That's the job.'

Rajesh raised his glass to Sajid before hesitatingly taking a sip. The drink tasted sour and almost medicinal. Despite his best efforts he grimaced, and his neck muscles strained as he swallowed it. It burned his insides, and his breath felt like it was on fire culminating in a coughing fit as his body rejected the homemade concoction.

'This stuff is lethal,' Rajesh croaked, looking back at Sajid, who was trying and failing to keep a straight face.

'So, tell me,' Sajid continued, ignoring Rajesh's discomfort. 'I'm happy you're continuing with the story, but I hope you aren't telling me this because you need me to cover for you? I already have enough on my plate. I requested another crime reporter to reduce my workload, not add to it.'

Rajesh shook his head. 'No, no, it's okay. Jaskiran has offered to help me investigate the story. I will do what I can while I work on whatever Sabeena assigns me next.'

Sajid's brow furrowed. 'Jaskiran? You brought her onto the story?'

'Yes, we are going to share the byline.'

'Oh dear,' Sajid said, looking disappointed. 'And you were doing so well.'

'What is it?' Rajesh asked, confused by Sajid's reaction. 'She's a good journalist.'

'She's also very ambitious and has a point to prove. What's stopping her from digging up the next piece of the puzzle and going straight to Vinod to get the story all to herself? That would leave you out in the cold.'

'She wouldn't screw me over like that … would she?' Rajesh said, suddenly worried. He realised that in his haste to accept Jaskiran's offer, he did not stop to think about the possibility that she would want more than a shared byline.

'Young man, you have a lot to learn,' said Sajid. 'A bit of advice from a grizzled veteran: make sure you're the lead reporter. Get the big scoops; that will keep you in the driving seat.'

'Thanks, I will.' Rajesh felt unsure even as he spoke the words.

Sajid knocked back the rest of his whisky, leaving Rajesh contemplating the swirling brown liquid in his glass.

13

As soon as Jaskiran arrived home, she could smell the enticing aroma of frying onions, ginger, garlic and cumin. Following her nose down the cool tiled hallway into the kitchen, she found her mother passing instructions to the cook, who was diligently nodding his head while he put the finishing touches to a tadka before pouring it atop a boiling pot of dal. A plate of succulent-looking kebabs sat on the kitchen counter, still sizzling fresh from the tandoor oven they kept outside. Jaskiran suddenly realised how hungry she was, and she reached over to tear a piece for herself.

'Not yet!' Jaskiran's mother said, slapping her hand away. 'I thought you were never coming home. Go and change quickly.'

'Why?' Jaskiran responded, baffled.

'Because we have people coming for dinner, that's why,' said her mother, 'and you'd look better in a salwar suit instead of this.' She gestured disapprovingly at the shirt and jeans Jaskiran was wearing.

Jaskiran didn't like the sound of this. 'Who's coming for dinner?' she asked.

'Your chacha, chachi and the kids too,' her mother answered before picking up the kebabs and the chutney bowls. 'Here, make yourself useful and put these on the table before you change. They were supposed to be here half an hour ago, so they should be here any minute.'

Jaskiran took the plate from her mother and was reluctantly about to do her bidding when she caught a closer look at her mother's appearance. She was wearing an expensive cotton salwar kameez and a gold necklace given to her by Jaskiran's father as a wedding present. It was a chunky band with black and gold raindrop-shaped embellishments across the front. She only wore it on special occasions.

'Wait, why are you so dolled up?' Jaskiran asked her mother, who hesitated and averted her gaze.

'No reason,' she said quickly, but Jaskiran's mother had always been a terrible liar. It was a consequence of her pious upbringing, and Jaskiran was suddenly hit by a sinking feeling as the realisation washed over her.

'You haven't?' she said despairingly to her mother. 'You promised me you wouldn't do this again. I can't stay for this. I'm going.'

She turned to leave, only to be blocked by the gigantic form of her elder brother, Gurvinder, in the doorway. The tip of his red turban almost touched the top of the doorframe. 'Where are you going?'

'I'm not staying for dinner,' she said defiantly. 'I've lost my appetite.'

'Then you can sit while the rest of us eat,' retorted Gurvinder. 'We have family coming over. Is this any way to behave?' He folded his arms like a bouncer at a club. His forearms tensed together, straining against the half-inch thick steel kara on his right arm.

'Save me your fake fury. I know what you have planned. Who is it this time?' She looked at her mother and brother in turn.

Gurvinder said nothing but continued to fix her with a cool stare that worked so well when forcing his employees into submission, but Jaskiran wouldn't be subdued so easily. It was their mother who broke the standoff. 'Just a friend of your cousin Ravi,' she said. 'His name is Bobby Chana. He moved to America a few years ago and has a good job in finance. Ravi says that he lives in a big house and drives a Porche.' Jaskiran's mother looked at her before continuing, 'He's in India on holiday for two weeks, and Ravi thought he'd bring him over for dinner. See, there's no harm in that, is there?'

'And let me guess,' Jaskiran shot back, 'he's single and just so happens to be looking for a good Punjabi girl to marry and whisk away to America to be his domestic goddess?'

Her mother tutted her annoyance. 'You do get such silly thoughts in your head,' she said. 'You haven't even met him and are already judging him harshly.'

'I don't need to meet him,' Jaskiran said, exasperated. 'I don't need to meet anyone until I'm ready. Marriage is the last thing on my mind right now.'

Her mother audibly gasped, closed her eyes and muttered a prayer. The cook, fearing a full-on argument, turned down the flame on the stove and slipped out of the side door into the garden.

'Now you've upset Maa with your childish rubbish,' said Gurvinder angrily. 'You're twenty-eight now. You need to start thinking about your future and settle down.'

'It's not my future you're worried about. You only care about me marrying someone you approve of.'

'If we don't approve of them,' said her brother, 'it's because they're not good enough for you or this family.'

'Funny, nobody sought my opinion when you got married,' Jaskiran replied bitingly. Gurvinder's eyes flared with anger and his thick moustache twitched with rage. He would have struck her if he could, but he knew his father would deal him a worse beating if he did so. Before he could articulate a response, Jaskiran was already heading out the side door.

Gurvinder began to charge after her, but their mother held up a placating hand. 'Let her go,' she said.

Outside, Jaskiran followed the path down the side of the house towards a concrete courtyard where her father was manning the tandoor oven. Despite the cook's protests, Jaskiran's father refused to let anyone else use the oven and took a great deal of pride in cooking kebabs himself using a recipe that he had honed to perfection over a lifetime. Jaskiran saw him sitting with a glass of whisky and soda while a skewer of mutton chops roasted over hot coals in the terracotta clay barrel.

'Papa, did you know?' Jaskiran asked softly as she came up behind him. Despite her anger, she couldn't bring herself to shatter such a peaceful scene. Her father looked up as she took a seat across from him. His white beard flowed down to his chest and almost blended with his impeccably white kurta.

'I did,' he said, almost in apology. 'They only want the best for you, Jaskiran. Don't be angry.'

'And you?' she asked.

He paused for a second, peering into his glass as if he were studying tea leaves. 'I just want you to do whatever makes you happy,' he eventually answered with a smile. Jaskiran couldn't help but smile too. Her father was still on her side. With some effort, he got up from his chair. His large frame weighed heavy on his weary knees. Despite this, he cut a formidable figure when he stood upright as he did now, stoking the coals in the tandoor. In his youth, Jaskiran's father had been a champion wrestler. His eyes still lit up like a young boy's when asked to recite the story of how he, at the tender age of nineteen, defeated Balu Ravachandran, the Tiger of Tamil Nadu, at the national championships. He returned to Punjab to a hero's welcome and was treated like a celebrity for years. Even to this day, whenever he made a trip to his ancestral village of Pharwahi, there would undoubtedly be a few grey-haired men and women who fondly remembered the victories of his youth.

The smoke from the tandoor made the old man's eyes water. He patted them dry with his handkerchief as he looked at his daughter. 'No one is forcing you to like this man, Jaskiran,' he said. 'You don't have to see him again after this night if you don't want to. But do it for your mother. She worries about your future. It keeps her up at night. She needs to feel like she is doing something.'

'I've told her that I'm not ready, but she acts like I'm some old crone who will never find anyone if I don't get married right away.'

'Well, what do you expect? In our day, women got married a lot younger than you are now. She has a hard time adjusting to the modern way.' He eased himself into his chair once again and lifted his glass.

'Couldn't you talk to her?' asked Jaskiran. 'Make her understand?'

Her father smiled at the thought. 'You know, your mother asks the same from me,' he said. 'To talk you into finding a husband. But I didn't get to this age without learning a few things. And choosing between a wife and a daughter is no choice at all. So, the best I can do is to remain neutral.' He smiled and took a sip from his glass before continuing, 'And you're not the only one who has to endure a difficult evening. You know your chacha can't handle his drink but will insist I open a bottle of Johnnie Walker. And when he's drunk, all he'll want to discuss is starting a business. He thinks that if he gets enough whisky in me, I'll help him to open his own wholesale business in Jalandhar. As if I have that kind of money to throw around.'

He held up his glass to Jaskiran, indicating that he wanted a refill.

'You know the doctor told you to cut down on the drinking,' she said. 'It's not good for your liver.'

'When a man can't even enjoy the simple pleasures of food and drink in his own home, it's time to light the pyre and be done with it all,' he responded in mock anger.

Jaskiran rolled her eyes. 'Fine, no need to be so melodramatic,' she said, smiling warmly. She took his glass and walked back towards the house.

When she returned to the kitchen, she was glad to find only the cook preparing a salad; her mother and Gurvinder were nowhere to be seen. As she made her way to her father's alcohol cabinet in the dining room, she couldn't help but reflect on her situation. If her father was of the same mind as her mother, she might already be married to a man of their choosing. What was the alternative? Run away and live alone, shunned by those she loves? What kind of choice was that? The doorbell rang, and she shook the thought from her head. Her mother's footsteps echoed down the hallway, followed by a chorus of greetings as she opened the door. Jaskiran took a gulp of the whisky.

14

IT WAS LATE IN the evening, and Rahul Yadav was at home in Delhi's exclusive Golf Links neighbourhood sipping on his obligatory peg of single malt he enjoyed most nights. Sitting on the veranda, all was quiet. Having served dinner and scrubbed the kitchen, his cook had retired to her room in a purpose-built annexe away from the main house. Only the housekeeper, Neha, remained. She would stay within earshot until Rahul went to bed. Rahul surveyed the garden, tended by gardeners over the years into an idyll of serenity and order. It was the antithesis of the city that surrounded it.

Rahul remembered a time when sitting with a drink in his hand in the evening air would bring him a real sense of joy. But now he just felt nothing. *Is this what it is to be content or is this apathy?* he wondered. *When was the last time I felt any real pleasure?* The only thing he ever felt these days was anger – at the stupidity of others, at the broken system he toiled within and at a society that rewarded those lesser than him simply by virtue of their caste, family name or inheritance. It was an anger without end. There was always something to rage against.

Perhaps if I had chosen differently in life – married, perhaps had children – I could have fought off this creeping indifference to life's pleasures. He stopped himself from taking the thought any further. Rahul refused to regret the choices he had made. It was a dangerous game to have second thoughts and self-doubt. He had always done what he needed to do to survive. As a boy toiling on his father's fields in the rural backwaters of Bihar, it would have been impossible for Rahul to ever imagine he would end up in such affluent surroundings.

'Sir,' said Neha softly, bringing him back to the present. 'There is a police officer here to see you – Deputy Commissioner Arvind Sagar.'

'At this hour?' Rahul was annoyed. He knew what the greedy, fat crook wanted.

'I'm sorry, sir. He insisted. He is coming up the drive now.'

'Fine, I will see him out here. Bring me the sealed envelope from my desk. You know which drawer.'

Neha nodded and went inside. She soon returned with a brown envelope and placed it on the table beside Rahul. A few minutes later, she led the deputy commissioner out onto the veranda.

'I'll have a peg of whisky before you run away,' said Sagar to Neha as she retreated. 'There you are, Rahul Saab. You are a hard man to get hold of at times.' He was still in his uniform. Despite his protruding belly, Sagar still cut an imposing figure. He was over six feet tall, with strong arms formed from his youthful years in the army. He was in his late fifties but still had an impressive head of black hair.

'This couldn't wait until the morning, Arvind?' Rahul asked, noting the slight twitch on the policeman's face. Sagar didn't like people omitting his official title, which was precisely why Rahul did it. Regardless of Sagar's official position, Rahul viewed him as an employee, albeit an expensive one. The deputy commissioner's ties in the police force were invaluable and the sole reason Rahul had ever done business with him.

'I called your office as soon as the press briefing was concluded,' said Sagar. 'I thought you'd want to know how it went.' He took a seat beside Rahul. Neha reappeared with a generous measure of imported Scotch whisky and handed it to the deputy commissioner.

'Thank you, dear,' said Sagar, looking up at Neha, who averted her eyes and left. He watched her go before turning back to Rahul. 'I can see why you have not married, saab. I bet she takes care of you very well. Where did you find her?'

Rahul ignored the question and asked one of his own. 'So, how did it go?'

'It went well,' replied the policeman, not sounding too convincing.

'There's a problem?'

'It's nothing, really. But one journalist, a boy from the *Delhi Daily*, said that someone claims they saw Anjali leave in a car the night she died, contradicting our version of events.'

Rahul's brow furrowed. 'How is that possible? You said your men spoke to the neighbours, and no one saw a thing.'

'They did, so I'm not sure who told him. But it doesn't matter, really.' Sagar tried to sound reassuring. 'I have dealt with it. He won't be causing any more issues.'

Arvind's eyes now fell on the envelope. 'Is this for me? May I?'

Rahul nodded, and Arvind picked up the envelope and wasted no time opening it.

'What about her phone? Have you located it?'

'No, that's a strange one actually,' said the deputy commissioner, counting the rupee notes inside the envelope. 'The phone's last known location shows it at the girl's home, but we have searched the place twice now and have found nothing. The parents have no knowledge of where it could be either.'

Rahul resisted the urge to swear. The phone could not be allowed to surface. It held evidence that Rahul was desperate to keep from falling into the wrong hands. He tried to remain impassive in front of the senior officer, not wanting to reveal how dangerous the small device could be to him.

'And the boy you arrested?' Rahul asked, watching him closely.

'At first he refused to cooperate,' said Sagar. 'But we made it clear if he didn't do as he was told we would arrest his family for trying to help him cover up the crime. We painted a very graphic picture of what life in a juvenile home would be like for his sisters. That seemed to do the trick. Now we will keep him locked up awaiting trial.'

'Trial?' Rahul repeated, his brow furrowed. 'That's not what I said. He needs to be finished off.'

'Saab, you worry about nothing. A trial could be years from now. We could still get a conviction, but I think it's more likely that he will go free. But by then, no one will care about reopening the case, and the boy gets to go on with the rest of his life. Everybody wins.' Sagar raised his glass and took a large swig of the whisky.

'You pick a strange time to grow a conscience, Arvind,' Rahul said sharply.

'You know I don't have a problem with such matters when you are talking about low-life criminals,' replied the officer. 'In their case, we are doing society a favour by taking matters into our own hands. But this Vivek Trivedi? Let's be honest, he is innocent. He hasn't done a thing.'

'What's your point?' Rahul asked, unmoved.

'If we kill him, it's cold-blooded murder. Plain and simple.' Arvind's tone was now more severe.

'And that's your limit, is it?'

'It is for what's here.' Arvind gestured toward the envelope in his hand. 'You came to me for help, and I didn't ask any questions. I still don't want to know what happened. But you understand my discretion – my friendship, even – comes at a greater price than what can be stuffed in one envelope.'

‘What is it you want?’ Rahul asked. He was growing tired of Arvind’s company.

‘I know you operate lucrative schemes for your friends,’ said Sagar with a smirk. ‘I am simply asking you to bring me into the fold.’

Without even considering the proposal, Rahul’s response was to the point. ‘There is nothing in the pipeline I can offer you, Arvind. Perhaps another time.’

The abrupt response angered the deputy commissioner. He didn’t like the feeling of being looked down on, especially by a wily old man like Rahul Yadav. He clenched his teeth to prevent himself from reacting adversely to the rejection. He finally managed a jovial smile and downed his whisky quickly. Standing to leave, he looked down at Rahul. ‘Yes, another time then.’ He turned and left through the expansive hallway, his smile now replaced with barely contained resentment.

15

Rajesh awoke to the morning sunlight cascading through the threadbare curtains of his family's one-bedroom apartment. His mouth was dry, and he could still taste the liquor from the night before. As his eyes adjusted to the light, his head still felt heavy with sleep. He heard the sound of soft footsteps approaching him, but before he could react, a figure leapt at him with a sinister giggle and landed heavily on his abdomen.

'I won. You didn't see me coming!' his sister Roopa shouted in triumph, bouncing on his stomach.

Winded and feeling like he might retch, Rajesh exclaimed, 'OK, I give up!' Roopa looked down at him, a little disappointed. Rajesh had not come home before she had gone to bed last night, and she had missed out on spending time with him. It was only when her eldest brother was around that their small, cramped apartment felt like it had any life within its walls.

She attempted to stand up, but Rajesh grabbed her, pulled her close and began tickling her mercilessly. 'What are you going to do now?' he cried as she broke into a fit of laughter.

'No!' she yelled in glee. 'Stop!' She eventually dropped to the ground, her sides hurting from laughing so much.

Their mother, hearing the ruckus, stepped out of the apartment's only bedroom she shared with her two younger children and looked on with some concern.

'Roopa! Get off the floor. And look at the state of your hair now! Go and sit down. I'll have to fix it again.'

Rajesh looked up at his mother, who was already preparing the stove to cook breakfast. There was a time when she would have joined in the fun, but no longer.

His father's passing five years ago had been hard on the whole family but particularly so on his mother, who was left to bring up three children by herself in Delhi. Her own family was hundreds of miles away in a village in Uttar Pradesh. Despite her hardened exterior, there were occasions when the mask would slip. Rajesh would come home at night and hear the soft sounds of longing and grief coming from the bedroom as his mother wept for her late husband and the life they would never share.

Rising from his charpoy, he walked across the room to put a comforting arm around his mother as she began kneading dough for puris. Rajesh noticed his mother wasn't wearing the small pearl drop earrings that had been given to her by his father and that she had worn every day since his death.

'Ma, where are your earrings?'

His mother seemed irritated at Rajesh's proximity, and pressing her fingers to her lobe, she answered brusquely, 'Yes, the pin was loose. I gave them to Mr Khurana downstairs, his son-in-law works at a jeweller's, and he said they will get it fixed for me.' She now waved him away. 'You stink of alcohol. Just go and wash, or you'll get late for work.' He kissed her on the forehead and did as he was instructed. She kept berating him even as he went into the bathroom. 'You're out every weekend with your friends, drinking and partying, and now you've started doing it during the week too!'

'It's not like that, Ma,' Rajesh responded, shutting the bathroom door behind him. When he came back out a few minutes later, he found a stack of deep-fried puris and a steaming bowl of spicy aloo sabzi waiting for him on the table. He began eating while shooting his sister a disapproving look as she played with her food while their mother plaited her hair. She was only twelve years old but already thought that she had to watch what she ate to stay slim like all her favourite stars.

Rajesh then looked across the table at his brother, Amit. He was gleefully tucking into his favourite breakfast, nimbly folding the puri with one hand while completing equations in his textbook with the other. His brow arched in concentration over his black-rimmed glasses.

'What are you doing?' Rajesh asked.

'Homework,' answered Amit.

'Homework?' Rajesh responded with irritation, his mouth still full. 'How many times have I told you to do it as soon as you come in from school?'

'I forgot,' Amit said with a shrug. 'It doesn't matter. It's easy anyway.' He said, not taking his eyes off the page he was reading.

'Let me see,' Rajesh said, spinning the book around. What he saw may as well have been written in hieroglyphics. 'This makes sense to you?' he asked, unable to hide the admiration in his voice. His brother nodded, the grease from the puris smeared across his lips. Rajesh reached over and attempted to ruffle his brother's impeccably neat side-parting, but Amit batted it away with a strong forearm.

'Ma, you have a genius here,' Rajesh quipped. 'Which university shall we send him to?'

'Whichever one he wants,' his mother responded. 'His big brother will surely be paying. As you seem to have so much money for partying, I'm sure you've already put aside enough for your brother's higher education.'

Rajesh felt a pang of guilt and wondered what his mother would say if she knew the truth. While his salary and whatever his mother earned as a seamstress were enough to pay the bills, there was little to spare. He had long ago turned to other means of financing to pay for his needs.

'I wasn't partying last night, Ma. I was working. I've been promoted to crime reporter now.'

'Does that mean you'll get a raise?' his mother asked, suddenly sounding interested. Rajesh nodded, and his mother's expression brightened. Reassured, she kissed the back of Roopa's head and prompted her to get ready for school.

Rajesh had managed to hide just how dire their situation had become from his mother, and the events over the past few days had put it out of his mind, but Rajesh knew a reckoning was coming. He needed the raise, but to get it he had to do as Vinod ordered. That meant not chasing after the Anjali Mangal story, no matter how beneficial it could be for his prospects. It was too much to think about so early in the day. Rajesh sighed heavily and checked the time. He would need to leave soon to pick up Karishma.

'Amit, get your books,' he said. 'If you want a ride to school, we must leave now.' He rose from the table.

'But I'm nearly finished,' protested his brother.

'You can do it on the way to school. Let's go!'

Rajesh grabbed his messenger bag, kissed his mother goodbye and led his siblings to his beat-up scooter outside. It had belonged to his father, who had bought it brand new over twelve years ago. Over the years, Delhi's harsh, pot-hole-filled roads, extreme heat, dust and powerful monsoon downpours had taken their toll. Its original paintwork had faded and much of the body was covered in rust. The wheels were misaligned and the motor misfired regularly. If it hadn't held such sentimental value, Rajesh would likely be embarrassed to ride it.

As he drove his siblings to school, Rajesh wondered if maybe Vinod was right – a little boy wasn't a reliable witness, certainly not one to stake a career on. But he couldn't help but feel that Roshan wasn't just a child making up stories. Growing up with two younger siblings, Rajesh was well-versed in the types of lies younger children can tell. They can be believable, at times well-meaning, but often vague.

Children are so busy thinking about the big lie that they forget to invent the smaller details. But when Rajesh had asked about specifics, Roshan had the answers. He said that the car he had seen only had two doors. He had even recalled that Anjali had promised to buy him a pack of cards to replace the ones that he had lost at school.

Sitting astride the scooter now, his sister sitting in front between his outreached arms and Amit behind him, Rajesh was suddenly aware he had missed a detail from Roshan's account. The boy had claimed Anjali was going to replace his cards; yes, Rajesh remembered that clearly. But Roshan had also mentioned the name of the store Anjali said she would visit. Rajesh sat motionless while he tried to remember. Then, after some thought, it finally came back to him.

'Toy Kingdom,' Rajesh muttered triumphantly.

16

JASKIRAN ENJOYED HER VISITS to Delhi University and the South Campus most of all. She had visited in connection with a story several times in the past and loved walking through the pristine gardens surrounding the many department buildings. The students all looked so happy that it was impossible not to be caught up in their exuberance and view life more optimistically. From her phone calls the previous day, she had learnt that Anjali had been studying at the Department of Financial Studies.

After she located the department, Jaskiran was disappointed to find that it was housed within a drab-looking grey building. Inside, she soon found a board listing the names of faculty members and their office numbers. She scrolled down until she found the name she was looking for: Professor Gopal Randrapathy, room C12.

She knocked on the door of the professor's room. A voice from inside told her to enter. The professor was sitting at his desk marking papers. He did not look up when Jaskiran entered. The professor was middle-aged and balding, with thick black-rimmed glasses and an even thicker moustache. Jaskiran thought that he looked like the stereotypical professor, down to the three different coloured pens in his shirt pocket.

Professor Randrapathy eventually set aside the paper he was working on and looked at Jaskiran over the top of his glasses. 'Please sit,' he said, pointing with his pen to the chair in front of his desk. 'I believe you are the girl from the *Delhi Daily* who called yesterday?'

Jaskiran disliked being referred to as a girl but decided to let it go. Her tone remained cordial as she replied, 'That's correct, professor. I'm Jaskiran Sohal, and I wanted to ask you a few questions about Anjali Mangal.'

'Why?' the professor asked, looking genuinely bemused. 'You think a few extra words on a page will make a difference now?'

'Yes, professor, I do,' Jaskiran replied, a little taken aback. 'I believe people have become so used to hearing about these crimes against women that it's difficult for them to care about each case. Perhaps if our readers look at Anjali as a person they could identify with rather than just another stranger, it will make them care a little more.'

'And what good would that do now?' Randrapathy asked, examining Jaskiran as if she were a student in his class.

'Well, only when we care can we demand real change to prevent such crimes from happening again.'

'Change!' the professor retorted derisively. 'You believe you can change the savage impulses that drive people to murder?'

Jaskiran had not expected such an interrogation and to have her own motives questioned. 'I believe that we can change the culture of our society,' she persisted. 'It is a society that seems to accept such violence with little resistance. That finds ways to deflect guilt away from the perpetrator to the victim. And if we don't try and change things, professor, then we are part of the problem.'

The answer seemed to satisfy the professor. He nodded slightly before placing his pen on the desk.

'I'm sorry,' he said. 'I didn't mean to belittle your craft … it's just that in the aftermath of such an evil and senseless act that robs the world of a talented young woman like

Anjali, one grows cynical about how much humanity is actually left in our godforsaken race.'

'I know that this must be difficult for you, so I'll try not to take too much of your time,' said Jaskiran. 'You said that Anjali was talented?'

'Yes, and I didn't do her justice. To put it plainly, she was brilliant. The hardest-working student I've seen in years. She aced every paper and never seemed too busy to help her peers. And she was always smiling. Even when I set her a difficult task, she enjoyed picking it apart piece by piece, as if she knew the answer would reveal itself to her eventually.'

'You must have really enjoyed teaching her?'

The professor smiled tenderly. 'Yes, very much,' he replied. 'She was the kind of student every teacher dreams of – the right balance of receptive and inquisitive. She challenged me and made me try harder. She made me a better teacher.' He looked away, almost embarrassed at the sincerity of his revelation.

'The way you describe her, she sounds like she would have been popular with her classmates,' said Jaskiran. 'Did she have a lot of friends?'

The question pulled Randrapathy away from his recollections of Anjali. 'Well, like I said, she helped her fellow students with their coursework,' he replied. 'I would see her studying with them around campus. As for friends, I can't say I take much notice of such things. She certainly didn't parade around with the girls who spend their time giggling at whatever it is they find so fascinating on their phones.'

'Are there any classmates of hers that I could speak to?'

The professor thought for a moment before saying, 'All those who were close to Anjali or were deeply affected by her death have been given a special leave of absence. Anyone who does show up to class most likely did not know her very well.'

Jaskiran couldn't help but be disappointed at the response, but she persevered. 'Did you ever see her with her boyfriend, Vivek?'

A look of disapproval appeared on the professor's face. 'Yes, a couple of times,' he answered. 'I had no idea that Vivek and Anjali were an item until I saw the news that they had arrested him.'

'They weren't in the same class?'

The professor shook his head emphatically. 'No, my class is for the crème de la crème of Delhi's young minds. I believe Vivek was taking business management or some other mediocre course.'

'Did you ever see Vivek or Anjali travel in a car to or from campus?'

Randrapathy looked a little confused at the question. He shook his head. 'No, I can't say that I did. Why is that important?'

'No particular reason,' Jaskiran said quickly before switching to her next question. 'Do you remember if you ever saw Vivek and Anjali with anyone else, like another close friend?'

The professor became thoughtful again. 'No, I think it was always just the two of them,' he said after a while. 'I could be wrong, but it was months ago that I last saw them together. However, I don't take much notice of what my students get up to outside of my class. I know that's not a popular thing to say nowadays, but it's the way I prefer it. I don't pry into their personal lives, and I don't share intimate details of my life with them. I think it's better for all concerned.'

'I understand,' said Jaskiran. 'I just have a few more questions. This won't take much longer.'

The professor gestured for her to ask away.

'Did you see her at all on the day she died? Did she look upset about anything?'

'I'm afraid I didn't. Anjali didn't have lectures that day on account of her work placement.'

'Work placement?'

'Yes, every student is sent on a summer placement at the end of their first year. Anjali was taking hers at Delhi Financial Corporation. They were so impressed by her that she was offered a part-time position when the placement ended. Students usually work part-time jobs at retail stores or as waiters. But Anjali was working at one of the most sought-after firms in the city!'

'It's never been mentioned that she had a job,' said Jaskiran. 'Do you have a contact at the corporation?'

'As a matter of fact, I do,' said Randrapathy, turning to a cabinet behind him. 'The individual who offered Anjali the part-time position is the same one who offered her the summer work placement. We would have his details on file.' He flicked through a folder until he found the correct page. 'Ah, here we are. Deepak Rao. He's a manager in their commercial accounts department. Unfortunately, we don't seem to have a telephone number.'

'That's fine,' said Jaskiran. 'I can take it from here.' Jaskiran felt she had all the information she was likely to get from the professor and stood to leave. 'Thank you for your time, professor. You've been very helpful.'

'I hope so,' he replied. Jaskiran had reached the door when Randrapathy spoke again. 'Thank you,' he said, his voice little more than a whisper.

Jaskiran turned to face the professor. He suddenly looked weary.

'Excuse me?' she said, unsure of how to respond.

'I said thank you. Thank you for asking about Anjali,' he said. 'Since they arrested Vivek, they don't talk about her anymore. She doesn't deserve to be forgotten. She really was an amazing student and an outstanding young woman. I hope you won't let them forget her.'

A feeling of immense responsibility swelled within Jaskiran. 'I won't,' she said, shutting the door behind her.

17

IT WAS MIDDAY BEFORE Rajesh managed to leave the newsroom without arousing suspicion from Sabeena or Vinod. The traffic was heavy on the way to the toy store, which was in Rohini's Pocket 21 district. Rajesh felt a sense of relief when he finally parked his scooter outside the shop's entrance. He looked up at the yellow sign emblazoned with red letters that read 'Toy Kingdom'. Painted plasterboard had been used to make the entrance resemble a castle door. The display windows were packed with soft toys, remote-controlled cars and large dolls.

Rajesh stepped through the transparent PVC curtains at the doorway and was greeted with a blast of cold air from the overhead air-conditioning unit. It was a small store, but they made use of every available inch. Among the shelves sat assorted bubble machines, water guns and board games. There were figurines behind glass cases, rotatable racks of keychains and magnets, and stuffed toys suspended from the ceiling by pieces of string.

Rajesh approached the only employee in the store, a Sikh man with a short beard standing behind the counter. His red turban matched his checked shirt, and Rajesh wondered for a moment if it had been a conscious decision.

'Hi, are you the owner?' Rajesh asked as he approached. The man was slouched over the counter fiddling with his phone. His eyes darted up and viewed Rajesh with distrust, wondering if he was another angry customer demanding a refund for a faulty electronic toy. 'Why?' he asked. 'What's the problem?'

'No problem,' Rajesh replied. 'I'm a reporter with the *Delhi Daily*, and I'm researching a story for the newspaper. I just wanted to know if you saw this woman in here last Friday night.' Rajesh held out his phone to show a picture of Anjali at a recent family gathering that the media had been using in their coverage.

Rajesh's explanation did little to ease the man's suspicions, but he eventually relented and took a long look at the photo. Finally, he shook his head. 'No, I don't think so,' he said. 'But let me ask my brother. He works most evenings.' The man called toward the door at the other end of the counter. 'Hardeep! Come here for a minute.'

A man wearing a blue turban, also matched to his shirt, emerged from behind the door. He was still chewing on a mouthful of food and was wiping his hand on the back of his jeans.

'This guy is a reporter,' the first man told his brother, gesturing toward Rajesh. 'He wants to know if this girl was here a few nights ago.'

Hardeep glanced at Rajesh before taking a look at the photo. 'Yes,' he nodded. 'She was here. I sold her some cards.'

Rajesh was dumbfounded. 'Are you sure it was her?' he managed to ask.

'Yes, I remember because I had already closed for the night,' said Hardeep. 'She arrived as I was leaving and said that she needed to buy some cards. I have it on tape if you want to see.' Hardeep pointed to the corner behind him, where a security camera was fixed to the wall, almost obscured by stacks of lunch boxes piled high on a shelf. A few minutes later, the three of them were standing in the back office amidst boxes of unsold stock and cabinets of paperwork. On a desk cluttered with invoices was an ancient-looking computer covered in dust.

Hardeep pulled the CCTV footage from that night and fast-forwarded through the grainy video. The daily routine of his life took on a comedic element as he and the customers sped through the store, handing over their money in record time.

When he began to play the video at regular speed, the shop was dark, and they could see Hardeep's silhouette outside locking the door, the only light coming from the streetlamps. Suddenly Hardeep was illuminated. He turned and seemed to be speaking to someone. A woman then came into view.

'That's her,' Hardeep confirmed.

Rajesh noted the time on the screen: 9.28 p.m. 'And the light there, that's from a car?' he asked.

Hardeep nodded. 'Mercedes C-Class cabriolet, very nice car. Actually, it's the reason I let her in. I thought she must be rich, and I could get her to buy a few more things.'

Hardeep's brother flashed a wry smile. 'And did you?' he asked.

'No, she was in a hurry.'

The red-turbaned brother clicked his tongue. 'It's because you don't know how to talk to women.'

Hardeep made to raise the back of his hand. 'Chutiya. What do you know about it? The only woman you speak to is our mother.'

Rajesh ignored the squabbling brothers and focused on the footage. The pixelated form of Anjali, dressed in a white blouse and sky-blue jeans, moved through the aisles. Her hair was tied in a ponytail, which fell to her lower back. Even in the grainy footage, Rajesh could see she possessed a certain elegance. Rajesh took a picture of the screen with his phone. After a swift transaction at the checkout, Anjali left with the cards. Rajesh watched her disappear beyond the shopfront. A few moments later, a silhouetted car drove past.

'There!' shouted an excited Rajesh. 'Rewind that and pause it just as the car drives past.'

Hardeep did as he was told, and the three of them crowded in for a better look. Straining their eyes at the frozen pixels, they eventually conceded that it was impossible to make out any further detail.

'Did you get a look at the driver?' Rajesh asked Hardeep.

Hardeep shook his head. 'No, the glare of the headlights meant that I couldn't see the driver. Why? What is this all about?'

Rajesh was unsure how much to tell them but, in the end, reasoned there were already enough lies about what happened that night to Anjali that he didn't want to add to them. 'The girl, she was murdered that night,' said Rajesh. 'We don't know who the driver is, but I believe they must be involved. If you remember anything, please give me a call.' Rajesh handed his card to a dumbstruck Hardeep, who took it solemnly.

Walking outside to the scooter and away from the cool air of the store, the sudden heat made Rajesh's head feel heavy. There was no way Anjali could have been on the bus at the time the deputy commissioner had stated in the press briefing. Rajesh looked again at the grainy photo he had captured on his phone, before composing a message to Jaskiran. He added the image as an attachment and lifted his finger towards the 'send' button. But then he wavered, lowering his hand. He put his phone back into his pocket, the message unsent.

18

RAHUL YADAV LOOKED CLOSELY at Ayesha Begum as she sat placidly across from him in his office. She had seemingly mastered the art of elegant modesty with a hint of seductiveness. The pallu of her crisp cotton saree clung to the toned curves of her body, revealing flashes of her bronzed skin. Her hair was tied in a tight bun, which accentuated the graceful lines of her neck and highlighted the expensive diamond earrings that she wore. She had dark, penetrating eyes, but it was her lips that stole his attention. They were full and ripe in a dark maroon shade of lipstick. He wondered how soft they would be to touch.

The lips now parted, and it took him a moment to realise she was smiling at him.

He averted his eyes, aware he had lowered himself to his most base animal desires just as she had likely wanted him to do. He felt a stab of anger at the knowledge that her strategy had worked and thrown him off balance.

'Yadavji, is everything alright?' asked Ayesha.

The bitch, Rahul thought, *she enjoys watching men squirm*. She was turning the screw. He looked her right in the eye. 'You wished to meet me today?'

'Yes,' replied Ayesha. 'Thank you for taking my request. I understand men of your stature are extremely busy.'

Rahul almost rolled his eyes. *These cheap compliments*, he thought, *do they work on anyone?* He had heard things about Ayesha Begum, the young MLA leading the Democratic Union Party's attempt to overthrow the Indian Workers' Party in the upcoming Delhi elections. She was building a brand based on a pious public-facing persona. But behind the scenes, she was forming alliances with Delhi's powerful elite. There were rumours, too, of the lengths she was willing to go to in order to cement these new relationships, using her sexuality as leverage over men and as a battering ram against the most obstinate of opponents. Rahul abhorred such cheap tactics that relied on the most carnal desires of men.

'I see that your star is rising within the party,' said Rahul, his tone even and flat.

'The party's lacked a figurehead for some time,' said Ayesha. 'It needs someone whom the voters can get behind.'

'And that's you, is it?' Rahul barely disguised the condescension in his tone.

'Yes,' she responded. 'You said yourself that you took the meeting out of interest. We've never met, but you haven't failed to notice me. The people of Delhi are doing the same. I must be the most recognisable MLA in Delhi.'

'We have established that I have heard of you,' said Rahul curtly. 'Now let's discuss how you found your way into my office. I highly doubt you wish to take out a loan.'

'Well, I was quite surprised to see your name appear on a list of the most generous donors to candidates from the Indian Workers' Party.'

'There is no such list,' Rahul shot back.

Ayesha smiled. 'I am a resourceful woman, Yadavji,' she said. 'I mean no disrespect. In fact, it's quite the opposite. You have done well to keep such a low profile. I must admit it's the first time I have seen your name mentioned anywhere. Yet, you command a post of such authority at the behest of the Delhi government.'

Rahul took a moment to ponder Ayesha. She was beautiful, of that there was no doubt. But she had weaponised her beauty, and this debased her in his eyes.

'If you already know that I have made donations to a rival party, what are you doing here?'

'I understand you are quite prophetic when it comes to your political alliances. Many of those you backed in the last election won their seats.'

'I back winners.'

'Then back me,' said Ayesha immediately.

Rahul made a dismissive gesture. 'The Democratic Union Party is not taking Delhi.'

'I think we can.'

'Your party is racked with infighting and weak leadership.'

'Yes, there is much work to be done,' Ayesha agreed. 'But in terms of would-be leaders, you can look to me. I speak for women and have a good rapport with students and the middle class. Voters back personalities, and my popularity has been surging for the past few months. It's the perfect time to be riding a wave of popularity into an election.'

Rahul sighed. He was growing tired of sparring with Ayesha.

'Then what is it you want from me?' he asked. 'Your party has plenty of money.'

'You're right,' she said. 'I don't need your money. But I could do with you denying it to those whom you helped in the past. They have probably already come asking for your donations and will come again before the election is over. I'm asking you to refuse their requests.'

Rahul laughed scornfully. It was a ludicrous proposal. She either thought that he was stupid or couldn't comprehend the danger such a move would put him in. 'You expect me to turn my back on those I have helped elect – the incumbents in power – and throw my lot in with you?' he scoffed. 'Your party had just a handful of seats at the last election!' Before Ayesha could respond, Rahul continued, the vitriol rising in his voice, 'You think that because you dress seductively, I will fall at your feet and do your bidding in the hope that you will sleep with me in return? That is how you operate, isn't it?'

Ayesha remained impassive, not rising to the bait.

'I can see you'll need some time to think it over,' she said, rising from her seat before heading for the door. However, once there she couldn't resist the urge any longer and she turned to face him once again.

'I almost forgot to thank you.'

Rahul's brows furrowed, but he held his tongue.

'I understand you paid for the Mangal family to stay in a five-star hotel out of town to grieve for their daughter away from the media. That was very considerate of you.'

'She was an employee.' Rahul spat the words as if they were explanation enough.

Ayesha smiled. 'Yes,' she said slowly, 'I'm sure that's it.' She opened the door and left, leaving Rahul seething with rage at the unspoken threat. He had misjudged her.

19

ASHOK CHOPRA STOOD IN the Char Bagh garden looking along the central pathway to Humayun's Tomb, a red sandstone structure with a white marble dome. It seemed to reflect the gentle light from the sun, which now hung low in the hazy afternoon sky.

'Hi, sorry if I'm a little late,' Jaskiran said as she came up behind him. Ashok seemed to have been lost in reflection and now looked to Jaskiran as if waking from a dream.

'Hi,' he said, finally breaking the spell that seemed to have been cast over him. 'No need to apologise. There are few places in the city better for spending time alone.' Jaskiran was about to disagree with him but, looking around, she realised the crowds of people that she had expected to see were nowhere to be found. It was oddly quiet, with only the odd visitor snapping pictures on their camera and gardeners tending the grounds.

'Yes, the crowds of tourists and schoolchildren are gone for the day,' said Ashok. He smiled at her, but Jaskiran could see that it was half-hearted. *He looks tired*, she thought. Sensing her eyes studying him, Ashok turned away again towards the tomb. 'It really is beautiful, isn't it?' he said, looking first along the narrow water channel that ran down the centre of the path towards the base of the tomb, then to the mausoleum itself, which sat resolutely at the centre of a vaulted terrace; it's simple, symmetrical exterior seemingly carved from a single piece of stone rather than assembled piece by piece over seven long years. 'I may be a little biased, but I've always preferred it to the Taj Mahal.'

Jaskiran found herself agreeing with him. While the Taj Mahal was certainly grander, it was built to a scale that demanded attention and respect. Humayun's Tomb and the surrounding gardens had been constructed to a more human scale.

'Did you know a father-and-son team designed it?' Ashok asked. 'Haji Begum, Humayun's widow, oversaw the construction herself. She brought in a well-known architect, Mirak Mirza Ghiyas, to design the final resting place of her beloved husband. Mirak had begun his career as a stonecutter under Emperor Babar. As his experience and expertise grew, he went on to construct buildings all across Afghanistan and India. Humayun's tomb was to be his final masterpiece, the pinnacle of his life's work. But unfortunately, he died before the tomb was ever finished, and it fell to his son, Sayyid, to complete his father's work.'

'Does that resonate with you?' Jaskiran asked.

The question brought a genuine smile to Ashok's face, and he turned to look at her again. 'How foolish of me to forget that I'm in the presence of an inquisitive journalist,' he said. 'I guess it does to some extent. My father was just a small-town politician with very little formal education. But he was also a man of vision. He wanted India to build itself out of poverty. He saw it as the responsibility of those in power – men like himself – to build the infrastructure the people needed to reach their potential. My father wanted to do great things, Jaskiran, but he never got a chance to see his plans come to fruition. I hope, just like Sayyid, to continue his work. Look at this place,' Ashok continued, making an expansive gesture toward the tomb. 'For hundreds of years, people have marvelled at the beauty of their work, and they will admire it for hundreds of years to come. Can you name me a son that has left a greater gift to his father than this?'

'No, I can't think of another example,' Jaskiran replied, looking at the structure again as if for the first time. After a moment, Ashok turned away. 'I thought we could walk through the gardens,' he said. 'Maybe even venture as far as some of the other tombs. Their enclosures are even quieter than the Char Bagh here. You wouldn't believe you were in the middle of a city of almost twenty million people.'

Jaskiran followed Ashok away from the main path, and they began to walk along the perimeter of the thirty-acre grounds that surrounded the tomb. The garden itself was laid out in a grid system, with the paths enclosing the square lawns on all sides. The water channels that ran through the centre of the paths culminated in small fountains at each junction. Trees dotted the perimeter of the lawn, so in the low afternoon sun, their shadows stretched across the orange-hued dust beneath their feet. It would have been easy to simply walk and enjoy the last hours of sunlight, but Jaskiran had an important job to do. She took the voice recorder from her bag and hit record, folding her arm so that it could rest level with her shoulder.

'Down to business,' said Ashok on seeing the recorder. 'So, what do you want to ask me?'

'I guess the first question is: why politics?' responded Jaskiran. 'It seems that you would be a better history teacher.' She smirked at Ashok.

'Ouch, you take no prisoners, Jaskiran,' he laughed. 'You're lucky I'm not offended and call this whole interview off,' he joked.

'Seriously though,' Jaskiran prompted. 'What made you want to pursue a career in politics? Was it simply to follow in your father's footsteps?'

'In part, yes,' replied Ashok. 'It was the desire to make a difference. It's as simple as that.'

'You don't think our politicians are doing that now?'

'They're certainly making a difference but I'm sure few would say that the changes are for the better.'

'That outlook can't endear you to your political masters considering they're the ones in power,' pointed out Jaskiran. 'I mean, surely that puts your nomination for chief minister at risk?'

Ashok made a dismissive gesture. 'They're happy because my rhetoric is focused against our opponents,' he said. 'That's who I take aim at now. Anyway, there's a long way to go and I have a lot of work to do before I can even begin to think about all that. Right now, the people of Delhi are my focus.'

'But even you must admit that you have not been in politics long enough to be handed such a position when there are more experienced candidates within your party?'

'Yes, but they are the old guard,' responded Ashok. 'They have been around too long and have been indoctrinated in the politics of the past. It's toxic. It puts the individual's desires before the good of the party and the party's interests ahead of the welfare of the people. Voters are fed up, and that's why they support me. I am young and offer a new way to do things. The party can see how popular I am becoming, and they realise that it is time to embrace new-age politicians like me. Otherwise, they will see those votes go to their rivals.'

'Do you mean that you'd defect to another party if you weren't nominated to stand for chief minister?' ventured Jaskiran.

'I didn't say that.'

'Perhaps you *are* a true politician,' Jaskiran quipped, and Ashok laughed.

She could see that he was more relaxed than he had seemed when she first spotted him at the entrance. The same easy-going, charismatic manner that she had witnessed at the rally was returning. *He's slipping into character*, she thought. *The outward face of the politician.*

'In all seriousness, I'm not here to play party politics,' said Ashok. 'Shouting down opponents, stalling legislation, sit-ins, walkouts – these are the reasons why progress happens at a snail's pace in this country.'

'Do you really think that one man can change that?' Jaskiran asked. She couldn't hide the lack of conviction in her voice.

'I have to,' Ashok replied resolutely.

She recalled that this was the same rhetoric he had used at his rally. There, his words had sparked excitement and joy; here, they were robbed of gravitas and seemed naive and idealistic. Despite his self-belief, Jaskiran, in all her cynicism, couldn't help but feel that he was just a man and one man couldn't change a whole lot in India, not anymore.

As they continued to walk through the gardens, Jaskiran noticed small green parrots darting over the lawns. The mausoleum itself, partially hidden from view behind the greenery of the trees, would reappear a few steps later, shaping the horizon as resolutely as it had done for five hundred years. Ashok continued to speak of politics and his desire for change. However, Jaskiran realised that she still had little idea of who he really was – like someone staring at a shadow, unable to set their eyes on the form from which it had been cast.

In a pause from his recital, she tried to change the subject. 'What did you do before politics?' she asked. 'When we last spoke, you had mentioned that you were successful outside of politics.'

'I did say that, didn't I?' said Ashok. 'I apologise if I came across as arrogant, but I was only trying to convince you that I wasn't in it for myself. The truth is I've been very fortunate. I started my construction company some years ago, building hotels, data centres, that sort of thing.'

‘You’re in construction?’ Jaskiran asked teasingly.

‘You wouldn’t think so, would you? While you won’t find me mixing cement, every worthwhile project needs men in suits to turn it from a dream to something real.’

They sat down on the steps of the terrace. From there, Jaskiran could see the western gate to the grounds from where they had begun. She noticed that the sun had fallen past the treeline, and the light was fading. *We will soon be asked to leave*, she thought, feeling disappointed.

‘Running my own company has taught me a lot,’ Ashok was saying now, ‘and not just about the construction business. It was the first time that I witnessed the outright corruption that is endemic in our country.’ He shook his head in disapproval before continuing, ‘It was so widespread and rampant that it seemed to be woven into the very fabric of the people. Everyone from the government officials down to the labourers wanted more of the profit for themselves. If I refused, there would be labour shortages, stealing of supplies and delaying of permissions. I had to work twice as hard because half my profits disappeared in payouts.’

Ashok turned to Jaskiran. ‘How many other people are there like me in India, desperate to change things for the better?’ he asked. ‘And how many never reach their goal because of the society that we belong to?’ Ashok shook his head. The emotion was clearly visible on his face. ‘Unrealised potential – there’s nothing more tragic, Jaskiran.’

They talked some more, and not just about Ashok. He asked Jaskiran about her life, family and career. She was aware that it was now less of an interview and more of a conversation, but for once she was happy to relax and not feel the need to be so officious. She decided to enjoy the moment. Eventually, guards approached and asked them to leave so they could lock the gates for the night.

Ashok stood and looked around at the darkening shapes of the surrounding garden. 'Perhaps we can visit the other sites another time?' he asked. 'Sure,' Jaskiran agreed. Even in the failing light, she could see a smile spread across his face. 'For another interview, perhaps?' she added, causing his smile to falter.

As they made their way to the gate, she asked him about his upbringing.

'You mean after my parents died?' he said, his face seeming to take on a look of deep concentration as he recollected distant memories.

'There's not much to say. They passed away when I was very young, and I had to go on without them.'

'And you were raised by your extended family?'

'In a way, I guess. When I wasn't at boarding school, I was bounced around between my uncles and aunts. It is a common misconception that an orphan has no parents. It may be true in the traditional sense, but in my experience, an orphan has many mothers and fathers. And they're all desperate to leave their mark on the child, like scars,' he added almost bitterly.

'Was it an unhappy childhood?' Jaskiran prodded, feeling like she had finally peeled back the hard exterior to his core.

Ashok's eyes filled with sorrow, and he nodded before he spoke. 'It was tough and a lonely way to grow up,' he said, 'but it ultimately made me into the man I am today, so there's that.' He smiled. 'You're good, Jaskiran. You've got me speaking about a time in my life that I would rather forget. But perhaps we should stop, if for no other reason than not to end a pleasant afternoon on such a sour note.'

'Of course,' said Jaskiran. As they approached the gate in silence, Jaskiran admired the deep red glow on the horizon, the last hurrah of a retreating sun. When she looked up at him, she smiled slightly.

'I almost forgot,' he said impulsively. 'I'm throwing a party this weekend. There will be a lot of important people there. I'd love for you to attend. I can introduce you to everyone.'

'A party?'

'It's to celebrate the success of the rally. But, in fact, the truth is, it's more of an excuse to get some very influential people together. Even the very rich will turn up if they know there will be free food and alcohol.'

'Sounds like fun,' said Jaskiran immediately. 'I'd love to come.' She was unsure if her delight was at the prospect of rubbing shoulders with celebrities or to see Ashok again.

'Sounds like a deal,' Ashok said. He hesitated awkwardly, not knowing how best to say goodbye.

Jaskiran felt it too and held out a hand. 'Well, until we meet again, Mr Chopra.'

They both began to laugh as Ashok took her hand gently. 'Yes, until we meet again, Ms Sohal.

20

ACROSS THE ROAD FROM the gates of the Rohini bus depot, Rajesh straddled his scooter while tucking into a bowl of aloo chaat from the nearby street vendor. As he ate, he swiped a hand at the mosquitoes that menaced under the light from the streetlamps. He felt his pocket vibrating, and taking the phone out with his free hand, he saw a message from Jaskiran: 'Where are you? We need to talk.' He slipped his phone back into his pocket, the message unanswered. He felt guilty keeping Jaskiran in the dark about what he was doing but felt as if he needed to stay in control of the story. He wasn't ready to share what he had just yet.

Rajesh looked a little way down the street, where the vendor was busy serving a line of bus drivers waiting for a cheap meal. The vendor knew the drivers well and had told Rajesh that the driver for the 167 bus five nights ago was likely a man called Suraj Babu, and he was still out on his route. Deciding to wait for his return, Rajesh had been stationed across from the entrance for almost an hour before finally seeing the lime-green 167 bus turn the corner and approach the depot.

Discarding the paper bowl, Rajesh quickly crossed the road, dodging motorcycles and rickshaws in order to follow the bus as it entered the depot. Past the gates was a large expanse of dirt and gravel with row upon row of buses that had completed their routes for the day or had returned to the depot to switch drivers. Several low-level concrete buildings were dotted around the periphery, including a toilet block, prayer room and another that housed the cramped offices of the clerical staff. Drivers mingled in small groups everywhere. Some stood around smoking, sharing stories and laughing together, while others sat in circles on the floor, eating their dinners from plastic carrier bags and metal containers before they headed off on their routes once again. Drivers slept on the roofs of buses while others fitted fans to the inside of their cabs.

The 167 was parked at the far end of the depot. The driver jumped out of the cab, stretched and spat on the floor.

'Suraj Babu?' Rajesh asked as he approached the short, scrawny figure.

The driver peered up at Rajesh, his eyebrows arched as he tried to identify the stranger. And then, all of a sudden, his eyes were full of fear. He struck out an arm and slapped Rajesh hard across the face before turning and running in the opposite direction.

'Fuck!' cried Rajesh, staggering backward while raising a hand to his stinging cheek. It had caught him completely by surprise. By the time he had recovered his composure, there was no sign of the driver. 'Shit,' he muttered under his breath, his anger flaring as he began running to the end of the bus. He stopped again, looking left and right, but there was still no sign of Suraj. Standing still, he listened and could hear the faint sound of running feet somewhere to his right. He ran in that direction, slowing to check between the rows of buses until the narrow path ended and he was out in the open. Scanning the grounds, he thought he saw a figure slip between two buses across the forecourt. Rajesh ran after him, but by the time he reached the buses, there was no sign of anyone.

Rajesh began to feel desperate. He hurried through the rows of buses, looking underneath and inside the vehicles but to no avail. Suraj had disappeared. He asked some drivers standing nearby if that they had seen Suraj, but they simply shrugged and gave little indication that they even understood the question. Rajesh was aware there must have been a camaraderie between the drivers, and he was an outsider. They would be reluctant to help him. He kicked the side of a bus and swore. Catching his breath, he touched the side of his cheek, which was still tender.

It was at that moment that he heard something. Not the sound of feet on gravel as he had been expecting, but the soft thud of metal straining and shifting. It was coming from over his right shoulder, but Rajesh resisted the urge to look. Instead, he made a show of shaking his head in frustration and walking away. He took a left turn and passed two buses before suddenly taking another left, using the buses as cover to double back to where he had heard the noise.

Rajesh stopped close to where he suspected the sound was coming from. Kneeling in the shadows, he listened in silence. After just a few moments, Rajesh heard the sounds again as Suraj appeared on the roof of the neighbouring bus. The sound had been the aluminium roof plates bending under his weight. Rajesh watched the driver creep to the edge of the roof.

Rajesh waited in the shadows for the right moment to pounce.

Suraj tentatively lowered himself down from the roof, his slight frame landing softly in the dirt. Almost immediately, Rajesh emerged from the shadows and ran full speed toward him. Suraj turned in terror as he heard Rajesh's hurried footsteps approached, but there was no time to run. Rajesh held out his arms and readied himself to collide with Suraj, but there was nothing. Rajesh, overextended, lost his balance and fell to the floor, his momentum sending him crashing through the gravel.

He looked to the spot where Suraj had been standing, but there was no one there. It was as if Suraj had evaporated before him. He then saw the shuffling shadow beneath the bus and realised that the driver had dropped to the ground and crawled away. He was already on the other side of the bus and getting to his feet. Rajesh sprung up as fast as he could, ignoring his aching muscles and scraped knees. Out in the depot forecourt, he caught up with the fleeing Suraj and intercepted him by the toilet blocks.

Rajesh grabbed him by the collar and pinned him to the wall. 'Calm down!' he yelled. 'I'm not here to hurt you. I just want to ask you some questions!'

'I'm sorry, sir, they made me do it!' cried Suraj. 'They made me!' He was almost in tears.

'What are you talking about?'

'They told me that you had killed your girlfriend,' sobbed the driver. 'I had to give a statement that you were on my bus at a certain time, or they threatened to have me fired if I didn't do it. I can't afford to lose my job, sir!'

'You think I'm Vivek?' Rajesh asked.

Suraj stopped struggling. 'You're not?' His arms went limp as he looked at Rajesh, confused.

'I'm a journalist. My name is Rajesh.'

Suraj let out a sigh of relief. 'Sir, I thought Vivek had escaped and was looking to get his revenge.' He laughed nervously, which angered Rajesh.

'Behenchod, there's an innocent man in jail because of your testimony.'

Suraj's expression quickly turned back to one of contrition. 'I know, sir, I know, but what could I do? They would have had me fired and beaten me too!'

'Who? The police?'

Suraj nodded.

'What were their names?'

'Sir, do you think they tell me their names?'

Their altercation was gathering attention from other bus drivers nearby, and a small group began to approach for a closer look.

'Ai, Babu!' came the call behind Rajesh. 'What's going on?'

Rajesh realised that he still had hold of Suraj's collar. He let go and stepped away from the bus driver.

'You should go,' whispered Suraj. 'I shouldn't be speaking to you. If this gets back to them, I could get into a lot of trouble.'

The group of men stopped a few feet from Rajesh and Suraj. The apparent leader was a middle-aged man with an unshaven face and dark complexion. He came closer and squared up to Rajesh. Taking the beedi from his mouth, he blew the smoke toward Rajesh provocatively.

'What do you want with Babu?' asked the man.

'Nothing, uncle,' Rajesh said casually, ignoring the hostility. 'I was on his bus earlier today, and now I can't find my phone. I thought he stole it, but it was my mistake.'

The man turned towards Suraj, who was still standing against the wall.

'Is this true, Babu?'

'Yes, he thought I stole his phone, but I would never do that,' Suraj answered quickly. He smiled nervously.

'Well, if that was all, you can leave,' said the man to Rajesh. 'Now.'

'Of course, uncle. I'm leaving.'

Rajesh shuffled away toward the main entrance. At the gate, he looked back and saw that the group of men was still watching him. The leader was speaking to Suraj. Rajesh walked to his waiting scooter, his head spinning. He now knew for certain that the police were covering up the truth. But the question was why.

He took out his phone once again. There was no delaying the inevitable any longer. He needed to tell Jaskiran everything that he had discovered.

21

IT WAS EIGHT-THIRTY in the evening when Sabeena arrived outside Thai Garden on the edge of Champa Gali. She joined Jaskiran at a small table outside. The streets were still relatively busy as commuters gathered to share a meal with colleagues before the long trip home. Sabeena ordered herself a diet Coke and removed the sunglasses she wore despite the sun having long since set.

'Sorry I'm late,' she said as she arrived. 'I had to return this really vulgar sweater Karan's mother bought me the other day. It's a turtleneck – I mean, who wears a turtleneck anymore?' She made a disgusted face. 'It was an obvious ploy to make me appear more modest, but she couldn't have got it more wrong – that sweater makes my chest look huge.'

Jaskiran couldn't help but laugh. 'It's okay, I didn't mind,' she replied. She looked at her phone, but still no reply from Rajesh. She had hoped to tell him what she had discovered while speaking to Professor Randrapathy. His silence frustrated her and demonstrated a lack of professionalism. *Perhaps I was wrong to partner up with him*, she thought.

'What's wrong, babe?' asked Sabeena, studying Jaskiran's face. 'Somebody giving you the cold shoulder?'

'No, it's nothing,' replied Jaskiran. She put her phone away. 'I've just been so busy with work, and home is ... well, home,' she smiled. 'It's actually nice to have some time to myself.'

'I hear you, babe,' Sabeena said with a nod. 'Sometimes I have to get away from Karan and his family. I mean, I love them all, but there are times when I'm just sick of having to deal with their bullshit. Some advice – when you get married, make sure you and your husband get your own place. Don't move in with his family. Until I made that mistake, I had no idea that Karan was such a mummy's boy. He's always taking her side over mine. It's pathetic.' Sabeena took a breath and then continued, 'Speaking of useless creatures, has one managed to steal that big heart of yours?'

'No, not yet, despite my family's best efforts. They actually tried to set me up with a guy last night. They even invited him over for dinner.'

'Shut up. Who was he?'

'Just some friend of a cousin. A financial analyst who emigrated to America. Now he thinks that he's better than us. He spent the whole evening talking about his life in New York and how much money he earns. I guess he thought it would impress me.'

'And did it?' Sabeena asked, flashing Jaskiran a naughty smile. 'I mean, a man with a big paycheque should not be dismissed lightly.'

'Please. The only one who looked aroused was Gurvinder. He wants me to marry him, no questions asked.'

Sabeena tutted. 'I hope you put him in his place?'

'Yes, but ever since he took over the family business after my father stepped down, he behaves as if he runs the whole house. I know that he's the one putting crazy ideas in my mother's head, making her worry about me becoming a spinster or, worse, marrying the *wrong type*.' Jaskiran used her fingers for air quotes.

'Show me a mother's definition of the right husband, and I will show you a bored wife,' Sabeena declared.

They ordered their meals and then continued catching up. Jaskiran always looked forward to these casual dinners with Sabeena. She had only ever met a handful of women as confident and self-assured as Sabeena, and none were as young. They tended to be older, their confidence growing with age and their positions of responsibility, but Sabeena seemed to have been born with an unwillingness to concede when she was in the right no matter the foe. She would have made a great lawyer, but she had other plans.

When the young waiter returned with their food, Jaskiran looked on with relish as he placed a plate of prawn satay with a sweet and sour dipping sauce on the table, followed by a colourful pounded papaya salad with ruby-red slices of chilli. A selection of crispy fried vegetables in a tamarind sauce sat beside a bowl of white sticky rice, and finally, there were slices of chicken with green chilli and basil leaves. They ate in silence, savouring the flavours of each dish. By the time they finished, Sabeena raised another topic.

'Did Rajesh tell you what happened with the Anjali story?'

Jaskiran looked at her plate, unsure how to respond. She finally said, 'He mentioned that Vinod has reassigned him.'

'Did he say anything else? He snuck out this afternoon. I have a feeling he's disobeying Vinod's orders.'

'He didn't say anything to me,' Jaskiran said quickly with a growing sense of frustration. They hadn't been teamed up for an entire day, and Rajesh was already working the story solo.

'I can sense that you're being coy with me, dear,' said Sabeena, putting on an expression of mock hurt. 'I never would have thought your friendship with Rajesh took precedence over ours, but I shouldn't be surprised. I suppose he's not bad-looking in a boyish kind of way.'

'What?' Jaskiran asked in genuine confusion. 'Rajesh and me? Please, there's nothing going on between us. It's just that …'

'It's just what?' Sabeena prompted with an eyebrow arched.

'Okay, fine. Yes, he's still investigating the story. But I honestly don't know where he went today.' Jaskiran shook her head at her inability to hide the truth from Sabeena.

'Good,' Sabeena replied emphatically. 'I was hoping he would. Any journalist worth his salt would do the same thing. What he's talking about – a second killer, incompetent cops – it's a big story. A career-defining one.'

'Hang on, but Vinod ...?' Jaskiran began.

'I'd be the first to tell Vinod when he was in the wrong,' said Sabeena, 'but this time he actually had no choice. I'd have done the same thing in his place, publicly anyway. You see, Rajesh is definitely on to something, but he made a rookie mistake: he revealed his hand too early. The cops know that he doesn't have enough and are trying to shut the story down before it gains momentum. It happens all the time. The trick is to make sure that you have something to dangle over them to ensure that they don't get too heavy-handed. Proof of a scandal, a recording, compromising photos – that sort of thing. It helps keep them in line. Rajesh was too eager; young men always are. So Vinod reassigned him hoping that was the end of the matter. But I'm glad to see that Rajesh has shown some initiative.'

'Well,' said Jaskiran, 'then you'll be glad to hear that I'm also on the story.'

'What?' Sabeena exclaimed in genuine surprise. 'You're working on it together?'

Jaskiran nodded, smirking.

'How did you manage to convince him? What am I saying, of course he gave you the byline,' Sabeena proclaimed.

'What's that supposed to mean?' Jaskiran replied.

'I'm not judging, Jaskiran. Far from it. It's about time that you used some of those feminine charms to get ahead. We have to use all the weapons at our disposal.'

'Rajesh needed help with the story, and I offered to help him. I didn't flirt, there were no fluttering eyelashes – and there's certainly nothing going on between the two of us,' Jaskiran answered categorically.

'Whatever you say. Here's to you anyway. If you and Rajesh are right, you'll leave Vinod no choice but to put you back on the crime beat.' Sabeena lifted her glass ceremonially before taking another sip.

Jaskiran looked almost ashamed, recalling the emotion in Professor Randrapathy's final words to her that afternoon. 'That's what I thought when Rajesh first told me what he knew. Now I'm not sure that was the right reason.'

'How so?' Sabeena asked, distracted as she motioned for the waiter to bring the bill.

'I mean, at first, I wanted the story to bring it to people's attention. But when I heard how Vinod had mistreated Rajesh, I remembered how he had done it to me too. I took the story to prove Vinod wrong. Anjali became secondary to my own career and office politics. I was treating her death like an opportunity for myself. I'm not sure that's the kind of person I want to become.'

Sabeena rolled her eyes. 'It's not your job to get emotionally involved with every story, Jaskiran,' she chided. 'God, if you did that, you'd be a wreck by the end of your first week on the crime beat. What you're doing is normal. All reporters – all good reporters, anyway – need to be able to stay detached from the stories they cover. It helps you see all the angles and keeps you open-minded.'

Jaskiran half-heartedly nodded. Sabeena reached out and placed a hand over Jaskiran's. 'I'm not saying that you shouldn't feel a connection,' she said. 'Just don't bloody well turn it into a crusade. It won't end well.'

Sabeena was about to begin speaking once again when a phone vibrated. She instinctively reached for her phone only to see a blank screen. 'It's not me,' she said, looking up at Jaskiran, who began rummaging through her bag to find her phone. Taking it out, she read the message.

'It's Rajesh. He says that he has to meet me now. He must have found something important if it can't wait until the morning.'

'I'm sure that's it,' Sabeena said with a wry smile. 'Fine. Go. I'll take care of the bill, but you better give me a full briefing tomorrow. If you're on to something real, I'll make sure that you're given the time to work on it.'

'Thank you,' said Jaskiran, reaching over and clutching Sabeena's hand before grabbing her bag to leave.

She took an auto to the Old City. Rajesh had requested they meet at a coffee house not far from the entrance to Jama Masjid. Even at this hour, the roads, side streets and alleyways were heaving with people, and the auto struggled to progress through the ever-increasing obstacles and pedestrians who walked out across its path. Eventually, Jaskiran told the driver to stop and made the remainder of the journey on foot through the maze-like avenues.

Entering the dimly lit Jain Coffee House, Jaskiran spotted Rajesh sitting alone at a corner table. 'What the hell Rajesh? Where have you been all day?' Jaskiran asked reproachfully. 'We're supposed to be a team, but I found out from Sabeena that you're sneaking out of the office. That is just the kind of attention you're not supposed to be drawing to yourself.'

'I'm sorry,' said Rajesh. 'I just needed to be one hundred per cent sure before I told you.'

'What are you talking about?' Jaskiran asked, sliding onto the plastic bench opposite Rajesh. 'Tell me what?'

'It's big, Jaskiran. Anjali was never on that bus with Vivek. The bus driver lied because the police threatened him. He admitted that to me himself. In fact, Anjali had been to a toy store, which matches Roshan's story. This afternoon, I went to the store that he had mentioned.

The owners confirmed that she was there the night she was killed. They even have her on the recording from the security camera.'

Jaskiran was struck by the news. Sitting up to attention, her mind raced through the ramifications of what Rajesh had just said. 'But if all that's true, then the confession—'

'Exactly,' cut in Rajesh. 'That's why it makes no mention of a car. Not because Vivek is trying to protect an accomplice …'

'… but because the police are trying to frame Vivek,' Jaskiran concluded.

'It's also the reason why the deputy commissioner was so eager to get me to stop investigating,' said Rajesh. 'It explains why he put Vinod under pressure and why they told the neighbours to not talk to the press.'

'Did the bus driver say anything else? Will he go on record?'

'I don't think so,' said Rajesh with a shake of his head. 'He's too scared of the police, and I think, of some of the other drivers, to come forward himself.'

'What about the store owners? Did they see who Anjali was with?'

'No, but they identified the car. It's a silver Mercedes, a C-Class cabriolet. There can't be too many people in her circle of friends who could afford such a car – and the protection of the police.'

'But maybe a colleague could,' Jaskiran replied.

Rajesh's brow furrowed and he looked confused.

'What? You think you're the only one with new leads?' Jaskiran allowed herself a satisfied smile. 'Anjali had a job at the Delhi Financial Corporation. They're a government body that awards loans to small business enterprises. She worked in their accounts department and was being lined up for a permanent position. How much would you bet that one of her colleagues drives a silver Mercedes?' Jaskiran was pleased her breakthrough at the university was looking to be even more helpful than she had hoped. 'I'll pay them a visit tomorrow morning,' she added.

'And I want to go and speak to Vivek's parents,' said Rajesh. 'Maybe Vivek has had an alibi all along, but it's being ignored. Might be worth following up.'

'There's one more thing,' Jaskiran said. 'Sabeena knows that we're investigating the story.'

Rajesh made a face to convey his surprise, but Jaskiran cut him off before he could formulate a response.

'Don't worry,' Jaskiran continued, 'she's on our side. She wants to be kept updated on our progress. And when the time's right, she'll make sure Vinod runs the story.'

'Fine,' Rajesh replied, placated if still a little confused. He then exhaled loudly and placed his hands behind his head. 'I have to pinch myself that this is actually happening.'

'We're not done yet, but remember one thing, Rajesh,' Jaskiran said sternly. 'We are working on this story together. So that means I need to know what you know when you know it. No more radio silence and doing it alone.'

'Understood,' Rajesh replied sincerely.

Satisfied she had made her feelings clear, Jaskiran stood to leave.

'Good, we should get home. Tomorrow is going to be a busy day.' Jaskiran was aware that it was late.

'You're right. Let me drop you home,' offered Rajesh.

'No, it's fine. I'll catch an auto,' Jaskiran replied, knowing full well the commotion it would cause if anyone was to see her being escorted home so late by a male companion.

'Come on, it's late,' insisted Rajesh. 'It's the least I can do for dragging you all this way.' Rajesh pushed further, and reluctantly Jaskiran relented.

Outside, Rajesh brought the scooter out from the rear courtyard of the coffee shop and gestured for Jaskiran to get on. Riding pillion so close behind Rajesh, she could smell the fading scent of aftershave from his shirt and the more pungent aroma of sweat. Rajesh fired up the motor, and they were soon on the move, while Jaskiran allowed herself to get lost in the nightly spectacle of the old city.

22

ARRIVING AT HER HOME in West Punjabi Bagh, Jaskiran let herself in through the main gate. Waving to Rajesh while he turned the scooter, she made her way up the path to the front door. The garden lights had been left on for her, and the house seemed quiet. She expected her family to already be in bed, so was caught off guard by the sight of Gurvinder standing by the door. He was about to say something, then stopped for a moment as if he had only just recognised her.

'Why are you home so late?' The hostility was clear in his voice. Jaskiran glanced at him before passing down the hall towards the stairs. His eyelids looked heavy, and his lips were wet. It was clear he had been drinking.

'What's it to you?' she retorted. 'I already told Maa I was having dinner with Sabeena.'

'That wasn't Sabeena on the scooter though, was it?' Gurvinder said triumphantly as if it were his ace card.

Jaskiran stopped and turned to face him. 'No, that was a colleague of mine who offered to give me a ride home,' she snapped. 'Or would you prefer that I get in an auto with a stranger?' The contempt was clear in her voice.

'Don't get smart with me.'

'What are you even doing waiting up for me? It's not your job to police my whereabouts. In fact, it's not anyone's job.'

'Don't flatter yourself. I wasn't waiting for you. I was having a drink.'

'Where's Nisha?' Jaskiran asked, sensing there was more to the story.

Gurvinder didn't answer right away. Instead, he brought the glass to his lips. 'Out,' he replied finally before taking another gulp.

The situation became clearer to Jaskiran. It had been obvious for some time that her sister-in-law was spending more time outside the house and away from her husband's company. The time they did spend together seemed to be filled with awkward silences or blazing rows. Gurvinder had been waiting for Nisha; Jaskiran just happened to come home first.

Gurvinder didn't like the look his sister was giving him. It looked like pity.

'Don't try and deflect to Nisha,' he said, approaching her on unsteady legs and waving a finger. 'I know where she is. But you? You're out late at night, who knows where, lying about who you are with. Don't disgrace the family, Jaskiran, or not even Papa can protect you.'

'Fuck you, Gurvinder! Don't you dare threaten me!'

Before he could reply, a light came on from the upstairs hallway, and they could hear the sound of footsteps.

'What's going on down there? Is Jaskiran back?' It was their mother's sleepy but concerned voice.

'Yes, Maa,' Jaskiran replied. 'Go back to bed.'

Jaskiran met Gurvinder's gaze defiantly before turning and heading up the stairs, her brother's heavy breathing audible behind her.

23

By the time Rajesh reached home, he was exhausted. He wanted nothing more than to collapse on his charpoy and sleep a dreamless sleep. Opening the apartment door, he entered to find his mother sitting at the table. 'You're back so late,' she said, it almost sounded like an accusation.

'Yes, work, like I told you before. Why did you wait up?' Rajesh was in no mood for his mother's chiding.

'You must be hungry,' said his mother. 'Sit down. I'll make roti.'

'No, it's fine,' protested Rajesh. 'I ate earlier.' But his mother waved him away and fired up the stove. Realising that there was no talking her out of it, he went and washed up. When the food was ready, Rajesh ate greedily, realising that he was hungrier than he had thought. Street vendors, he surmised, were no substitute for a mother's cooking.

After his meal, he sat back in the chair and thought of Vivek Trivedi. *How long will it be before Vivek can enjoy a home-cooked meal again?* he wondered. The thought took him by surprise. Rajesh wasn't accustomed to bringing his work home with him. Would it always be like this, or would he learn to block it out? He thought of Sajid and the way he had looked in the bar. The sorrow that seemed to surround him gave Rajesh his answer.

He was brought out of his contemplation by his mother's presence beside him. Looking down at him, she placed a letter onto the table without saying a word.

Rajesh's heart sank; it was from Credit Today, one of the lenders he had used to borrow money. The content of the letter was a demand for missed payments and threats of debt recovery. His embarrassment that his secret had been exposed in such a way now turned to anger.

'You opened my mail?' he snapped at his mother.

'Look again before you take that tone. It was addressed to me,' his mother responded, not suffering any insolence. Rajesh saw now that she was telling the truth. The letter was indeed addressed to his mother. The company was vowing to pursue her for the unpaid debt if Rajesh couldn't find the money.

'They can't do this,' Rajesh cried. 'Ma, they don't have the authority. We can fight them.'

'With what?' she snapped. 'We don't have the money to beat them in court. You think I don't know what these people do? They will come here causing trouble. Soon all our neighbours and friends will know that we borrow money that we can't pay back. The banks will find out as well. They'll make it so no one will ever lend us money again. We won't be able to send Roopa and Amit to university or pay for their weddings. You'll ruin their futures just as you have ruined yours.'

The accusation hit Rajesh like a punch to the chest. 'You think that I meant for any of this to happen?' he asked, his voice little more than a whisper.

'You made me believe that things were going well with your job,' she said. 'How else could my son afford to go out drinking and partying with friends so often, I thought. I believed you when you said that things would be okay, but it was all a lie. You are living a lie.'

'It's not that bad, Ma,' he said unconvincingly. 'I can repay this.'

'How?' she asked, her voice rising. 'You owe them twenty thousand rupees! And that's on top of what we need to pay the bills here. Amit's school is already asking for money for his books for next term.'

'I never asked for this!' Rajesh erupted. 'I never wanted this responsibility. I did everything you and Daddy wanted of me. After years of humiliation, I graduated, got a job and I still don't have anything to show for it. Everything I earn goes to get us by – just surviving to the next month.'

'That's how your father and I had to live to get you through school.'

'At least you had a choice, Ma. No one ever gave me that.'

'I didn't choose this either,' his mother retorted. 'Raising you children without your father and with no money was not my choice.' She got up and walked across the room towards the kitchen. Taking a spice tin from the rack, she pulled out a wad of rupee notes. 'Still, I put you first because all we ever wanted was the best for you.'

Rajesh looked at the roll of money and then at his mother's face. Her eyes were wet with tears.

'Your earrings?' Rajesh asked. His mother's silence only confirmed the truth. Chastened by her tears and the thought of his father, Rajesh felt contrite. 'Daddy got you those. If you had come to me, I would have found a way.'

'I have my responsibilities too. I will pay these people their money.' His mother dabbed at her eyes with the edge of her dupatta and, placing the money back in the spice tin, retreated to her bedroom.

'With this promotion, things will be easier for us,' Rajesh said after her.

She looked back at him and, unable to muster a smile or offers of reassurance that she believed him, bowed her head and closed the door, leaving Rajesh alone in the silence.

24

THE NEXT MORNING, JASKIRAN briefed Sabeena on everything Rajesh had discovered. Even as she made the revelations, Jaskiran got the impression Sabeena was more intrigued than her muted response led on, but Jaskiran put it down to experience. She correctly assumed that everything loses its ability to shock the more you witness it. Jaskiran went on to tell her senior of Rajesh's wish to visit Vivek's parents and her own desire to visit the Delhi Financial Corporation. True to her word, Sabeena waved both requests through without hesitation, and Jaskiran was soon in an autorickshaw on her way to speak to Deepak Rao.

The corporation's headquarters were housed in a modern office block in a little lane off Sewa Marg, nestled in an enclave between world-renowned banks, government buildings and the shadow of Tihar Jail. The reception desk was staffed by a couple of young women who Jaskiran thought had been rather liberal with the makeup brush that morning. 'Good morning, madam,' one of the receptionists chirped. 'Are you here for a meeting?'

'Good morning,' Jaskiran replied. 'Actually, I don't have an appointment.' She noticed the smile vanish from the woman's rose-red lips. The two receptionists exchanged looks.

This must be a daily annoyance for them, Jaskiran thought, *people just turning up hoping to talk to someone immediately for a loan*. 'My name is Jaskiran Sohal and I'm a reporter with the *Delhi Daily*,' she quickly continued. 'I'm here regarding one of your employees, Anjali Mangal. I'm sure you've seen the news reports. I was just wondering if I could talk to her manager, Deepak Rao.'

Jaskiran again noticed the sideways glances between the two colleagues, but this time the look was less of contempt and more of concern.

'Oh, madam,' said the first young woman, 'I'm afraid that would not be possible.'

'Look, I'm not here to cause trouble. I was just hoping for a few words from Mr Rao as I understand he was impressed with the work she was doing here.'

'Madam, you don't understand. Mr Rao is no longer with us.'

Jaskiran could see that the woman now looked genuinely upset.

'What do you mean? Does he no longer work here?'

The receptionist's lips began to quiver. 'No, madam,' she said quietly, 'he's dead.' She began distracting herself with some papers on her desk in an attempt not to be overcome with emotion and ruin her mascara.

'I'm sorry to hear that,' Jaskiran managed to say as she processed the unexpected news. Her instincts were telling her that something wasn't right. 'If you don't mind me asking, how did he die?'

'He was struck by a car two weeks ago,' said the other receptionist. 'The driver didn't even stop to help. Such cruel people in this world,' she added shaking her head.

Alarm bells began ringing in Jaskiran's head. 'Listen to me, it is very important that I speak to someone who worked with Deepak and Anjali right away,' she insisted. Jaskiran's urgency startled the receptionists, who seemed unsure about how much authority someone in Jaskiran's profession commanded. Finally, the second woman relented and reached for the telephone.

'Okay, I'll see what I can do,' she said. 'Please take a seat.' She pointed to a line of chairs against the far wall.

Jaskiran sat on one of the chairs and tried to make sense of what she had just heard. Two colleagues dead only two weeks apart seemed more than coincidental. Whatever the connection between the two, she was sure that the answers could be found here.

25

RAHUL YADAV WAS SITTING in his office going over a report on the corporation's monthly unsecured lending when the phone began to ring. He lowered his glasses and placed them on the desk beside the telephone before answering.

'Good morning, sir. I'm sorry to trouble you, but we have a reporter downstairs from the *Delhi Daily* requesting to speak to someone who worked with Deepak Rao and Anjali Mangal.'

'Why?' Rahul replied simply.

The receptionist answered in a hushed tone, 'Sir, she said that she had come to speak to Deepak about the work Anjali did here. She was very surprised to hear that he had also recently passed away. Would you like me to ask her to leave?'

'No, that won't be necessary. I will send someone down in a few minutes.'

'As you wish, sir.'

Rahul slowly put the receiver back down and contemplated his next move. *The reporter was surprised to hear of Deepak's death*, he thought. *Then there is no need to panic.* No one else in the building knew anything more about Deepak's death or had any reason to believe that the recent deaths of their colleagues were suspicious. Rahul would send someone with experience in talking to the press and have them repeat the same few publicly known facts.

Rahul picked up the telephone once again and was dialling the number for Manjot Thakur, one of the senior managers he was sure would be more than equal to the task, when he suddenly stopped. *Did she say* Delhi Daily? *Isn't that the same rag that the reporter who started asking questions at the briefing worked for?* If they were working together, that meant they were getting closer to the truth and to him. He slammed the receiver down in anger. This meant that greedy, incompetent Sagar hadn't scared away the journalists like he claimed he had. Fine, if the deputy commissioner couldn't manage it, he would have to take matters into his own hands. He swiftly picked up the receiver again and began dialling another number. Thakur could wait; he had a more important call to make.

26

RAJESH ALIGHTED FROM THE scooter in front of a small row of hole-in-the-wall stores to ask for directions to Vivek's home. A barber, who was sitting by his vacant chair smoking a beedi, pointed to a small alleyway further up the lane.

'Just turn there. You will find it,' he said before shaking his head slightly as Rajesh thanked him.

Following the directions, Rajesh made his way down a litter-strewn alleyway. On one side, the rear entrances to shops and down-market restaurants faced a line of dilapidated two-storey apartment buildings on the other. Rajesh's phone vibrated in his pocket, and he took it out to read an update from Jaskiran: 'Anjali's manager died two weeks ago. Hit by a car. Suspicious.'

'The plot thickens,' Rajesh said. He turned toward the apartment building, entering through a narrow gap in the wall where there used to be a gate. In the concrete courtyard, he spotted a man disposing of a garbage bag in one of the municipal bins. 'Excuse me,' Rajesh said, approaching the man. 'I am looking for Vivek Trivedi's home. Could you point it out?'

The man closed the lid of the bin and looked silently at the young reporter before asking, 'What business do you have there?'

'I'm a reporter with the *Delhi Daily*. I would like to speak to Vivek's parents about the circumstances surrounding his arrest.'

The man rubbed the sweat away from his forehead with the back of his hand and quietly assessed Rajesh. Finally, he responded. 'They do not want to speak to any more press. They just want to be left alone.' He began to walk towards the exterior staircase that led up to the upper-level apartments.

'You must be Vivek's father?' Rajesh asked, taking a step forward. He had seen pictures of Vivek in the paper and thought he could see similarities with the man standing before him. The thin upper lip and angular nose looked to be features he had passed on to his son. He was a small, thin man with a full head of hair, albeit greying on the sides.

The man stopped on the second step and looked back. 'Yes, I'm Mohan, his father. Please, leave me alone. I've had enough of the press.'

'But Mr Trivedi, sir,' Rajesh pleaded. 'I don't believe Vivek committed the murder. I think he is innocent. I just need to find a way to prove it. Please help me.'

Mohan Trivedi looked on again silently, deliberating whether he could trust Rajesh.

'Okay,' he said softly. 'Come upstairs.'

Inside the apartment, towers of cardboard boxes, some covered with drapes, lined the hallway. Leading Rajesh into a small living room, a look of embarrassment was clearly visible on Mohan's face. He was a proud man, and it pained him to present the cluttered surroundings as the culmination of his life's work. He pulled back the threadbare curtains to allow in more light. 'We have not been here long,' Mohan said as a way of explaining his current situation. 'We haven't even finished unpacking.'

He gestured to Rajesh to a sofa adorned with torn seat cushions while seating himself on a plastic garden chair set against the opposite wall. 'Where did you move here from?' Rajesh asked.

'Punjabi Bagh,' he replied with some pride. 'No other families walking over my head, no listening to their arguments through the walls.'

'If you don't mind,' Rajesh began, 'why did you move?'

Vivek's father clenched his teeth in anger. 'Because I trusted the wrong people,' he said. 'I ran a furniture store in Kirti Nagar with a business partner. Things were very good until the day my business partner cleared out our accounts and disappeared with the money. He left me with all the debts and the headaches of trying to run the business on my own. In the end, the debts began to pile up, and I had to sell my home just to keep the business open. But the final insult is that I later found out my business partner had set up his own furniture store and signed deals with all our old suppliers.'

'Did you not go to the police?' asked Rajesh.

'Yes, but he paid them off, and that was the end of it. Justice costs money in this city, and he has more than me.'

Rajesh shook his head in disgust before realising that it was best to change the subject. 'Will Vivek's mother be joining us?' he asked.

The anger drained from Mohan's face and his shoulders slumped. He shook his head slowly. 'She has taken the news of Vivek's arrest badly,' he said. 'Her sister has taken her to their family home for a while.' He paused before adding, 'There was no room to have them all here.'

'I understand that this is a difficult time for you, and I appreciate you agreeing to talk,' said Rajesh.

'I've talked to all you journalists,' Vivek's father retorted bluntly. 'I kept saying that my son is innocent, but they all just twisted my words, making it seem like I was trying to cover for him. The police say that they have a confession from Vivek. They threatened to arrest me if I kept fighting the matter.'

'Can you tell us how you know Vivek didn't commit the murder?' Rajesh asked.

'Because Vivek was here at home that night. He never left.'

'Can you be sure that he didn't sneak out after you had gone to sleep?'

'There's no way he could have,' explained Mohan. 'I lock the door at night. None of my children can leave after dark without my permission. Vivek and his sisters are good children, but I know that sometimes at their age they get crazy ideas.'

Rajesh studied Mohan's face and felt certain he was telling the truth. Vivek did indeed have an alibi for the night Anjali was murdered, but the testimony of the accused's father was never going to be enough to convince a judge. The sofa creaked as Rajesh sat forward and asked, 'Did you know about Vivek's relationship with Anjali?'

'I knew as much as a father would know,' replied Mohan. 'I saw the changes in his behaviour.' He began to smile at the recollection. 'He took more care in his appearance,' he continued. 'Always playing with his hair in the mirror, buying hair products that made it stiff like cardboard. I would smell the scent of my aftershave on him as he left to go to university. But no more than these small things. He never talked to me about it.'

Rajesh nodded and then asked, 'Do you know when Vivek last spoke to Anjali?'

Mohan shook his head. 'You should speak to Ritu,' he said. Before Rajesh had a chance to ask who Ritu was, Mohan called out in the direction of the narrow hallway. A few seconds later, they heard the bedroom door open, and a young girl no more than ten years old emerged into view.

'Yes, Papa?' she said before she was suddenly overcome with shyness at the sight of the stranger sitting on the sofa. She lowered her eyes and played with her long pigtails.

'This is Ritu, my youngest,' said Mohan. 'She is closer to Vivek than anyone else in the family. Ritu, this man is a reporter and wants to bring Vivek home. Help him by answering his questions.'

'Yes, Papa,' she said, nodding to her father before looking at Rajesh with the singular concentration she usually reserved for quick-fire quizzes at school.

'Hello, Ritu. My name is Rajesh. I have some questions about your brother. I'm sure you can tell me all I need to know.'

Rita didn't hesitate and nodded eagerly. 'I will do my best.'

Rajesh smiled. 'Good, that is all I want. You were with Vivek on Friday night, correct?'

'Yes,' she fired back, happy at what she perceived was the right answer. 'He helped me with my homework that evening.'

'Good,' Rajesh answered. 'What did you study together?'

'Maths,' Ritu beamed. 'Bhaiya is so clever with numbers. There is nothing that he can't work out. He shows me how to do it also.'

'And once you finished your studies, what then?' Rajesh enquired gently.

'We ate dinner, and then Bhaiya went to his room. He stayed there for the rest of the night.'

'Do you know what he was doing in there?' Rajesh added.

'He was studying. He has exams at the end of the month.'

Rajesh now sat forward and spoke slowly, 'Did your brother ever talk to you about his girlfriend, Anjali?'

The question troubled Ritu, and it was clear she was finding it hard to answer.

'You know your brother was dating a girl named Anjali, correct? They were boyfriend and girlfriend?'

'Yes …' Ritu began before hesitating.

'What is it, Ritu?' Rajesh coaxed.

'Sir, Bhaiya and Anjali broke up months ago.'

'What?' Rajesh exclaimed. He looked across at Mohan, who looked just as shocked.

'Bhaiya was very upset at the time. He would sit in his room and hardly speak to anyone. But after a few days, he became his old self again.'

'I remember that,' Mohan proclaimed. 'I'm such a fool. I thought that he was upset at the prospect of us moving here. I didn't realise it was …' he trailed off, clenching his teeth in a bid to contain his emotion.

'Are you sure, Ritu?' Rajesh asked. 'Is it possible that they got back together?'

Ritu shook her head categorically. 'Sir, Bhaiya would never lie to me. He said that he wanted to focus on his studies and get a job. Only then would he look for a girl to date.'

'If I had known this earlier,' Mohan said, 'I would have shouted it to all the papers!'

'Don't blame yourself. The police seemed to have wanted Vivek to be guilty. They would not let such details get in their way,' Rajesh replied. 'Have you had any contact with Vivek since his arrest?'

'No, none,' Mohan replied sullenly. 'I've been asking to talk to him, but they say that Vivek does not want to see me. I know that is a lie.' He looked up at Rajesh. 'But now you know the truth,' he said, growing agitated. 'You can publish that they lied about him being her boyfriend and that he was here the night of the murder. Tell everyone that my boy did nothing wrong!'

'We are investigating the murder, Mr Trivedi, but we do not have enough proof of Vivek's innocence yet,' Rajesh explained. 'If I publish what I have heard now, it could jeopardise our ability to continue investigating. The police could shut us down, and Vivek would remain in jail awaiting trial.'

'Then what are you doing here?' shouted the old man. 'You said that you wanted to help free my boy, but you won't tell people the truth!'

Rajesh noticed a growing resentment emanating from the father. He understood it would seem to Mohan that he was refusing to help. To Mohan, the only thing that mattered was that Vivek was innocent and should be freed. Unfortunately, Rajesh did not have that luxury, and he had to keep his eye on the bigger picture; if Vivek was innocent, it meant that someone else was guilty. Unable to take the awkwardness in the room any longer, Rajesh stood to leave.

'I am doing everything to get to the bottom of this, and the truth will come out. The whole truth.'

Rajesh turned to leave before Mohan spoke softly, 'If you do speak to Vivek, tell him that his father loves him very much. I can't remember the last time I said that to him. He's my son, and I should have protected him from the evils of the world. I failed him.' He seemed close to tears.

Rajesh stopped, struck by Mohan's emotion. He knew how difficult it was to love someone so completely and yet be utterly incapable of helping them. He lingered, not knowing how to say goodbye and leave. The aching silence became deafening as Rajesh struggled to find words for an appropriate response. Thinking of his own father, Rajesh recalled a quote from the Sufi mystic Rumi that his father had recited to him not long before he died. 'Do not despair,' he said quietly to Mohan and Ritu. 'Where there is ruin, there is hope for a treasure.'

27

IT WAS CLOSE TO an hour before someone finally came to speak to Jaskiran. During that time, apart from offering her a refreshment, the receptionists went about their business as if she wasn't there. Finally, a stocky man in his fifties approached and introduced himself as Mr Thakur, a senior manager at the firm. He shook her hand firmly and sat down beside her right there in the foyer, as if to emphasise that he didn't expect this to take long.

'Ms Sohal, you want to speak to me about Deepak and Anjali?' he said, leaning back on the sofa, his maroon tie curving over his protruding belly.

'Yes sir,' replied Jaskiran, 'I was hoping you could tell me about the work they did here.'

'Well,' he replied before wiping the corners of his lips with his thumb and forefinger before continuing. 'Deepak reviewed loan application cases,' said Thakur. 'He decided whether someone was a sound candidate and gave his recommendation for approval. This would be passed on to a committee that would make the final decision. Anjali would help him with these duties by analysing accounts and forecasting, that sort of thing.'

'So they would also be responsible for rejecting applications?'

'Of course, many. We get thousands of applications a month, and we reject the vast majority of them. But I can't tell you any more than that. We have to respect the confidentiality of our clients, even the ones we reject.'

Sensing she was getting off track, Jaskiran decided to focus on Anjali.

'So I take it you would have seen Anjali around the office quite regularly?'

'Yes, quite often,' replied Thakur. 'I work on the same floor, just down the corridor from Deepak and Anjali's office.'

'Excellent,' she replied. 'Then you would know who she was close to here?'

Thakur hesitated momentarily before tilting his head as if the answer were written on the ceiling. 'No one that I can think of.'

'Oh,' exclaimed Jaskiran, exaggerating her surprise. 'You never saw her chatting with any of her colleagues, not even on lunch breaks?'

'No, I'm sorry,' he replied bluntly.

Jaskiran construed his answer as evasive. Despite the initial warm welcome and convivial tone, Jaskiran now got the impression Thakur didn't want to be sitting here speaking to her. She decided to push him further. 'Didn't anyone at the firm think it a little suspicious that two employees – from the same team, in fact – both died just a couple of weeks apart?'

'I don't think "suspicious" is the word I would use, but it was certainly a tragic coincidence,' answered Thakur coolly. 'From what I have seen on the news, Anjali's boyfriend is guilty of her murder, while Deepak was the victim of an accident.' He then pointed to the notebook open in Jaskiran's hands and said, 'Please add that our prayers go out to their families.'

Jaskiran nodded before asking, 'Have the police not come to speak to anyone at the company since Anjali's death?'

'Not that I know of,' answered Thakur.

'Well, I guess they are not even aware of Deepak's death. I mean, a hit-and-run isn't going to make headlines.

Do you not think someone should inform them, even just for the sake of conducting a thorough investigation?'

Thakur again looked momentarily stumped before shaking his head to dismiss the question. 'I think if the corporation or Deepak were mentioned in the confession from Anjali's killer, then they would have already been here. Otherwise, I don't see why it would be necessary to bring it up. I mean, we have to think of Deepak's wife and family too. They are trying to move on with their lives. They don't need to read wild speculation about his death. It wouldn't be fair, would it?' Thakur now looked at his watch. 'I'm sorry, Ms Sohal, but I will have to bring this interview to a close,' he said. 'I have a meeting to attend. I'm sorry I couldn't have been of more use. If you have any further questions, then please do give me a call. The receptionists will put you through to my office.' He said this as sincerely as he could, but to Jaskiran his words rang hollow.

Jaskiran rose from her seat along with Thakur, hiding her frustration at the abrupt end to the interview as she shook his hand and watched him leave through the double doors at the end of the foyer. Trying to find a way to salvage something from her visit, she returned to the reception desk. She was greeted again with the same unfamiliar broad smile as if she had just walked in for the first time.

'Hello, madam,' said the first receptionist. 'I hope you got everything you needed from Mr Thakur?'

'Yes, he was very helpful, thank you. There was one last thing. Could you give me Deepak's home address?'

'I'm sorry, madam, but I cannot give out personal information, even for former employees,' the receptionist added apologetically.

'No, you don't understand. Mr Thakur said it's fine,' Jaskiran lied.

The receptionist hesitated and then reached for her phone. 'This is very peculiar, madam. I will have to get confirmation from Mr Thakur himself. It totally goes against company policy.'

The woman raised the receiver to begin dialling before Jaskiran put her finger down to cut the connection. 'It was worth a shot,' she said with a shrug before walking out.

She left the artificial climate of the office building and stepped into the heat of the midday sun. Before getting much further, she stopped and began rooting through her bag. Unable to find what she was looking for, she took out a pencil, and with a few expert twirls, she fixed her hair into a messy bun behind her head to expose her slender, olive-toned neck to what little breeze there was. Rather than stick to the main road, she opted to take a shortcut through the tree-lined side streets. She enjoyed the shade beneath the trees as she made her way across a narrow path lined with wild shrubs.

Jaskiran began to think of Anjali and Deepak. No matter what Thakur had told her, their deaths were suspicious. The fact she wasn't able to get any more information from Thakur only made her more distrustful of the firm. She got the impression that he had no intention of being open with her, and his unwillingness to share any information on who Anjali was close to in the office was a deliberate attempt to stop her from speaking to anyone else. *But why?* she wondered. *What could possibly be going on in there that they don't want me to know?* Whatever it was, Jaskiran knew she wouldn't have any luck speaking to anyone at the company again. What she needed to do was find a way to speak to Deepak's widow.

Jaskiran had been so lost in her thoughts that she didn't hear the footsteps approaching from behind her until it was already too late. A pair of arms grabbed her around the shoulders and shoved her into the trunk of a jamun tree before she even had a chance to turn around. Grazing her palms against the rough trunk, she managed to steady herself and not fall to the ground. Turning quickly, she faced her attacker. He was tall and lean. His pockmarked face was fixed in an almost apathetic expression at the mismatch before him.

'When will you learn that there are places you should not visit in this city?' he said as he walked, almost casually, towards her. Jaskiran froze as he then pushed himself against her and brought his face close to hers. His greasy hair fell almost to his eyebrows.

'You're beautiful,' he said as he began to run his fingers down her face and then her neck. Jaskiran pushed his hand away before he could get any further.

'Don't you have any shame!' she said, her fear turning to indignation. She slapped him hard across the face and he winced in pain. She then pushed him back with both hands to create some space between them before attempting to turn and run. She made it a few feet before she felt his grip on her arm as he yanked it back causing her bag to fall from her shoulder.

'You want to play rough?' he said pulling her close to him as she fought to loosen his grip. 'Fine, I'll show you how rough I can get.'

Before he could act on his threat, a loud voice bellowed from behind him: 'Madarchod! What are you doing?' They turned to see a uniformed police officer racing towards them. The attacker looked back at the approaching figure and narrowed his eyes. 'Look at this,' he said coolly, turning back to Jaskiran. 'It must be your lucky day. But remember,' he said now, drawing his face down to hers. 'I'll be watching you.'

He then set off at speed in the opposite direction to the police officer, leaving Jaskiran to watch the officer slow down as he reached her. Anger was pulsating through her body and Jaskiran did everything she could to not let her emotions get the better of her as the officer now placed a consoling hand on her shoulder.

'Are you okay?' he asked.

'Yes,' she said, looking up at the concerned face before her. 'But thank you.'

'No need to thank me, I'm just glad that I saw it. What was that all about?'

'Nothing, really. I guess you can call it an occupational hazard.'

The officer's brow furrowed and his expression turned to one of confusion.

'I'm a reporter,' explained Jaskiran.

'You wrote an article about him that he didn't like?' he asked, picking up Jaskiran's bag and handing it back to her.

'Not quite.' Jaskiran thought about how she could possibly explain the situation, seeing as she wasn't exactly clear on what was going on herself. 'Look, it's a little complicated,' was all she could manage. As if in compensation for her curt reply, she extended a hand. 'Jaskiran Sohal.'

'Inspector Imran Shah,' he said, shaking her hand gently. His name seemed familiar, but Jaskiran couldn't be sure where she had heard it before. 'Let me walk you back to the main road. Do you have a car?' he asked.

'No,' she replied. 'I took an auto to get here.'

'I'll see you into another one,' he said, taking his place beside her as they walked toward the main road. 'What were you doing in such a secluded spot?'

'I was visiting the Delhi Financial Corporation and decided to cut through here for the shade,' she said, gesturing to the trees dotted around them. 'I didn't expect to run into such a gunda.'

'Delhi Financial Corporation?' asked the policeman. 'What was your business there?'

Jaskiran looked at him suspiciously. That was when she realised where she had heard his name before.

'Inspector Imran Shah … you're the one who arrested Vivek Trivedi!' She began backing away from him. 'You're involved in this too.'

The inspector held up his hands. 'Yes, I arrested him, but I had nothing to do with that,' he said, pointing to the spot where he had found her. 'I came here to visit the corporation too. There are some questions that I need answering.' Jaskiran looked unconvinced and continued to back away. 'Look,' he tried again. 'If I was here to harm you, why would I have chased that gunda away?'

This seemed to work, and Jaskiran stopped, unable to think of a logical answer. But the suspicious look on her face remained. 'Okay, so what questions do you want to answer?' she asked.

'Probably the same as you. The reporter at the Anjali Mangal press briefing from the *Delhi Daily*, you work with him?'

Jaskiran nodded.

'When he raised the question about the car the night Anjali was murdered, I saw the way the deputy commissioner reacted. He was worried. From then, I did some digging and found out she worked here, and now I'm here to find out if anyone has seen her in a similar vehicle like your colleague described. And you?'

'The same,' Jaskiran replied. 'Weren't you the one who got the confession out of Vivek? Was it a real confession or not?' Jaskiran probed.

'The truth is that I wasn't even working the case,' admitted Imran. 'One morning the deputy commissioner calls me into his office, hands me the confession and tells me that I'll get the credit for obtaining it if I just keep my mouth shut. Fine, I thought. I was happy to go along with it until I found out the confession could be false. Now I want to find out the truth. But right now, I have nothing but what I've heard from your colleague.'

'Then who interrogated Vivek?'

'I didn't ask. These things happen from time to time. Some officers with questionable pasts are kept away from sensitive investigations, so the media or the defence team don't use it against us later.'

His openness seemed to have the effect of easing Jaskiran's suspicions, and she appeared content to continue speaking with him.

'Is there anything that I should know about the firm?' the inspector asked Jaskiran.

Jaskiran thought for a second about how to respond. 'Anjali's manager died two weeks ago,' she said slowly, studying the police officer's reaction.

'Died? How?' Imran replied as surprised as anyone who dealt with death on a daily basis could be.

'Hit and run, if you can believe it,' Jaskiran replied, her words heavy with insinuation while Inspector Shah absorbed the news with an expression of growing concern. 'You really didn't know?'

'No,' he replied. 'But I don't like it. What else did they say?'

'Nothing, but I don't think they were completely open with me.'

'Here,' Imran said, taking a card from his pocket and handing it to Jaskiran. 'If you find out anything else, it will be in both our interests to share that information with me. We are working towards the same goal.'

Jaskiran took the card and looked at it for a few moments. 'Fine,' she said finally. 'I'll help you. But if we really are on the same side, there's something I need from you first.'

'What?'

'I want to speak to the widow of Anjali's manager, Deepak Rao,' explained Jaskiran. 'I need you to find out his home address. Do that, and then I'll know I can trust you,' she said, handing him her own card.

The inspector couldn't help but smile. 'That's a fair deal, I'll get you the address.'

Jaskiran was about to continue on her way, but she felt compelled to convey her gratitude once again. Despite playing it down, she had been at the mercy of that thug and shuddered to think what would have happened if the inspector hadn't shown up. 'Thank you again, Inspector.'

'Please, call me Imran,' he replied and watched her walk to the end of the lane and onto Sewa Marg.

Once Jaskiran had hailed another auto, she sat back, relieved to be once again among the noise and crowds of Delhi. There was a comfort in being able to lose yourself in the masses. She exhaled loudly in relief.

28

JASKIRAN DIDN'T HAVE TO wait long to hear from Inspector Shah again. The very next morning, he sent her a text message with an address for Annie Rao, Deepak's widow. She was still looking at her phone when Rajesh walked into the office.

'Something juicy?' asked Rajesh.

'For your information, it's a new lead.' Jaskiran turned to face Rajesh as he sat down at his desk. 'I couldn't get anything out of the contact at the corporation, but I've just got the home address of Anjali's manager. I'm going there now to see if his widow knows anything useful. The two deaths have to be connected.' She decided not to mention being attacked or her subsequent encounter with Inspector Shah. She wanted to verify the address was correct first and hopefully get something that could take the story forward to attribute to Shah's assistance.

'What about you?' she continued. 'Did you speak to Vivek's parents?'

'Yes,' said Rajesh. 'His father is certain that Vivek never left the house the night Anjali died. In fact, Vivek's younger sister says he broke up with Anjali months ago.' Rajesh's mood now darkened. 'The police, they've destroyed that family, Jaskiran.'

'Don't get so down,' Jaskiran replied, remembering Sabeena's advice. 'We'll solve this, and Vivek will be free again. Now, wish me luck.' She grabbed her bag and headed towards the exit. Before she could disappear through the doors, Rajesh called out, 'Good luck. By the way, who's your source?' Jaskiran closed her eyes. The office doors were only a few feet away. *So close*, she thought.

'What?' Jaskiran replied, turning back to Rajesh.

'Have you got an insider at the corporation?'

Jaskiran hesitated. 'It's Inspector Shah,' she said finally, defeated.

'Inspector Shah?' A look of confusion passed across Rajesh's face, and then it dawned on him. 'You mean the one who arrested Vivek? What are you doing speaking to him? He's probably got something to do with all of this!'

'He's not what you think. A guy tried to attack me on the street yesterday, and Shah came and chased him away.'

'What!' Rajesh could barely get the word out. A few people looked up from their desks to see what the commotion was about. Rajesh lowered his voice. 'You were attacked? Are you alright?' he asked, his concern now trumping his initial shock.

'I'm fine. He was just trying to scare me. The inspector chased him away before anything happened.'

'And what was Shah even doing there anyway?' Rajesh said, still mistrusting.

'He was on the way to visit the corporation himself. He told me that he never interrogated Vivek, and the confession was given to him by the deputy commissioner. But after he heard what you said at the press briefing, he knew something wasn't right and wanted to get to the bottom of this too. So, he's on our side.'

Rajesh let out a loud exhalation in disbelief. 'Don't tell me you believe that?'

'Then why would he help me?' asked Jaskiran. 'Why would he tell me that Sagar lied about the confession, and why would he just send me the only other lead we have to actually find some proof about what happened to Anjali and Deepak?'

'I don't know, but I'm not going to let you find out alone,' Rajesh declared.

'*Let* me?' It was Jaskiran's turn to get angry. 'I'm so sick of the backward, macho bullshit in this office! Look outside at the world around us. Believe it or not, I can do things without a male chaperone, thank you very much.'

'Okay, I'm sorry,' Rajesh said, taking a step back. 'I'm just looking out for you.' He knew that Jaskiran had felt hurt at being sidelined from the crime beat because of Vinod's view that she couldn't handle herself. It was bad enough to have a superior think of you as weaker than your colleagues; it was worse still to have those same colleagues share that view.

'Fine, if you think Shah is on our side, then I'll believe you, but you have no guarantee that the police or whoever is involved hasn't got someone waiting for you to show up at that address.'

Given the reasoning, Jaskiran had no choice but to accept he was right. The anger on her face dissipated as she looked at Rajesh's concerned expression. 'Fine, you can come. But only because you'd follow me anyway. At least this way, you can give me a ride.'

Passing the security gate, Rajesh slotted the scooter among a row of parked cars on the narrow lane in Saket. The sun had passed behind the lane's collection of townhouses and low-rise apartment buildings, silhouetting a circling black kite overhead. Distant car horns and the rumble of engines could still be heard from the main road, but the lane itself was relatively peaceful. Only the sound of two maids chatting while they pounded a rug in some unseen corner could be heard, and a pressure cooker whistled violently into life through one of the open apartment windows.

Rajesh walked around looking at the address plates in front of the houses. He eventually motioned to Jaskiran.

'Over here,' he called. 'Rao, number 11.' He pointed to the closed gate of an impressive house.

'Great,' Jaskiran said, catching up with him, happy to be vindicated in her trust for Inspector Shah's information.

Approaching the gate, they both couldn't shake the feeling that the house looked out of place in its current setting. With its brilliant white walls, decorative arches and ornamental balcony railings, it looked more like a European villa than a traditional Delhi house. 'Wow,' said Rajesh, genuinely impressed. 'I didn't realise Rao was such a big shot to be able to afford to live in a place like this.'

'I didn't either,' Jaskiran frowned.

The gate creaked wearily on its hinges as they pushed it open. The garden path was lined with potted plants. Where the path forked, they took a left toward the front entrance while the alternative route continued to a small garden at the back of the house. The veranda on which they stood had been embellished with shrubs, plants, potted flowers and a circular metal table and chairs complementing the Mediterranean ambience.

Stepping through an archway to a small porch adorned underfoot with painted tiles, Jaskiran rang the doorbell. After no one came to the door, she knocked again and stood listening quietly for the sounds of footsteps or hushed voices. Nothing.

'Doesn't seem like anyone is home,' Jaskiran said, disappointed.

'Didn't Shah feel the need to tell you that when he sent you the address?'

'Evidently not,' Jaskiran said, moving away from the door to peer through the windows. 'The shutters are drawn from the inside. I can't see anything.'

Rajesh noticed that one of the horizontal shutter panels had moved out of place, exposing a slender gap through which he could see into the room beyond if he pressed his face against the glass. It took a moment before his eyes adjusted to the darkness of the room inside and a few more for him to comprehend what he saw. 'Jaskiran, you're going to want to see this,' he said, moving aside for Jaskiran to view the scene herself.

'What is it?' Jaskiran replied, peering through the glass.

As her eyes adjusted to the dark, shapes began to pull themselves into view, but what should have been a familiar scene was one of chaos and disarray. Cupboard doors and drawers had been flung open, their contents spilling out onto the floor around them. Sofa cushions had been cut and their stuffing removed. A lamp lay shattered on its side, with shards of glass shimmering in what little light there was. A table had been overturned, and its legs stood defiantly erect among the devastation around them.

'The place has been trashed,' she said out loud.

'Has Inspector Shah been inside?' Rajesh asked gravely.

'He didn't say,' Jaskiran said, backing away from the glass. 'Come on, let's head to the back. There must be another way in.'

'What? You actually want to go in there? We should get the hell out of here,' Rajesh protested.

'Look, we don't know if Annie is still in there. She could be hurt and need our help.'

'Then let's call the police …' Rajesh realised almost as soon as he had said it that it wasn't a viable option. With his suspicions about Inspector Shah, there was no telling whether the police were responsible for the scene inside. 'Fine,' he surrendered. 'But let's make it quick.'

Following the path, they came across several windows, all locked shut from the inside with their shutters drawn. 'There must be another way,' Jaskiran said reassuringly.

They moved to the other side of the house, where Jaskiran stopped by a small window that looked into a utility room. At the same time, Rajesh inspected a door that led into the kitchen.

Jaskiran tried to prise the window open, but it wouldn't budge. She now saw the handle on the other side of the glass in the locked position.

'The window is locked,' she called out to Rajesh.

'The back door too,' he replied, testing the handle.

Jaskiran, out of ideas, now began to think about Inspector Shah. *Was he responsible for vandalising the home, or perhaps he simply left when there was no answer at the door?* She was still thinking about it when she caught sight of a strip of blue rubber lying at her feet. She bent over and picked it up. Even in her hand, it coiled to make a circular shape the size of a dinner plate. She looked up now to a point in the top corner of the window where an exhaust fan was installed. She held the rubber up in front of her face to frame the circular fan jutting out awkwardly from the window.

'Rajesh, I need a boost.'

'Why?' he asked, walking over.

'You'll see,' Jaskiran replied, placing a hand on his shoulder and raising a leg, whereupon Rajesh duly cupped his hands around the sole of her shoes. Jaskiran was now level with the fan installation, and she could see that it had been dislodged from its secure position, causing the strip of rubber that acted as a frame between the unit and the window to fall to the ground. She placed both hands on the circular fan and pulled. With a rattle of moving parts, it shifted completely out of the window, with only one electrical wire tethering it to the inside of the house.

'Someone removed the fan before. That's what caused the frame to fall out,' she called down to Rajesh. 'I think I can reach the handle of the window.'

'Well, make it quick. I hate to tell you, Jaskiran, but you're a lot heavier than you look,' Rajesh said, gritting his teeth.

Jaskiran ignored him as she reached through the hole where the fan had been and manoeuvred her arm towards the door handle. She gripped it as hard as she could and twisted it open. The effort caused her whole body to shake and brought on more protests from Rajesh.

'Almost there,' she called as she gave the handle one final push, and the panel moved slightly away from the larger frame as the lock was released. 'Got it,' Jaskiran said elatedly.

She placed the fan back in place before squeezing through the window. Rajesh raised himself in after her, closing the window behind him. Through the utility room door, they entered the kitchen to find that it had been completely ransacked. All the cabinet doors were open, and smashed bottles and upturned containers lay all over the marble floor. The two reporters avoided stepping on the spilled oil and milk as they walked across the room. Pieces of glass crunched underfoot.

Although no one had answered the door, the pair had lowered their voices as if in deference to the silence around them.

'Whoever did this was searching for something,' Jaskiran whispered.

'How do you know?'

She pointed at the lower cabinets. In some places, the wooden panels at their base had been smashed, exposing the untiled concrete beneath. 'They were looking for any false bottoms in the cabinets. My father keeps my mother's jewellery in hidden compartments under our kitchen cabinets just like that.'

'Good to know,' Rajesh quipped.

They moved on from the kitchen, past the breakfast table, and into a tiled corridor. A noxious smell of alcohol filled the air. As they passed the bar cabinet, they noticed several bottles of liquor lying smashed on the floor. A corridor led to a large entrance hall from which doors led off to other parts of the house. A staircase curved to the upper floor.

'Go check the rooms that way,' Jaskiran said, pointing towards a door to the left. 'I'll check upstairs.' Rajesh looked at her in silent protest at the idea of splitting up. 'You want to get out of here quickly, right? We'll search the place a lot faster if we split up.'

Unable to argue with her reasoning, Rajesh had no choice but to follow her instructions. 'Be careful, and call if you need me,' he said, turning towards the door at the other end of the hallway.

'You too,' she replied. As he passed through the door, Jaskiran suddenly felt very alone and regretted proposing that they search separately. She gingerly walked up the stairs past a shattered vase that lay across the steps.

At the first-floor landing, Jaskiran turned into the closest bedroom. Inside, she found that the mattress had been overturned. Boxes that had probably been stored beneath the bed had been pulled out and emptied on the floor. The wardrobe doors stood open, their contents in disarray.

Finding no sign of Annie, Jaskiran backed out of the bedroom when she noticed a light coming from a room at the far end of the hallway. The door to the room was partially closed. She walked over and gently pushed the door open to reveal a study.

Unlike the rest of the house, the room was carpeted. A desk sat to her left, littered with open folders and a lamp that had been left on. Behind the desk, there was a glass cabinet containing a number of pictures and trophies, all of which had escaped the destruction wrought on the rest of the home. Jaskiran moved around the desk to sit in the chair to better see the files. She sifted through folders labelled with what appeared to be the names of clients of the Delhi Financial Corporation.

The pages contained loan applications, decision letters, company accounts and repayment plans.

Jaskiran couldn't see the significance of them. Growing increasingly frustrated, she tried to disengage from the details and think about what the person who had ransacked the house could possibly have been looking for. Whoever it was, they had sat in the very chair Jaskiran was sitting in and had looked through the same papers that lay in front of her.

'Whatever it was you were looking for, you expected it to be here,' she said aloud. She suspected they must have been looking for files concerning a client of the Delhi Financial Corporation. And they must have thought it important enough to believe Rao would have hidden it within his home. Why else would they have gone to such extreme lengths to search for it?

Jaskiran sat back in the chair as she mulled over her theory, her eyes fixed on the opposing wall where three black-and-white pictures hung in thick frames.

It wasn't long before something struck Jaskiran as odd about them. It was the way they were hung on the wall, with such a large gap between the picture furthest to the right and the other two. It suddenly dawned on her that it wasn't a gap at all. She leaned forward in her chair to see over the desk, and, just as she had assumed, on the floor beneath the empty space sat another picture frame. She got up and walked around the desk to the far wall. She picked up the frame and turned it around in her hand. It was empty. She looked again at the bare space on the wall and found the protruding nail from which the frame would have hung. She looked at the other three photos again.

Despite being in black and white, they were not of that era but perhaps only a decade or two old, from Deepak's younger days. The one on the far left showed him smiling proudly in his graduation cap and gown, clutching a scroll between both hands. The next one, taken even earlier, was Deepak as a thin, lanky teenager, with acne visible on his cheeks and the first downy hair above his lip. He was dressed in cricket whites with a bat resting on his shoulder. Scanning past the space on the wall where the missing picture would have hung, she came to the last picture on the right. It seemed to be the most recent of the three, showing an adult Deepak and his wife, Annie, smiling together outside this very house. The front door was bordered with garlands, and a picture of Lord Ganesha was pinned to its centre.

Suddenly Jaskiran heard the door to the room creak. Before she could turn around, a hand covered her mouth. She was about to bite it when Rajesh whispered in her ear, 'It's me. There's someone here. We need to get out.' His voice was filled with fear. He removed his hand from Jaskiran's mouth, and she turned to face him, her eyes wide.

'Who?' was all she could utter.

'There are at least two men,' Rajesh whispered, peeking out from the door toward the staircase. 'I was coming back to get you when I heard voices from the kitchen.' Then Jaskiran could hear them too. The voices and footsteps were getting louder as they approached the stairs.

'I had locked the window before I put the fan back,' a voice was saying. 'Someone opened it.'

'You don't know what you did,' a second, deeper voice responded.

'Well, the guard said he let the boy and the little Rani in, so they have to be around here somewhere,' the first voice spoke again.

'But where are they? I'm telling you, the guard lied to us. He just wanted more money. I'm going to give him such a smack for this.'

'Enough already. Just go and check upstairs.'

Rajesh and Jaskiran simultaneously held their breath as they backed away from the door. With no chance of escape via the stairs, Rajesh dashed to the room's only window and slid it open. The window was positioned at the side of the house and looked out onto the neighbour's garden. There was a ledge a few feet below the window frame. If they could climb down to it, they could jump across to the top of the boundary wall and into the neighbour's yard. He wasn't confident of their chances of success, but it was their only option.

'Quick, give me your hand,' he whispered to Jaskiran.

'Are you serious?' Jaskiran cried.

'Do you see another way out?'

Jaskiran could hear footsteps climbing the stairs. She steeled her resolve and placed her hand in Rajesh's. He helped her onto the window frame and then held her arms as she lowered herself to the ledge, which was little more than the width of her foot. She pressed her back as firmly as she could against the house. Even looking down could throw her off balance.

Looking up, she could see Rajesh's legs dangling from the window frame as he lowered himself to the ledge. Now beside her, he tried to slide the window shut, but before he could do it, he heard the door to the study swing open. Rajesh quickly ducked below the open window. Looking at Jaskiran, he placed a finger over his lips.

They could hear the footsteps in the study from the open window as their pursuer approached the desk. They listened to the click of the lamp switch as it was turned off. There was then a momentary silence. *The man must be looking around the room*, thought Jaskiran. The footsteps began again, only this time they seemed to be coming towards the window.

Rajesh readied himself to be discovered when a loud banging sound erupted from the front door.

'Who's in there!?' a lady's voice cried. 'You bloody thieves, I saw you go in there!'

The man in the study swore, his voice directly above Rajesh and Jaskiran. His footsteps receded as he walked back towards the door. Rajesh risked a look inside and saw the back of a man's muscular frame leave the room.

'Let's go,' he whispered to Jaskiran. He looked out over the gap in front of them to the boundary wall. Pushing himself off the ledge, his long, athletic frame made up the distance with little difficulty. He placed one foot on the wall before dropping the remaining height into the neighbour's yard. Looking back, he knew it would be more difficult for Jaskiran. She was shorter than him, making the distance to the wall all the more considerable.

Jaskiran counted to three before launching off the ledge. She felt as if she were in slow motion, her outstretched leg pointed outward, every fibre of her being willing her to make it.

In her mind, she was transported back to a different time when she would play with Gurvinder in their village in Punjab as a child. The two of them raced along the narrow streets and alleys, pursued by the other kids in games of tag. Often finding themselves atop the little single-storey homes, they would jump from one roof to the other. Back then, it had all been for fun. It had never dawned on her that it could have been dangerous.

Placing the tip of her shoe on the top of the wall, her immediate elation soon turned to fear as she lost her balance and barrelled head-first into the yard. But rather than the sickening thud of her head cracking against the ground, she felt Rajesh's firm grip as he grabbed her around the shoulders and pulled her into his embrace. Catching her breath, she looked up at him, his expression full of concern. 'Thank you,' she said.

But before Rajesh could reply, a wooden pole swung through the air and caught him squarely across the shoulders. Crying out in agony, Rajesh arched his back and fell to the ground. Despite the pain, he had enough sense to open his eyes to better see his attacker. To his surprise, it was a middle-aged woman, and she approached him where he fell, bearing a fierce countenance and waving a large broom above her greying hair.

'You bloody gunda!' she yelled. 'The poor woman loses her husband, so you think no one will stop you from taking her things?' she cried, readying the broom for another swing.

Jaskiran was frozen where she stood, shocked and confused to see such a diminutive woman strike Rajesh so violently. It then quickly occurred to her that she must have been the same woman knocking on the front door moments earlier. Jaskiran sprang into action.

'Auntyji, no!' she yelled.

With her arms still poised above her head, ready to deal Rajesh another painful blow, the woman looked at Jaskiran and was momentarily confused about why such a decent-looking young woman would want to burgle her neighbour's home. She looked over again to where Rajesh lay prostrate on the floor, and another thought crossed her mind.

'You filthy whore,' she said, grimacing in disgust at Jaskiran. 'You can't go and do it at your own house; you have to break into people's homes to do your dirty deeds?' She brought the broom down again, striking Rajesh's leg, which he failed to move out of the firing line. He yelped in pain and held out his hands in submission.

'Auntyji, you've got it all wrong,' he cried. 'We're newspaper reporters. We're here following a story.'

'Do you think I was born yesterday? You think I'm an idiot?' she asked Rajesh, threatening to strike him again for his impudence.

'He's telling the truth, Auntyji,' shouted Jaskiran. 'We're investigating the death of Deepak Rao!' The woman was momentarily halted in her assault as she digested this new information. 'Here,' Jaskiran said, handing the woman her card. 'See, we're from the *Delhi Daily*. My name is Jaskiran, and this is my colleague Rajesh.' She pointed to where Rajesh sat rubbing his shin.

The woman studied the card and eventually lowered her broom. 'What were you doing in there?' she asked. 'Annie isn't here.'

'We wanted to talk to her about her husband's death and the death of one of his colleagues at the Delhi Financial Corporation,' explained Jaskiran. 'We saw from the window that the place had been vandalised. We wanted to make sure that she wasn't inside in need of help.'

The woman continued to study Jaskiran long after she had finished speaking but evidently decided she was telling the truth. Then, turning to Rajesh, who was only now picking himself off the floor, she apologised.

'It's okay, Auntiyji,' he said, unable to meet her gaze. His pride was as bruised as his body.

'Actually, you helped us. The men who ransacked the place were inside there too. We were hiding from them when you frightened them away. If it wasn't for you, I don't know what we would have done,' Jaskiran said sincerely. 'Did you see anyone else?'

'No, no one,' the woman replied, disappointed at having missed the opportunity to distribute some more rough justice. 'Yes, the place has been trashed,' she said. 'I have a key, so I went over to check on the place and found it like that.' She gestured toward the house. 'Luckily, Annie had already left. Hasn't the poor woman lost enough that they have to destroy her home too?' she asked, anger stemming from every pore. Rajesh thought she might strike out again in frustration and edged slowly back out of range.

'Did you phone the police?' Jaskiran asked.

The woman straightened her back and looked affronted. 'Of course not,' she snapped. 'I have two teenage boys. The last thing I need is the police looking for convenient suspects to take down to the station and force confessions out of. No, I let it be. They can't undo the damage already caused.'

'Do you know where Annie has gone?' Jaskiran asked. 'We really need to speak to her.'

The look of suspicion returned to the woman's face. 'No,' she said. 'She just told me that she was staying with friends outside the city. She could be anywhere.'

'I see,' Jaskiran said deliberately, noticing that the woman faltered, before eventually continuing, 'well, Rajesh, we better go. It looks like we came too late.'

She then thanked the woman and said, 'Please keep my card. If you speak to Annie, let her know that we wish to talk to her. We only want to help.'

Jaskiran then walked away, followed by a limping Rajesh. As they approached the street, Jaskiran turned to Rajesh. 'She knows something,' she said.

'She knows how to swing a broom,' Rajesh replied, struggling to keep up with Jaskiran.

'How's the leg?' Jaskiran belatedly remembered to ask.

'It bloody hurts. I've got cricket practice this weekend. I'll be no good if my shin is still sore.'

'Maybe you can get that aunty to take your place,' Jaskiran said, smirking. 'She certainly knows how to hit a few shots!'

'You're hilarious,' Rajesh responded with a deadpan expression.

29

'HERE, THE ALCOHOL WILL numb the pain,' Jaskiran said, sliding a bottle of beer along the bar to Rajesh.

Rajesh lifted the chilled bottle and savoured the refreshing taste. The pain in his leg had, in fact, subsided and seemed to be little more than superficial bruising. Still, he wasn't ready to admit that to Jaskiran and squander the offer of a free beer.

He now looked around the bar. It was Jaskiran's choice, a place called Club Tropicana in Kailash Colony. The abundance of bamboo, along with the tropical plants and palm trees, evoked an exotic hideaway. It was early, and only a few young couples were seated amongst its tables along the ground and mezzanine floors. Unseen speakers played a mix of generic Indian and American pop music.

'Your sort of place?' Rajesh asked.

Jaskiran nodded. 'It's a little kitsch, but I like the crowd compared to some of the trendier places where men have such egos,' she said. 'They are all about flashing their cash and buying bottles of champagne to get female attention.'

'You won't have to worry about me flashing any cash,' Rajesh said, taking another swig of his beer.

'Everything okay?' Jaskiran asked, a little confused.

Rajesh wasn't sure where the comment had come from. He only knew he felt the urge to confide in Jaskiran. But something stopped him. Her family had money, and she wouldn't understand, he thought. 'Yes, it's fine. I'm just venting,' he finally said. 'You must remember what they pay junior reporters? Vinod hasn't raised my pay yet. He says I am still on probation.'

'Well, if we break this story, Rajesh, I'm pretty sure you can name your price.'

'Do you think that makes me a bad reporter, to think about the money? My own gain from people's misery? Because I didn't get into this thinking about the money.' He frowned at how naive he had been. *Wasn't it always the son's role to think about providing for his family?*

'Why did you want to be a reporter?' Jaskiran asked, tilting her head and looking at Rajesh as if for the first time.

'To be honest, I thought that it would be a pretty cool thing to do. I wanted to break big news stories. Travel and meet interesting people every day. I thought it would be an adventure. I didn't want to end up like my father, working every day, week and year just like the last until after thirty years of toiling, you're gone.' He snapped his fingers. 'And eventually, everything you worked for is gone as well. What was the point of it all?'

There was an awkward silence as Rajesh drank. Jaskiran had never seen Rajesh like this. He was usually quick to smile, with all the enthusiasm of someone who had life by the tail.

'I'm sure that if he was here,' she ventured, 'he would say it was all worth it to see you now. Crime reporter for the *Delhi Daily.* Not too bad, no?'

It seemed to work. Rajesh nodded in agreement and said, 'He actually would have.'

'And if you keep searching for the truth; if you keep asking the tough questions and going where others are too scared to go, all to uncover a truth that people are trying to hide, why shouldn't you be rewarded?'

Rajesh nodded in agreement again and held out his bottle to Jaskiran, who reciprocated and tapped her bottle against his, the glass gently clinking. 'Well said, I'll drink to that.' They both took long swigs. 'What about you?' Rajesh now asked.

'What about me?' Jaskiran replied.

'Why did *you* want to become a reporter?'

'Well, I don't know. I think I was attracted to the idea of having a voice. Maybe I could use that voice to bring stories to people's attention that they would otherwise miss. Give the voiceless a platform.'

'That's why you wanted the Anjali story?'

Jaskiran sighed, thinking back to her own guilt and Sabeena's comforting words over dinner. 'I thought I did,' she said, 'but it was also to get back at Vinod.'

'Getting back at Vinod, I can drink to that,' Rajesh said, raising his bottle to Jaskiran's once again. They both drank. An uneasy silence followed as they were both aware they had to address the elephant in the room.

Rajesh eventually broached the subject. 'Any idea who trashed Deepak Rao's place?'

'I'm not sure,' was Jaskiran's reply. 'Someone is obviously looking for something Deepak had. He may even have been killed for it. How that relates to Anjali, I don't know.'

'Maybe she found out something?'

'Maybe,' Jaskiran replied. 'By the way, I've updated Inspector Shah on the state of Annie's home. He said that he had gone there yesterday, but there was no answer at the door, so he left. He seemed genuinely embarrassed he missed what was really going on. He said he'll do what he can to find Annie.'

'And you believe that? He was most likely the person who wrecked the place.'

'Come on, Rajesh. Why would he give news reporters the address to a home that he vandalised himself?'

Before Rajesh could answer, he felt his phone buzz in his pocket. It was Karishma. Rajesh mimed an expletive. He had completely forgotten they had made plans to meet.

'Everything all right?' Jaskiran ventured.

'Yes,' Rajesh hesitated. 'I'm sorry, Jaskiran. I have to go. I'm supposed to meet someone.'

'About the case?'

'No … a friend. My girlfriend, actually,' Rajesh replied clumsily.

Jaskiran stifled a grin at Rajesh's awkwardness. 'You never mentioned you had a girlfriend.'

Rajesh was unsure how to answer. 'Well, you and I never really spoke that much.'

Jaskiran felt embarrassed, knowing her earlier preconceptions of Rajesh had been the reason she had put little effort into forming a friendship with him to this point.

Rajesh headed out, wondering why he had been so reluctant to tell Jaskiran about Karishma. In the end, he decided not to think about it. The last thing he needed was to complicate his life any further.

30

CATCHING AN AUTO BACK to the office, Jaskiran was heading toward the entrance lobby when she saw someone approaching from the corner of her eye.

'Jaskiran.'

'Inspector Shah,' Jaskiran replied, studying the tall figure as he approached.

'I wanted to see if you were okay,' he said. 'You seem to have a habit of putting yourself in harm's way.'

'I'm fine,' Jaskiran said. 'Rajesh took a beating, but he'll live.'

'Rajesh, the boy from the press briefing? Maybe I should meet him.'

'I wouldn't recommend it. He still doesn't trust your motives. Thinks you were behind what happened at Deepak's home.'

'Really? And you?' The inspector seemed displeased.

'I still have my reservations,' Jaskiran replied candidly.

The inspector looked down at Jaskiran. His stern, judging eyes slowly melted, and he was almost smirking. *He has a level of intensity about him*, she thought. Most likely honed from years of interacting with criminals and the dregs of society.

'As soon as I got your message about what had happened, I went back there and saw the place for myself. The neighbours were no help, but I spoke to the guard. The two intruders attacked him on the way out. He doesn't have a name but gave a good description and had a phone number.'

'What are you going to do next?' Jaskiran asked.

'I suspect the men are working for the deputy commissioner. They knew the two of you might come snooping around. I'll put the number through the police database and see if anything comes up. It may be a burner phone, but we might get lucky.'

'Good work, Inspector.' Jaskiran couldn't help but be impressed.

'Do you still have reservations about me now?'

She didn't answer, but he knew he had done enough.

'Good, because I'm done trying to convince you. I'm getting to the bottom of this with or without you. If you want any more information from me and want to break the real story, you need to start sharing any information you have. Do we understand each other?'

He held out a hand for Jaskiran to shake, and she took it.

'We do, Inspector,' replied Jaskiran.

'Good. Now what have you found?'

'Nothing but confirmation of what we expected. The confession that the police have obtained is fake and their version of events is a fabrication. The driver of the bus that the deputy commissioner claims Vivek and Anjali took to Jubilee Park admitted that he lied. He was forced to do it.'

'Will he testify to that?'

'I don't think so. Rajesh says that he looked pretty scared – but maybe if you speak to him and promise that you can protect him, he may agree.'

'Did he say who threatened him?'

'No, Rajesh couldn't get it out of him.'

'Looks like I need to pay him a visit. Where can I find him?'

'His name is Suraj Babu. He works out of the Rohini bus depot.'

'Anything else?' asked the cop.

Jaskiran was about to tell him about the CCTV footage Rajesh had found at the toy shop. But she stopped herself and decided that it was better to keep that from him for now. She could use it as leverage when she needed something more from Shah. It didn't do to give away all her findings with nothing in return. 'No, nothing else yet,' she replied calmly.

He nodded in acceptance, took a pair of aviator sunglasses clipped to his shirt and put them on. 'I'll update you as soon as I can.'

Jaskiran watched him as he climbed into his police Scorpio SUV. It coughed up black exhaust smoke as it manoeuvred around the busy road, avoiding the scooter riders, and headed towards Rohini.

31

'WHAT THE HELL, RAJESH!' Karishma cried as he slid into the booth across from her. 'I've been waiting for half an hour.'

'I'm sorry, something came up with work,' Rajesh offered in the way of apology. As usual, Karishma had chosen to meet at a sophisticated, upmarket venue, the Amour Bistro, close to her design studio in Chanakyapuri. They sat by the window, and Rajesh could see the hustle and bustle as people filled the streets, many heading for the Metro station across the two lanes of traffic where stalls selling fruit and vegetables, soft drinks and fried foods lined the entrance.

'Well, never mind. I have exciting news!' Karishma declared sipping on a cocktail. 'I spoke to Bhavna earlier today, and she told me that Vikram was planning to take her to Goa for New Year's and invited us to come along. So, I said what the hell, let's do it! Isn't that exciting?'

'Goa?' Rajesh couldn't hide his shock. 'Shouldn't we talk about this first?'

'What's there to talk about? It will be so much fun,' Karishma said gleefully.

'What about the cost?' Rajesh asked, beginning to panic. 'Goa is expensive around the holidays.'

'We can afford it. I have some savings, and you, with your promotion, should have no trouble.' Karishma waved away Rajesh's concern.

'And your parents? They would allow you to go with me?' Rajesh was beginning to clutch at straws.

'Of course not. That's why I'm telling the folks it's a girls' trip.' Karishma sipped her cocktail triumphantly.

'Great,' Rajesh tried to muster some enthusiasm. 'You've got it all worked out.'

How could he tell Karishma the truth about his money trouble? He wondered if she would even stay with him if she found out. She wanted to enjoy herself and live life to the fullest. He couldn't begrudge her that.

Rajesh's phone buzzed, and he was happy for the reprieve. He looked at the screen and saw it was Sajid calling.

'I have to take this,' Rajesh told Karishma before answering, 'Hello, sir.'

'Hello, Mr junior crime reporter,' said Sajid, sounding slightly inebriated. 'I have some good news for you.' He paused for dramatic effect.

'Yes?' Rajesh prompted.

'Anjali's family has returned,' Sajid announced. 'A local constable told me that they arrived home this morning.'

'That's great. I'll go over there and try to speak to them.'

'Hold on just a second,' Sajid said. 'After our last conversation, my curiosity got the better of me, and I did some digging on your friend Deputy Commissioner Arvind Sagar. He's quite the character. Do you know how he got his start?'

'No,' Rajesh replied.

'Well, he's not someone to mess around with,' said Sajid, before telling him a bit about Sagar's history. His early career in the police had been unremarkable. Things changed twenty years ago when a cabinet minister's son crashed his car late one night, killing the driver of another vehicle. Sagar had been the first constable at the scene. By the time his superiors and the media arrived, there was no sign of the minister's son, who later reported that his vehicle had been stolen. The driver of the other vehicle was also found with a bottle of cheap booze in his lap. There was no case to answer for the minister's son, and embarrassing headlines were avoided. Not long after that, the young constable Sagar had suddenly been elevated to the rank of assistant sub-inspector. His career has followed the same trajectory ever since.

'You're saying he's well connected?' asked Rajesh.

'He's an opportunist. A player of the great game here in Delhi,' Sajid said, blustering. 'He uses his power for those he can benefit from.'

'But how does this help me?'

'I'm getting to it,' Sajid said, followed by the sounds of what Rajesh assumed was Sajid pouring himself another drink. 'If Sagar is covering for someone, it must be a powerful individual. You need to understand what that means. You could be getting into something pretty heavy. Are you ready for it?'

'Do I have a choice at this point? I can't walk away now, knowing for sure that Vivek is innocent.'

'You always have a choice. Whether you continue with the story or give it a pass, either choice carries consequences. You have to be able to live with them. Something to think about.'

After the call ended, Rajesh felt deflated. Even though Sajid was trying to help, the veteran reporter's advice for caution worried him.

32

DEPUTY COMMISSIONER SAGAR LEANED back in his office chair and stretched his aching back. Glancing at his wristwatch, he noted that it was time for his late-evening treat. He gleefully heaved his considerable frame off his chair and approached the filing cabinet. Opening the top drawer and shifting aside some papers, he removed a small tumbler and a bottle of imported Japanese whisky. He eyed the bottle in the light. It had been part of a haul confiscated in a raid a few days earlier. The owner had failed to pay the correct import duties and, in turn, lost both his liberty and the consignment of three hundred bottles. He had requisitioned a crate for himself and made sure to send bottles to a number of his superiors and colleagues.

He poured himself a measure and returned the bottle to the filing cabinet before taking some ice from the chilled container his assistant placed in his office diligently every evening. Taking a seat once again, he opened a beige folder and scanned the report with interest. A wealthy Delhi businessman had contacted him personally to intervene in an ongoing investigation. The man had been accused of sexually abusing his house staff. Four of his employees, men and women alike, had accused him directly, while another two were acting as corroborating witnesses.

Sagar held a look of disdain as he read the sordid details contained in the investigating officer's notes. What was it about commanding authority over other human beings that made people behave in such a way? Sagar was convinced the wealthy and powerful all lived debauched lives filled with ungodly perversions. Was it boredom? Or perhaps the idea that they could get away with it that made the most heinous acts seem pedestrian. Scanning the victims' statements, he faltered at learning that one of the victims was just fifteen years old. She had been ordered to give the businessman massages in his private study, both parties would be nude, and the girl would be directed to touch and fondle the man's genitals and gratify him to orgasm. Sagar shook his head in disgust. The folder contained further incriminating evidence. There were photos taken from a camera phone showing the businessman in various stages of undress with the victims.

It would have pleased Sagar very much to see the man prosecuted. It might send a message to others in similar positions that they could not act with impunity. He almost laughed. Who was he kidding? It wouldn't make a difference. His thoughts now turned to the textile factory in Noida that the businessman had promised would be transferred to Sagar's son-in-law if the case was thrown out. He took another sip of whisky and savoured the deep oak flavour before yelling for his assistant.

When the man arrived, Sagar pointed to the folder on his desk. 'It is evident that there is no case to answer,' he said. 'The staff are obviously trying to blackmail their boss. Tell the investigating officer that he will be given a commendation for his thorough reports after he ensures that all copies of the indecent images are deleted. He must then make it clear to the accusers that they will be arrested for blackmail if they bring this up again. Understood?'

The assistant nodded and left with the file folder.

A little later, the deputy commissioner was enjoying some more whisky when he sensed a presence at his door. Looking up, he was pleasantly surprised by the sight of a beautiful woman. She wore a simple yet elegant embroidered saree in a way that made the garment cling to her curves. His eyes lingered on her shapely figure before shifting to her face. She smiled and greeted him with a namaste. Sagar thought he recognised her. 'Yes?' he asked.

The woman entered his office without being asked. 'Deputy Commissioner Sagar, it's an honour to meet you,' she said as she closed the door behind her. The thought of being shut away in his office with such a woman, away from prying eyes, filled him with ravenous thoughts. He was aware now of how quiet the building seemed this late at night. Only the whirring of the electric fan in the corner and the distant car horns from the open window punctuated the silence as he licked his lips and looked at her standing before him.

'And you are?' he finally found his voice.

'My name is Ayesha Begum, sir. I'm an MLA here in Delhi. May I sit?'

'Of course. Where are my manners? Please.' Sagar motioned to the seat in front of him. An MLA, of course. He had seen her on TV bashing the Delhi government and the police's handling of the Anjali murder case. A spike of irritation shot through him. Was she here to berate him?

'I see that you're enjoying a drink,' said Ayesha nonchalantly.

'Yes, it's late,' Sagar replied defensively, unsure if her tone was critical or friendly. 'I should have gone home hours ago.'

'I understand,' she said. 'I too enjoy a drink after a long day. Of course, we can't let the voters know.' She shot him a mischievous smile.

'Indeed,' Sagar chuckled, his earlier irritation melting away. 'Would you care for a glass? It's very good.'

'Well, I wouldn't want you to drink alone,' she said with another smile. Sagar rose immediately and poured them both a measure diluted with a splash of soda water for Ayesha's benefit.

Offering the tumbler before her, she took it from his hand. Sagar noted the way her slender fingers touched his own. It seemed deliberate, but he enjoyed it nonetheless.

Sagar sat once again and watched her sip from the glass appreciatively.

'You were right. It is good,' she said, her maroon lips now slightly wet and glistening.

Looking at Ayesha at that moment brought to mind the Bollywood sirens of Sagar's youth. Yes, he thought, she reminded him of a young Rekha in *Umrao Jaan*. She had the poise and confidence to have been at home in a Mughal court. It was clear to the policeman now that she wasn't here as an adversary. He had met with plenty of feminists and women's advocates over the years. They tended to be the shouty types and unattractive as a rule. Ayesha was neither of these things. His feelings towards her softened, the spark of irritation he had felt earlier completely doused. *But then why is she here?* he wondered. Coming here alone at this time of night didn't feel like official business.

'Madam, to what do I owe the pleasure?' he asked courteously.

'I came to offer my congratulations for your success in catching the killer of that poor girl whose body was found in the Yamuna. Such a speedy resolution must have been satisfying.' She tilted her head. 'One less perverted killer loose on our streets, and it restores much-needed confidence in the Delhi Police. It's a win-win for everyone.'

'Indeed, the police force has been much maligned lately,' said Sagar, giving her a deliberate look above the rim of his glass.

'Now, sir,' she said playfully, 'you cannot judge me harshly. I do what I must to remain popular with voters.

I've always backed the police force, and around the country, the police have no greater ally than the Democratic Union Party.'

The police officer nodded. 'I am very grateful that you came down here to convey your wishes in person,' he said, 'but surely you have better things to be doing. Isn't your husband waiting for you at home?' Sagar knew it was a transparent play, but he didn't care.

'There is no husband anymore. I'm a widow.'

'I'm so sorry to hear that,' Sagar responded with little effort to sound sincere.

'Don't be,' said Ayesha lightly. 'I find it liberating. To not be encumbered by a man, yet no one frets about you marrying. People actually prefer to see a woman unattached and independent when she's lost her husband. Of course, they also expect you to live a life of celibacy, but they can't have everything.'

Sagar guffawed and banged the table in delight with his fist, eyeing her lecherously. 'Indeed, indeed.' He panted before asking, 'There must be a boyfriend then?'

'That is a very personal question, sir. But perhaps I will answer it if you first answer a question for me?'

'Of course, fire away,' Sagar said immediately.

'The boy you have in custody for the murder … is he really Anjali's killer?' she asked, looking closely at the policeman.

Sagar returned her gaze for a moment before replying, 'We have a confession and the evidence. The rest is for the courts to decide. But I'm curious why you would even ask such a question. Do you doubt our ability, madam?'

'Not at all,' she replied. 'I have made my enquiries about you, sir. You're liked and feared in equal measure by all who know you. There is no questioning your ability.'

Sagar swelled with pride. He had worked a lifetime to garner such a reputation.

'But in my role,' continued Ayesha, 'it's necessary to have eyes and ears all over the city. Even if the Delhi Police is a sturdy ship, it has its leaks. And from what I've heard, there are still questions to be answered.'

'Such as?'

'Since the incident, why have you been regularly meeting with Rahul Yadav, the managing director of the firm where Anjali Mangal worked? Why did he pay to have Anjali's family moved out of the city and away from the media spotlight?'

The look of pleasure disappeared from Sagar's face. 'Rahul Yadav?' he said, keeping his tone even. 'You think he has something to do with Anjali's murder?'

'Sir, I'm well-versed in how this city works,' Ayesha said quietly. 'I've been playing these delicate games my whole life, and I think it's fair to say that I am an extremely adept player. I know men like Rahul Yadav like to stay out of the spotlight but use their money and influence behind the scenes to get away with things. Yes, I suspect Rahul Yadav had something to do with Anjali's death. If I were to lay out my suspicions, I would say that he had been abusing his authority over her for his sexual gratification. When she threatened to expose him, Rahul killed her. He hadn't counted on her body being discovered so soon and was not ready for the media storm it created. That's why he paid for Anjali's family to leave Delhi, and why he asked you to help him get away with it by framing some other poor soul and closing the case as quickly as possible.'

Sagar was enthralled. He had never faced such a lethal combination of brains and beauty before. 'That's an interesting hypothesis,' he said after a pause. 'Let's say I humour you for a moment. What is it you actually want, madam?'

'Your friendship, Arvind,' whispered Ayesha. 'May I call you Arvind?'

'It's never sounded better,' said Sagar, trying to stifle the erotic desire pulsating through him.

'Rahul Yadav is the golden goose of the Indian Workers' Party,' she said slowly. 'He funds candidates in marginal seats, and that money can make the difference between winning and losing. If I can remove him from the picture, it will leave a big hole in their election finances at the most critical time. We'll also make sure that the scandal tarnishes the party he supports by making them guilty by association in the eyes of the public.'

She stood and put her empty glass down before slowly walking around the desk towards Sagar. Perching herself on the edge of his desk, she looked at him and said, 'Help me, Arvind, and you can have whatever you want. Name your price.'

Sagar breathed heavily. He also noticed Ayesha's chest heaving under her saree. He could feel sweat forming on his brow. This was an offer unlike any he had experienced before. He tried to formulate the best course of action and contemplate each move and its repercussions, but his mind was clouded with desire for the woman mere inches from him. His world shrank to the four walls of his office. At that moment, nothing else seemed to matter except, peculiarly, the idea of humiliating Rahul Yadav, which was almost as appealing to him as the woman before him. His mind was made up, and there was no use in fighting it any longer.

The deputy commissioner swallowed hard and grabbed Ayesha's hand.

'You never answered my question,' he said. 'Is there a man in your life?'

33

THE FOLLOWING MORNING, RAJESH and Jaskiran arrived outside Anjali's apartment complex on his scooter. Approaching the gate, they found the security guard in his hut fiddling with his radio.

'Greetings, Iqbal,' said Rajesh. 'I'm here to make good on the money I gave you,' he added with a smile.

'What are you doing here?' Iqbal asked, turning to the reporters before placing the radio on the floor and rising from his chair. 'The family has not returned. You can't come in,' he said.

'That's a lie, Iqbal,' Rajesh interrupted. 'They arrived yesterday.'

Iqbal looked momentarily alarmed at Rajesh's knowledge but was not ready to give up that easily. 'It doesn't matter,' he snapped. 'You can't come in. I shouldn't even be talking to you. You'll get us both in trouble.'

Rajesh scoffed. 'Are you trying to tell me that you're still under orders from the residents not to let anyone in?'

'Not the residents, my young friend,' Iqbal replied gravely. 'The police.'

'What have they said to you?' Rajesh asked.

'To not let any journalists in,' replied the guard, looking carefully around the empty street. He seemed to be deliberating a decision with himself. 'So you can't come in. Unless …' he trailed off, looking at Rajesh with a gap-toothed grin.

Rajesh suddenly understood. 'I've already paid you,' he said through gritted teeth.

'That was before. Now there is increased danger for me. Increased danger means increased price.'

Rajesh swore under his breath and took out his wallet. Opening it up, he fingered the few sorry-looking notes he had and remembered what his mother had said to him. Could he afford to give up his last few rupees? Jaskiran noticed Rajesh's reluctance to hand over the money and his uneasy expression. She knew that his pride was most likely preventing him from explicitly asking her, so she took the initiative and extracted several hundred-rupee notes from her own purse and handed them to Iqbal.

He gratefully pocketed the money. 'Thank you, madam.' He backed away from the gate. 'I must go on my rounds of the compound,' he said. 'Wait here a moment, please.' He went to the hut and picked up his radio before walking away towards the far end of the apartment complex, whistling along to the latest hits.

The two reporters waited at the gate until he passed out of view before entering the complex, Rajesh leading the way to Anjali's apartment. He was disappointed not to have seen the boy, Roshan, here again. *Perhaps he had more to say, but he was likely at school.*

Reaching the apartment, the two reporters found a woman sitting in the shade of the veranda. She was looking out over the garden, but it was clear she was deep in thought.

'Excuse me,' Jaskiran ventured. 'Are you Anjali's mother?'

The woman blinked and looked at them as if awakening from a dream. 'Yes,' she replied softly.

'We are reporters with the *Delhi Daily*,' Rajesh announced. 'We were hoping to ask—'

'We wanted to express our sorrow for what happened to Anjali,' Jaskiran interrupted. 'I have been following the story closely and have spoken to Anjali's professor, and he told me how wonderful she was.'

A flicker of emotion appeared on the mother's face before it disappeared. She looked away again. 'I used to watch her play there when she was a child,' she said, pointing in front of her to the neatly manicured lawn that lay in the shade of a row of neem trees. 'She was our only child, but I made sure that she never felt lonely. She was everything to me.' Her voice fell to little more than a whisper.

Something about her slow, rhythmic breathing and speech seemed odd to Jaskiran. 'What happened to her is tragic,' she said quietly, stepping closer. 'We can only imagine your pain.'

'Pain?' Anjali's mother echoed. 'There is no more pain. No pain, no anger, no joy. There is nothing.'

Jaskiran and Rajesh exchanged looks. Just then, the door to the apartment opened and a man appeared carrying an overstuffed box. He was sweaty and his blue-striped shirt had come untucked from his trousers. He looked as if he had not slept in days.

'Who are you talking ...' he began before seeing the two reporters. 'Who are you?' he asked sharply. 'We are not accepting visitors.'

'Sir, we are reporters,' said Jaskiran quickly. 'We wanted to share our condolences.'

'How did you know we were here?' the man asked brusquely. Jaskiran was sure that he was Anjali's father. He seemed unsure of what to make of their presence.

'Sir, we are not here to cause you any distress,' Rajesh ventured, now aligned with Jaskiran's gentle approach. 'We only wanted to speak to you both about Anjali.'

'Like I said, we are not speaking to anyone,' said Anjali's father.

'Come inside,' said Anjali's mother suddenly, rising slowly from her seat. 'I will make tea. Anjali loved my tea.'

'We said no visitors,' Anjali's father said to her sternly.

'I want to speak to them,' Anjali's mother rebutted with the same soft tone. Then looking her husband in the eye, she asked, 'Or would you prefer I sit here mute all day?'

After a moment, Anjali's father sighed heavily. He placed the box gently on the floor and held the door open. 'You had better come in,' he said to Rajesh and Jaskiran.

Inside the apartment, the sweet smell of incense filled the air. The rooms were decorated with colourful flower petals and small statues of Hindu deities. Anjali's mother disappeared into the kitchen through the door at the far end of the room while Anjali's father led the reporters to a sofa. He then took a seat in an armchair and switched on the TV.

Jaskiran noted framed pictures of Anjali as a schoolgirl, among which was her playing Sita in a school rendition of the Ramayana. The news came on the TV, and Jaskiran's attention was diverted by the image of Ashok Chopra on the screen. She felt an involuntary rush of excitement, and she immediately felt embarrassed. *Was it the thrill of attraction?* she thought, slightly panicking. She watched with interest as the news segment cut to him at his recent rally. The voiceover commented that the development bill he was championing was being put to vote in the coming days. If it passed, it would surely propel him to an election victory in the coming months and a starring role within the party.

Rajesh, for his part, was aware of the uncomfortable silence in the room. It was clear that Anjali's father didn't share his wife's desire to speak to the two reporters. 'Are you moving?' Rajesh motioned to the boxes on the veranda in a bid to end the stalemate.

'No,' Anjali's father replied, rubbing his eyes. 'That's just a few of Anjali's things. The sight of them is unsettling for my wife. Since our return, she can't stand to pass her room without weeping. I had to get some medication for her to calm her down. Until she is able to handle things better, I thought it best to store those things at my brother's house.'

'Where had you been the last few days?' asked Rajesh.

'Staying with family,' the man answered quickly, avoiding eye contact. 'The press came here to hound us and we couldn't even leave the compound. It was shameful the way they treated us.'

A pang of guilt weighed on Jaskiran. 'I can imagine that it must have been difficult for you,' she offered. 'But for what it's worth, the media attention means that Anjali's death isn't in vain. People are demanding real change now in Delhi.'

Anjali's father exhaled a pithy laugh. 'Really?' he said scornfully, pointing at the TV. 'Because I watched a news report where they blamed Anjali for what happened to her. The important question for them was what she was doing out so late. My wife and I were blamed for raising her with loose morals. This city won't change.'

The three of them sat for a few minutes in silence, Anjali's father staring at the TV as if now oblivious to the company of the two reporters. Eventually, Anjali's mother walked in carrying a metal tray with glass cups of tea, a bowl of sugar and a plate of biscuits.

'We would usually have more food to offer,' she said. 'But I haven't been shopping in a while.' She sat down near them. 'You said you spoke to Anjali's professor,' she said, turning to Jaskiran. 'What did he say?'

'He told me how much she enjoyed her studies,' Jaskiran began tentatively. 'That she was kind and would help her classmates.'

Anjali's mother was nodding with the merest hint of a smile, but Jaskiran noticed that she was squeezing the end of her kurta between her fingers.

'I'm sorry,' Jaskiran said softly. 'I didn't mean to upset you.' Anjali's mother mustered a slight nod to indicate she was coping.

'Then why come at all?' Anjali's father muttered. 'Of course bringing up Anjali will upset her.'

'We can't all move on as quickly as you,' Anjali's mother said, looking at her husband. Her breathing had become heavy. 'Clearing out her room so quickly like it was just another chore to do.'

'I did it for you. It was upsetting you to see her things.'

'It was upsetting me to see what they did to it,' she retorted. 'It was Anjali's room. It was just the way she left it. They had no right to come in and disturb it!'

'Who are you talking about?' Jaskiran asked.

'The police,' replied the mother. 'They searched Anjali's room while we were away. They made such a mess!'

'What were they looking for?'

'Her mobile phone,' the father answered. 'They said that it could give them clues about where she was headed that night. I told them that Anjali probably had it with her, but they said that it was never recovered.'

'Did they find it?' Rajesh asked.

'No, even yesterday, they were asking us to locate it. Even now, when they have the boy arrested and his confession.' Anjali's father tutted.

The mention of Vivek made Rajesh curious. 'Did you know Anjali and Vivek were seeing one another?'

'No, of course not,' Anjali's father interjected.

But Rajesh noted Anjali's mother hesitate as if biting her tongue in the presence of her husband. 'She didn't tell me. But a mother knows. The days before she ...' Anjali's mother hesitated, unable to say the words. 'She seemed upset about something. She said that it was about her work, but I think it was because of that boy.'

'About her work?' Rajesh enquired. 'Did she say anything else?'

'No, that's all she would say. She would shrug it off and say that there was nothing to worry about.'

'Did she mention any new friends at Delhi Financial Corporation?' asked Jaskiran. 'Was she close to anyone there?'

Again her mother shook her head, and Anjali's father stared adamantly at the TV, refusing to cooperate any further.

'Did the police take anything when they searched her room?' asked Rajesh.

Anjali's mother looked unsure. 'It was such a mess …' she began before looking at her husband for support.

'They said that they didn't take anything,' he said after a moment of silence. 'From what I can see, everything is there.'

'Did this search happen before the police arrested Vivek?' Rajesh probed.

'Yes, I think so,' Anjali's mother replied. The two reporters shared a knowing glance.

'Why are you asking these questions?' demanded the father.

'We want to understand the timeline better,' Rajesh answered. 'There were two items of Anjali's jewellery found at Vivek's. Did you see Anjali wearing them before she left?'

'I wasn't here,' said the father. 'I was working late.'

Rajesh turned to look at Anjali's mother, who seemed to wilt under his gaze.

'What about you?' Rajesh coaxed.

Anjali's mother seemed to hesitate, doubt now clouding her memory. 'I, erm, I, well, no, I can't remember seeing her wearing them.'

'But the police claim you confirmed she wore them the night she left. Is that not true?' Rajesh asked.

'Well …' Anjali's mother began, her breathing growing erratic. She looked at her husband, whose face was reddening. 'But what was he doing with her things anyway?' she said suddenly, her voice defiant. 'He must have taken them from her!'

'Enough!' Anjali's father roared before Rajesh could say anything. Getting to his feet, he glared at the two reporters. 'I knew it was a mistake letting you into our home,' he shouted. 'You have come to poison our minds! You want to make that murderer the victim in this. *He* isn't the victim! My Anjali is the victim – he murdered her, and he must suffer. I won't let you help him get away with this! Get out! Get out of my home!'

The two reporters rose together; Rajesh looked ready to argue on Vivek's behalf, but he felt a hand grab him by the elbow. He turned to see Jaskiran looking contrite and urging him toward the door. He sighed and shuffled out of the apartment, leaving Jaskiran to make their apologies. 'We're truly sorry for your loss,' she said before walking away. At the door, she turned and looked at Anjali's father again, who had moved to place a comforting arm around Anjali's mother, who looked close to tears. 'You have to understand that some of us are still trying to find the complete truth,' said Jaskiran quietly. 'The justice you want cannot be served until we do.'

34

IT WAS ALMOST MIDDAY when Jaskiran and Rajesh arrived back at the newsroom, much to the annoyance of Vinod. The managing editor immediately called Sabeena to his office for an explanation.

Taking their seats at their desks, Jaskiran looked at Rajesh. He had been quiet the entire trip back from Anjali's apartment.

'What's on your mind, Rajesh?' she coaxed.

'I need to say it?' he replied. 'Anjali's parents are helping the police frame Vivek.'

'It's not like that,' Jaskiran countered. 'Think of what they have been through. Now all they have to cling to is the desire for justice to be served and for someone to be punished for the crime. So if the police tell them they have the killer, you have to imagine they will overlook the methods they used to catch him.'

'We should have told them what we know,' said Rajesh. 'If we can get them to make a public statement that they didn't see Anjali wearing the jewellery that night, it may be enough for them to release Vivek.'

'How can we convince them that Vivek is innocent when we don't have any solid suspects of our own? As I said, they want to see someone punished.'

Before he could respond, they heard Sabeena's stern voice behind them. 'A little discretion wouldn't hurt,' she snapped. They both turned to see their senior colleague glaring at them. 'I've just had Vinod asking why the two of you are strolling into the office together halfway through a working day,' said Sabeena.

'What did you say?' Jaskiran asked, chastened.

'I told him that I had sent you on an assignment and that Rajesh gave you a ride.'

'Right, so I'm the driver now?'

'Would you prefer that I told him the truth?' Sabeena shot back, surprised at the fire in his voice. Rajesh didn't reply and avoided her gaze. 'What is the truth, by the way, seeing as you didn't think to keep me in the loop?'

'We went to see Anjali's parents,' Jaskiran replied. 'They couldn't tell us anything about who Anjali was with, but they seemed unsure whether Anjali was wearing the jewellery they found at Vivek's apartment. But that's it.'

'That's it? What more do we need to release the story?' Rajesh protested.

'We don't have the killer, Rajesh,' said Jaskiran. 'We don't have a suspect or a motive.'

'I thought this was my story,' Rajesh muttered petulantly to Jaskiran's shock.

'That doesn't mean you get to publish a half-baked one,' Jaskiran shot back.

'Enough!' Sabeena intervened before Rajesh could respond. 'You both need to cool off. Jaskiran, you've got an interview you're going to be late for, or did you forget? Rajesh, Sajid has left some police reports that he wants you to write up for tomorrow's issue.'

'Sure, more police statements, because they won't be a bunch of lies,' Rajesh remarked sarcastically.

'Perhaps you'd prefer to go back to sorting the classified ads if you can't handle the jobs you've been assigned?' Sabeena gave him an icy stare before heading back to her own desk. Jaskiran thought it best to leave and picked up her bag. At the door, she paused and thought about turning back and saying something to Rajesh. Instead, she took a deep breath and walked out.

Rajesh sat alone riddled with guilt. He hadn't meant to upset Jaskiran, and he knew that he had no ownership of the story. It was an immature thing to have said. But after everything that they'd found out, he couldn't help but feel that he had to help Vivek and his family. Rajesh tried to push such thoughts aside. There was no time to dwell on it now when he had work to do. He picked up the stack of police statements that had been waiting on his desk.

Rajesh began reading the first report, which was an account of a successful police raid on a suspected money-laundering ring. The police had arrested seven men at the scene. The magistrate had remanded them to judicial lockup, with a date for trial yet to be set.

Rajesh paused and reread the sentence. An idea suddenly began to form in his mind. Perhaps there was one person who could help.

35

RAHUL YADAV HAD BEEN waiting in the Leela Palace hotel's lobby for over twenty minutes and was beginning to lose patience. He took in his surroundings again and noted the maroon Persian rugs, the wide Victorian columns and the crystal chandeliers. The hotel was a popular venue for state officials and industrialists to meet, discuss closer ties and, most importantly, grease palms. Rahul knew from experience that the energetic buzz of conversations around him was the sound of money.

While he was comfortable in such settings, Rahul still preferred the privacy and comfort of his office. There, he could always make it clear that he was the one in control. However, when he had requested a meeting with deputy commissioner Sagar, the officer had specifically asked to meet at the hotel. Rahul couldn't imagine that a man like Arvind Sagar would be at home in such surroundings.

'Rahul Saab!' called a booming voice. Rahul looked up to see Sagar walking towards him with a broad smile across his face. He was still in his uniform and darkened sweat stains were visible beneath his arms.

Rahul noticed that some of the other guests had turned to look at them. He squeezed the bulbous top of his cane as he felt anger flaring up through his chest. 'It's bad enough that you make me meet you here in public. Do you have to announce it to the world?' he snapped.

'Don't be so paranoid,' said Sagar dismissively. 'What do you think all these suits are discussing? Charity work?

Helping the poor?' Sagar let out a hearty laugh as he sat across from Rahul, one arm extending along the top of the sofa, his fingers cloying appreciatively at the leather. 'And as for choosing this location,' he continued, gesturing at the opulent room around them, 'I have another meeting here today, so it works well for me.'

'A meeting?' Rahul asked, slightly surprised. 'With whom?'

'Rahul Saab, I cannot say,' said the cop with a shrug. 'You know how these government types value their secrecy.' He smiled slyly, clearly enjoying having Rahul on the back foot.

'I see,' Rahul said simply, refusing to give Sagar the satisfaction of seeing him curious.

'What was it you wanted to speak to me about?' Sagar asked, still smiling.

'We have a situation with those journalists,' said Rahul in a low voice. He checked his surroundings again before continuing, 'They are still investigating the girl's murder and are getting closer. They visited her home today and spoke to her parents.'

'And what do you want me to do about this?' Sagar replied casually.

The policeman's tone angered Rahul. 'This has gone on long enough!' he snapped as forcefully as he could without attracting any unwanted attention. 'You told me that you had them under control. It's time you put a stop to this once and for all.'

'Impossible,' the deputy commissioner stated definitively.

'Sagar—'

'That's Deputy Commissioner Sagar, saab,' he replied with a cheerful expression, but his tone implied that he wasn't joking.

Rahul's knuckles turned white as he squeezed down harder on his cane. 'Of course,' he said, managing to maintain his cool. 'As I was about to say, we only find ourselves in this mess because you decided to bring in Vivek alive. If you had "encountered" him like I told you to, no one would have cared to prove his innocence.'

Despite Rahul's seriousness, the deputy commissioner maintained a jovial smile. 'You're in this position as a result of your own rash decisions. I mean, saab, she was just a girl. What need was there for that?' Sagar gave Rahul an accusatory look one might give an infant who had made a mess on the floor. 'Getting rid of the journalists would just make things worse. By extinguishing one torch, you'll invite the glare of a thousand more. I won't have anything to do with it.' Sagar got up from the sofa.

'Where are you going?' Rahul demanded. 'We're not done yet.'

The deputy commissioner was not used to being spoken to so abruptly, and there was anger in his eyes as he glared at Rahul before breaking out into a good-humoured laugh.

'Saab, my advice to you is to make sure you destroy any evidence connecting you to the girl. But, most importantly, leave the journalists alone. If I've learned anything from my dealings with them, it's that if you give them even a sniff that you are worried, it will only make them press harder. Eventually, they will lose steam and give up. I wish you luck, saab. Please let me know if there is something – how did you phrase it … *in the pipeline* – so that we may work together again.' Sagar then turned and walked away, leaving Rahul in a fury.

He cracked his cane against the floor with force as he rose and strode as fast as he could towards the exit. Even after all the money Rahul had paid him, the deputy commissioner was refusing to help. *Sagar is making new friends and thinks he no longer owes me*, Rahul thought. *I'll make sure he pays for this. But first, these journalists. They have gone too far. I can't let them get any closer.*

36

JASKIRAN HAD BECOME A victim of her own success. Her interview with Ashok Chopra had made waves within Delhi's political circles. The Democratic Union Party was particularly ruffled by her favourable portrayal of their rival's candidate and now demanded she interview one of their candidates as part of her journalistic duty to demonstrate her impartiality. Jaskiran had preferred to politely decline the offer, but Sabeena had forced her to reconsider.

'You can't get on your high horse just yet, darling,' she had said. 'It's like finding a man. First, you need to drive up demand before you can be choosy over who you decide to date. The same goes for interviews.'

With requests coming in from members of all parties wanting similar profiles for their rising stars and elected officials, Jaskiran found herself committed to another four interviews.

She was concerned about what was expected of her. She had wanted to genuinely understand Ashok Chopra and the man behind the claims and slogans. If the feature turned out to be a positive endorsement, it was because she believed in his vision for Delhi. Jaskiran wanted to research any other prospective interviewees thoroughly beforehand and have the freedom to ask difficult questions. However, she was beginning to understand that the other candidates would expect it to be nothing more than a PR exercise. They wanted an unashamedly flattering piece of self-advertisement to wave under the noses of their friends at future gatherings. Unfortunately, she was sure Vinod would have been pleased enough with this. 'At least they're waving our paper!' he'd be sure to say.

Jaskiran's interview that day was at Vaasu, an upscale restaurant housed within a converted haveli deep in the Old City. After she entered through the weathered wooden doors, she was led into the restaurant's sunlit inner courtyard. There was the soft sound of running water from a large fountain at the centre and groups of diners sat along the walls near blooming violet flowers. Jaskiran reflected on the juxtaposition between the antique facade of the building and its modern, sophisticated interior. It was symbolic of how much the city continued to change, that even in the stifling, crowded streets close to the Jama Masjid, steeped in hundreds of years of history and tradition, the city was reinventing itself once again as it had done countless times before.

A young woman approached Jaskiran. 'You must be from the *Delhi Daily*?' Shriva said. 'Ms Begum is very pleased to speak with you today,' the woman said with little sincerity. She had the demeanour and erect posture of someone who took their job seriously. She led Jaskiran to Ayesha Begum, who was busy texting. 'Will you require me for anything else, madam?' The young woman turned to Ayesha.

'No, that will be all, Shriva,' she said, finally placing her phone on the table and taking a long look at Jaskiran. 'I'm sure I can manage from here,' she said playfully, but it nevertheless made Jaskiran uneasy, as if Ayesha were indeed making a comment about her first impression of the reporter. Shriva nodded and retreated back toward the entrance.

'It's nice to meet you, Ayeshaji,' Jaskiran said, taking a seat across from the MLA.

'And you, Ms Sohal. Please let's get you a refreshment. It's deadly out there today.' She motioned toward a waitress who duly complied. Approaching with a large jug, she poured Jaskiran a glass of cucumber-and-mint-infused water. 'I'll be glad when the rains arrive. They were always such an occasion for celebration back in Calcutta. Until they turned to floods, of course.'

Jaskiran nodded in agreement. Her first impression of Ms Begum was one of cautious intrigue. She was an attractive woman, which was clear to anyone, including Ayesha herself. She had the easy confidence of women who know how to wield the power of attraction. Her hair and makeup were simple but faultless. Her expensive salwar kameez was designed to give the illusion of modesty but was nonetheless chosen to set her apart from the crowd. However, a sparkle in her eye said there was more to her than what could be perceived on the surface.

'You moved to Delhi when exactly?'

'Around ten years ago,' Ayesha replied succinctly.

'What brought you here?'

'I was involved in politics back home,' said Ayesha. 'I married, and my late husband suggested we relocate to Delhi to be closer to his business interests. I thought that it wouldn't hurt to be closer to where the real power lies. So here I am,' Ayesha replied matter-of-factly. It didn't seem to be a subject she was interested in discussing.

'What drew you to a life in politics?' Jaskiran followed her journalistic curiosity.

Ayesha's expression now turned into a wry smile. 'We all must work where our skills can be put to best use, Ms Sohal,' she replied.

'I see,' Jaskiran said.

'Oh, you seem disappointed. Was I to say something more romantic or poetic?'

'No, it's not that—' Jaskiran began.

'I am not Ashok Chopra, Ms Sohal. I will not deceive you by telling you what you want to hear. I prefer to speak the truth.'

The pivot to Ashok surprised Jaskiran. There seemed to be real animosity in her tone.

'I believe that he gave an honest account of who he actually is,' Jaskiran responded. She hadn't anticipated having to defend her work from scrutiny.

'Oh dear, it seems that you really did fall for his spin. Tell me, did you fuck him?'

Jaskiran was taking another sip of water and almost spat it out. 'Excuse me? No, of course not!'

'Shame. I was hoping to hear how he scored.'

'Then why don't *you* sleep with him?' Jaskiran shot back defiantly.

Ayesha appeared to give the idea some thought and then merely shrugged. 'Maybe I should,' Ayesha grinned, and Jaskiran got the feeling she was sitting across from a tiger who had just spotted its next meal.

'You think I go too far?'

'I think you want to shock me,' responded Jaskiran.

'And why would I want to do that?'

'I don't know.'

'Yet you assign motive without knowing why,' Ayesha continued as if a teacher speaking to a student. 'It is an affliction that blights many in your line of work. You must understand why people say and do the things they do before you can truly understand them. For those working in the media, I believe it is necessary. The same is true with politics. Ashok Chopra doesn't want to come to terms with this, so he surrounds himself with those such as yourself who inflate his ego and treat him like the messiah Delhi has been waiting for.'

'I see,' Jaskiran said confidently. She could see the point Ayesha was trying to make. It was the same argument that populists across the world had been making in recent years. 'So it's the usual media class and elites working against the rest of the population. Are you still banging that drum? Don't you think it's beneath you?'

Ayesha merely shrugged with the same playful expression on her face. 'It's ugly,' she agreed. 'But if our politics is ugly, it's because the views of our electorate are ugly too. We represent them, remember? If politicians are divisive, it's because they are giving voice to the divisions that people feel in their lives.'

Jaskiran looked on with open-mouthed surprise. 'You don't honestly believe that, do you? To take an extreme view is to pander to a minority in our society.'

Ayesha's head flew back in a scornful laugh. 'Mr Chopra might appeal to you and others like you – the educated and the rich,' she said. 'But he doesn't resonate with the working man. How could he? He isn't one. The masses need someone who reflects them. He can't even get the basics right. How many of those who live in the streets around here, the slums, the villagers on Delhi's outskirts, our millions of poor and uneducated are going to vote for a man of privilege who wears Western clothes and speaks English as much as he does Hindi? With a horrendous clipped accent, I might add.'

'People are waking up to how bad things are getting. They want change, and our politics must change with it,' Jaskiran replied simply.

'Politics will and has always remained the same. Only the politicians change, Ms Sohal.' Ayesha sighed as if she were talking to a child who couldn't understand the point she was making.

'And you are happy with that, with the way things are run?' Jaskiran felt this was no longer an interview but a confrontation.

'Of course not. Delhi needs to get rid of the Indian Workers' Party. They are ineffective and waste money on useless projects.'

'But they're currently passing the development bill. They're trying to change the city. What do you offer? More scapegoats and straw men to distract from your inability to govern effectively?'

Ayesha laughed again. She seemed to be enjoying the heated exchange and the emotional response she had elicited from Jaskiran. 'Yes, now we can see what you really believe. You have fallen for Chopra's bluster. Poor girl, his brand of politics preys on young minds like yours.'

Jaskiran had heard just about enough. She wanted to tell Ayesha what she really thought about her and the politics she peddled.

She suddenly felt her phone vibrate in her bag. Taking it out, she didn't recognise the number but took the call anyway, happy for the respite from Ayesha's company.

'Hello, Jaskiran here.'

'Nehru Park,' said a woman's voice. 'Be at the bench by the Lenin statue in forty-five minutes.'

'I'm sorry, who is this?'

'It's the woman you've been looking for. Come alone.'

'Who? Annie?' But it was too late. The phone went dead. Jaskiran sat staring at her phone, trying to comprehend what had just happened.

'Everything alright?' Ayesha asked, irritated that Jaskiran had dared to take the call in the first place. When the reporter failed to respond, she continued, 'Perhaps we should move away from Ashok Chopra and on to my interview now. I want it to be focused on my work for women and children, particularly ...'

'I'm really sorry,' Jaskiran interrupted, finally overcoming her initial shock. 'But I have to go,' she said, rising from her chair.

Ayesha suddenly looked incredulous. 'Go? We haven't even begun!'

'I have no choice. This is an emergency.' Jaskiran turned to leave.

'And what am I supposed to do? I took time from my busy schedule and was promised an interview.'

‘I’m sorry,’ Jaskiran apologised again as she backed away towards the exit. ‘I will call your office. We can finish the interview over the phone.’

‘This is highly unprofessional, Ms Sohal! You will regret this. I’ll make sure of it!’ Ayesha bellowed from her seat in anger toward the departing Jaskiran, shattering the tranquillity of the setting to the dismay of the waiting staff and the other diners.

Outside, Jaskiran’s head was spinning. She needed an autorickshaw immediately. But even if she found one, it would be impossible to reach Nehru Park in forty-five minutes. Even if she managed this minor miracle, she didn’t even know where, in its rolling expanse, she was supposed to find a statue of Lenin. Wasn’t he a Russian leader?

37

RAJESH STEERED HIS SCOOTER past the iron gates of the Karkardooma Court complex in the eastern part of the city. He was feeling nervous as he crossed the security checkpoint beneath the blue sign that spanned the width of the entrance emblazoned with the name of the court in both Hindi and English.

Rajesh smiled politely at the guards, who looked on with minimal interest or enthusiasm. They eventually waved him through, and he headed for the crowded parking lot that seemed to be the meeting place of choice for defendants and their legal representatives. Rajesh dismounted from the scooter close to a stone pyramid structure that looked like a giant arrowhead with a perfect circle carved out of its middle and made his way toward the seven-storey, whitewashed building that was the main focal point of the complex.

What am I really hoping to achieve? He contemplated heading towards a group of people huddled around a row of makeshift counters close to the entrance of the building. A plastic sign above the wire-mesh facade indicated it was the information desk. *Do I really think this is going to work, or am I just trying to make myself feel better by attempting a futile gesture?*

Rajesh managed to wriggle his way through the small crowd and, after a few words with the lady behind one of the counters, received directions to the office of Judicial Magistrate Sahil Pal. 'Room 18B, first floor,' he repeated to himself as he entered through the glass doors into the main building and a lobby teeming with people. It was sweltering. Electric fans bolted high on the walls whirred noisily but provided little relief. The crowds of people were impatiently awaiting their day in court, conspiring with their advocates, while others were simply looking for help navigating the labyrinth that was the Indian legal system.

Rajesh brushed past the crowds in the lobby toward the wide corridors and the stairs to the upper levels. Fluorescent lights lit the way from the low-suspended ceiling, and his footsteps echoed against the polished floor crisscrossed with innumerable scuff marks.

He ascended the stairs to the first floor and deeper into the Delhi court complex. Here too, the passageways were lined with people caught within the snares of the sputtering, slow-moving legal system, a look of muted desperation on their faces as they waited to be delivered from purgatory.

Rajesh entered the magistrate's anteroom. It was a windowless box with empty chairs lining three walls. A diminutive, middle-aged clerk looked up from behind a small desk positioned by the remaining free wall. 'Hello,' Rajesh said in the most well-mannered tone he could muster. 'I'm here to see Magistrate Sahil Pal,' he added warmly to the confused clerk, who stared at Rajesh long after he had finished talking before finally scanning the schedule for the day on the wall beside him.

'I do not have a meeting scheduled for this afternoon. There must be a mistake,' the clerk replied.

'I don't have a meeting booked, but it's urgent. I must speak to the magistrate. Is he in?'

The clerk shook his head and waved a hand to dismiss Rajesh. 'He is here, but if you don't have a meeting booked, you cannot see him. Sir is busy.'

'Look, this is important!' said Rajesh, losing his polite tone. He was tired of feeling blocked at every turn. 'If he is in, tell him that a reporter from the *Delhi Daily* needs to speak to him urgently.' Rajesh extended his card to the clerk, who outright refused to take it.

'Have you been hit in the head? Do you not understand? You cannot come in and start ordering me around!' the clerk fired back at Rajesh, whom he perceived to be a young interloper.

'Mukesh, what is this racket?' The irritated-looking magistrate now appeared at the doorway, his hand fixed firmly on the open door. Dressed in a shirt and trousers, the magistrate was a thickset man with a dark complexion, a thick bristling moustache and streaks of grey in his smartly combed hair.

'Sorry, sir, he is a journalist,' Mukesh began pointing at Rajesh. 'He was adamant he had to speak to you, but I was telling him you are extremely busy, and he must make an appointment.'

The magistrate now fixed Rajesh with a look of interest. 'You're a reporter?'

'Yes,' Rajesh began. 'Rajesh Gupta, with the *Delhi Daily*. As I was saying, I believe a confession you witnessed was false.'

The magistrate looked at him gravely before finally opening the door wider. 'Well, you'd better come in then.'

Rajesh followed him into a small office. The walls were lined with shelves of leatherbound legal tomes. There was a framed picture of Sathya Sai Baba on the wall above a recent image of the prime minister, looking every bit the Indian mystic with his long, flowing white hair and beard.

'Take a seat,' said the magistrate as he sat behind his desk littered with stacks of case folders. 'You'll have to excuse the mess. I have a full day of hearings tomorrow. Honestly, it feels like trying to clear a sandy beach one grain at a time.' He stroked his wrinkled forehead and removed his glasses, placing them on the dark faux mahogany table. His eyes looked weary and spoke of long hours, the processing of meticulous details and the heavy responsibility of his work. 'Tell me,' he said, now looking at Rajesh, 'which confession are you referring to?'

'Vivek Trivedi's,' replied Rajesh. 'For the murder of Anjali Mangal.'

The magistrate nodded along. 'Yes, yes. Of course, I remember. It was just a few days ago. And you mean to say the confession was false?'

'Yes, sir, I have heard evidence that Vivek never left his home that night.'

'Have the police corroborated this evidence?'

'I'm not sure, sir. I have not discussed this with them.'

The magistrate now furrowed his brow. 'You say he couldn't have committed the crime, but he confessed to me personally that he had. I witnessed the confession myself. The boy was morose but compliant. No officers were present in the room when I took down his statement of what occurred.'

Rajesh took a second before he replied. 'Sir, I believe that the police have arrested Vivek knowing he was not the one to commit the murder, but because he was simply the easiest suspect to blame. They have threatened or coerced him into making the confession. I can't be sure of their tactics because I have no way of contacting him. No one does. His father tells me the police say Vivek refuses to take his call or see him.'

'And what exactly do you want me to do, Mr Gupta?'

'Allow him to be released on bail until the trial.'

'That is impossible for me to do at this stage. He confessed to a non-bailable offence. The correct thing to do after somebody is presented to a magistrate following an arrest and confesses to a non-bailable offence is to send them to judicial lock-up until the trial. And that is what I did.'

'Couldn't you speak to him? He will tell you the same. They have forced him somehow.'

'He may well do, but that's the case for many defendants who sign confessions only to plead their innocence at a later date.'

The magistrate waved his hand dismissively, wanting no more to do with the affair. 'This really is a matter for his defence team,' he said. 'They can appeal for bail to the trial court. Or they can present all the evidence at the trial. If the evidence for his alibi is as strong as you believe, justice will be delivered. I'm sure of it.'

'And until then?' Rajesh replied passionately. 'Sir, we are still investigating the murder and have evidence that someone else was with Anjali that night. But until we get more evidence, the longer Vivek sits in jail, the more people will believe that he is guilty.'

'The court of public opinion is of no interest to me, Mr Gupta. I can't help what people believe, but you and those in your industry can play a role in that. If you have evidence, take it to the police or publish it in your paper and force the police to take a look at the evidence that you say they have overlooked. Why come to me?'

'It's …' Rajesh hesitated. Knowing he didn't have the authority to publish the story or any trust in the police, he felt trapped. 'It's complicated,' he said, feeling powerless.

The answer didn't satisfy the magistrate, and he frowned once again.

'I know this is not what you wanted to hear, Mr Gupta. The wheels of justice move slowly in India. That's true for Mr Trivedi as it is for the many tens of thousands of other prisoners sitting in jail awaiting trial. I can't begin releasing them just because I am petitioned to. If magistrates exercised such power before trial, how long do you think it would take before that power is abused in this country? Do you think I don't know how rotten and compromised our system has become? I'm fully aware that sometimes illegal tactics are used by some police officers, but – and I want to be crystal clear on this – I saw no wrongdoing when I witnessed the confession you are talking about. Therefore, it is imperative I don't jeopardise any impending case by seemingly taking sides based on evidence that hasn't been corroborated by the investigating officers. No, I'm sorry, it's important we stick to the rules that govern our practice to stop this rot from spreading any further.'

'So we do nothing while an innocent man sits in jail for a crime he did not commit. This isn't justice.' Rajesh rose to leave the magistrate's office.

The magistrate watched him head to the closed door before finally relenting. 'Okay. Okay, Mr Gupta,' the magistrate called out to the retreating Rajesh. 'I stand by what I said. If the boy is innocent and the evidence exists to prove it, he will have his day in court and be exonerated as he should be. But that being said, I agree that he should be able to speak to his family. I will call the jail personally and speak with him. If he wishes to see his parents, I will see to it that he does.'

'Thank you,' Rajesh said before walking out the door.

By the time Rajesh had navigated his way out of the building and its stifling, humid air, he felt as if he had escaped from the clutches of a spider's web. He looked back at the court building behind him and felt a shudder run down his spine, pitying those who found themselves trapped in its grasp.

38

ATOP A PLINTH BEARING his name stood a life-sized bronze statue of Vladimir Lenin. Smartly dressed in a three-piece suit, one hand casually placed in his pocket while the other clutched a cap by his side, the Russian communist revolutionary seemed perfectly at ease within the world's largest democracy. Jaskiran stood panting as she studied him, her forehead beginning to shimmer with sweat. It had taken her just under an hour to reach the statue; her search through the park had led her to several wrong turns and dead ends, but she had finally found her man. *Am I too late?* she thought as she looked around for any sign of Annie. But other than a family enjoying a picnic and an amorous young couple getting close beneath the shade of a tree, there was no one else around.

Jaskiran decided to catch her breath on a nearby bench before deciding what to do next. In her panic to find the statue, she had taken for granted the abundance of greenery and the soothing quiet of her surroundings. A gentle breeze offered some relief from the heat. A troupe of joggers went bounding past, dressed in a colourful mixture of nylon and lycra. While she began to lament on an opportunity wasted, a smartly dressed woman wearing a white tunic top over black trousers sat down beside her.

'You're late,' the woman said disapprovingly to Jaskiran.

'Excuse me?' Jaskiran replied, surprised.

'What took you so long?' the woman asked, irritated.

'Annie?'

'Who else were you expecting?' Annie responded resolutely. Despite Annie's oversized Gucci sunglasses, Jaskiran could see from the wrinkles on her forehead that she was frowning. She was a petite woman and clearly took pride in her appearance. Her hair was short and pampered, as if she had come straight from the salon. Liberal amounts of rouge had been applied to her cheeks to disguise the sunspots that were beginning to appear.

'Sorry, it took me some time to find this place. But I'm glad you contacted me,' Jaskiran said, trying to focus.

'I'm still undecided whether coming here was a good idea. You're just a girl. Why do you even want to get mixed up in all of this?'

'I want to find out the truth. I was investigating Anjali's murder, and it led me to your husband. I think their deaths may be connected.'

Removing her glasses, Annie let out a sigh and sat back. *She has pretty eyes,* Jaskiran noted. They made her appear more approachable, in contrast to her wide cheeks and arching eyebrows that gave her the look of a woman perpetually ready for confrontation.

'Of course they are connected,' said Annie. 'Only a fool would believe that Deepak's death was an accident. He was murdered, just like that poor girl. But at least Deepak knew what he was getting himself into.'

'Into?' Jaskiran asked.

'The scams of course!' came Annie's reply. Jaskiran looked confused, and Annie's face shrivelled again in annoyance.

'My God, what am I doing here?' Annie said, exasperated.

'So your husband was running scams at the corporation, stealing money?' Jaskiran tried to connect the dots.

'In a way. But not just Deepak. He couldn't do it alone. His boss, Rahul Yadav, first came to him with the idea fifteen years ago. They would approve loan applications in exchange for a bribe from the applicants. Together, they must have done this for hundreds, maybe thousands, of applications.'

'And no one at the company stopped them?'

'No, that was Rahul's doing. You see, Rahul sits on the board as the executive director. But what no one knows outside of the corporation is that Rahul actually runs the DFC like his own private kingdom. The board is powerless. They agree with whatever he says. Rahul recognised the opportunity this presented. He realised the system to approve applications rested on the recommendation of account managers like Deepak and final authorisation from the board, of which Rahul is the figurehead. If he allows an application to go ahead, no one would question him.'

'He had it all figured out.'

'Yes,' Annie scowled. 'He chose Deepak to be his partner, the one who would do his bidding. Rahul wouldn't trust anyone else. I remember the way we celebrated the day he came home and told me the news. I had never seen Deepak so happy. He said that it would change our lives forever.' She looked down at the jewellery adorning her hands. 'And he was right,' she concluded.

Jaskiran looked confused. 'So, if they have been running the same scam all these years, what went wrong?'

Annie's brow creased again. 'It was Yadav,' she said bitterly. 'In the beginning, things were good. We had more money than we had ever had. I mean, we struggled in the early years of our marriage, lived in a one-room apartment and shared a toilet with four other families. Back then, we could never have dreamed of the future we would have. The money, the jewellery, cars, foreign holidays. Rahul was the same. He came from nothing too. Both of them worked hard to get to where they were, and I thought the baksheesh was just a way for us to finally enjoy life without worrying about money. It's not like they were the only two in Delhi taking bribes. Everyone was doing it.'

'But Rahul …' She shook her head. 'He changed. It wasn't just about the money with Rahul. He began loving the influence it brought him.'

'What do you mean?' Jaskiran asked.

'I mean, Rahul wanted more than a comfortable life. He realised that he no longer had to wait for genuine applications to be submitted. Even fake applications could be approved. That meant that none of the money would be used for legitimate purposes, so it could all be shared around. Yadav would no longer just take a small commission but keep the lion's share. I'm talking crores. He started mixing with very big players such as politicians, the police and even criminals. They all loved him because he was their gateway to easy money. All they had to do was make fraudulent applications, and he and Deepak would do the rest.'

'And Deepak?'

Annie shrugged. 'What could he do? He went along with it because he continued to get his share. But Yadav pushed him too far. The day before his death, they got into an argument. I heard Deepak shouting on the phone with him, saying that Yadav was being reckless. They were running the risk of an audit on their finances, which would have exposed them both. Deepak said that he would not sign off on any new applications and hung up.'

'And because he wouldn't go ahead with it, you think Rahul Yadav had Deepak killed?'

Annie looked at Jaskiran with another annoyed expression. 'Of course, what else?' Annie replied.

'Do you have proof?'

Now Annie let out a cynical laugh. 'No, if I had that, I would have gone to the papers long ago. But I *know*. After the argument, Deepak had been restless. He couldn't sit still but didn't want to talk about it. That wasn't like him.

He would always tell me everything. I could see he was worried. The next day, he didn't go to the office. He said he was having back pain. Later that day, he said he was going out for some cigarettes. He put on his shoes, told me that he loved me, and that was the last time I saw him alive.' Annie wiped away a tear from her eye, and her expression hardened. 'The police called me to say that his body had been found on the side of the road. They never caught the driver of the car that hit him, but I know it was Rahul Yadav who orchestrated it.'

'Is that why you're in hiding?'

'Yes,' Annie nodded. 'After his death, I knew that I wasn't safe in my home any longer. I'm another loose end. I left the same night Deepak died, before it was ransacked. My neighbour phoned and told me about it. I can't bear to go back and see what they've done to my home.'

'What were they after?'

'Proof of their wrongdoing.'

'Deepak's laptop?' Jaskiran ventured.

'Yes, he communicated a lot through emails. I'm sure many of them would implicate Rahul and others in various scams over the years.'

'But the laptop would have been in the study. So why search the rest of the house?'

Annie couldn't help but smirk. 'Perhaps my first impressions of you were wrong,' she said before turning to her tan-coloured Chanel bag, placing a hand inside and pulling out a brown folder. 'They were also looking for this,' she said, holding the frayed folder out in front of her. 'It's the application Deepak was working on at the time. This is what he was fighting with Yadav about the day before he died. I've already looked through it and can't find any names. It's made out by a company, but someone obviously thinks it's important enough to destroy my home to find.'

She handed the folder to Jaskiran, who took it gratefully.

'Thank you,' she said, giving the pages a cursory glance.

'But,' Jaskiran hesitated, 'if Rahul killed Deepak because he wouldn't go ahead with approving the application, why kill Anjali?'

Annie shrugged. 'I'm sorry, I don't know why they would hurt that poor girl. But I know Rahul only used Deepak. If someone else approved the application, Rahul would have been behind it.'

'Did you know her? Anjali, I mean?'

'I met her a few times. I liked her. She wasn't the typical bimbo-type they hire as window dressing there. She was smart and idealistic, but perhaps a little gullible.'

'Did you know if she had a boyfriend?'

'Only what I heard on the news. That boy, Vivek something.' She clicked her tongue in disapproval. 'He's another victim in all of this.'

'Yes, we don't believe he had anything to do with it either. I was actually referring to someone at the corporation. We've had witnesses claim that they saw her getting into a Mercedes the night she died. Do you know anyone at the firm who drove such a car? Rahul Yadav, perhaps?'

Annie thought hard. 'No, Rahul still favours an Ambassador.' She shook her head. Then, as if remembering something important, she glanced at her gold chain-linked Cartier watch. 'Listen, I really must be going. I only told them that I'd be gone for an hour. They will worry.'

'Who will?'

Annie stopped to assess whether she should answer.

'I'm staying with some friends. Best I don't say any more.'

'Thank you again for giving me this.' Jaskiran indicated to the folder in her hands. 'I know it would have been easier for you to stay quiet. What you're doing is very brave.'

'It's just who I am,' said Annie, raising her chin defiantly. 'When you start life with nothing like I did, you know what it is to fight for everything. They have taken my husband.

Now I want to take something from them.' She stood and looked at Jaskiran. 'Now you have the folder. Probably best I stay out of sight a little longer. Good luck and,' she hesitated, 'make them pay.' She tucked her bag beneath her arm and walked away.

Jaskiran looked back at Annie, admiring the abundance of strength in such a small frame. She would never have guessed from the photo in Deepak's study of a young, demure Annie standing by the door of her newly purchased home that such an innocuous woman would have the fortitude to strike back against the forces that had wronged her. A thought suddenly interrupted Jaskiran's reflection, and she stood and called out, 'There was one thing.' Jaskiran moved in closer as Annie turned around.

'I was at your home, in the study, and I noticed a photograph had been taken from the wall. It was second from the left, between a picture of you moving into your home and one of Deepak as a teenager dressed in his cricketing gear.'

Annie looked confused. 'Yes, I know the picture. It was a group shot taken at our wedding, with our guests all around us. Why would anyone want that?' Annie asked aloud before smiling again. 'Of course, in the picture, you will see Rahul at the wedding party as one of our guests. Deepak was close to Rahul in those days. He was almost a father figure to Deepak. Perhaps he took it to hide any links to us.' She shrugged.

'Do you have a copy?'

Annie shook her head. 'No, I could only leave with a few valuables.'

Jaskiran nodded silently, a little embarrassed at her own question.

'But I can get you one. My parents have copies of their own. I can ask them to post it directly to you. It may take a few days. They still live in Kerala.'

‘That would be very useful, thank you,’ Jaskiran replied.

‘Good luck, Jaskiran, and for heaven’s sake, don’t get yourself into any trouble over this. Don’t make me regret giving you that folder.’ With that, Annie put on her expensive sunglasses and paced down the path, looking like just another carefree lady of leisure enjoying an afternoon stroll.

39

The Cinnamon Cafe at Connaught Place was a regular haunt for reporters looking to meet contacts away from prying eyes. Jaskiran had texted Rajesh to meet there. He arrived ready for another scolding. No doubt Sabeena would have told Jaskiran that he had again left the office without telling anyone where he was going. Besides, Jaskiran may even still be mad about his outburst that morning. He decided the best thing to do was to apologise immediately.

'Hi,' he ventured as he approached the counter where she sat sipping coffee, a ream of papers before her.

'Hi,' she replied excitedly, turning to face him. 'Rajesh, we have to talk.'

'I know,' he interrupted, taking a seat. 'I just wanted to tell you that I'm sorry for my outburst this morning. It was childish. This is your story as much as it is mine. I was upset that we couldn't help Vivek any sooner. But it's okay. I went to see the magistrate who witnessed his arrest. He agreed to speak to Vivek and get him access to his family.'

'You went to see the magistrate?' A flash of irritation passed across Jaskiran's face, but rather than say anything, she paused and looked at Rajesh anew. 'I understand you are frustrated, Rajesh. We both are. I want to help Vivek just as much as you do, but the only way we can really get him out of jail is to prove that someone else killed Anjali. We need a plausible suspect.'

Rajesh sighed while nodding in agreement. 'I know, I know. But who?' he replied, exasperated.

'Rahul Yadav. He's the managing director of the Delhi Financial Corporation. Both Anjali and Deepak reported to him.'

'Why him?'

'Because,' Jaskiran replied, trying to contain her excitement, 'I got a call today from Annie Rao, Deepak's widow.'

Rajesh looked duly shocked, much to Jaskiran's pleasure.

'That's right. She got my card that I left with the neighbour. Rajesh, she told me everything.' She leaned in closer. 'She says Rahul and Deepak have been scamming the company for years. Deepak got cold feet and wanted to slow things down. The next day, he was dead. Annie is convinced that Rahul is behind it.'

'But what does this have to do with Anjali?'

'She must have been involved somehow. Maybe Deepak told her what he and Rahul were up to, and Rahul found out.'

Rajesh exhaled loudly, his mind racing. 'This is big, Jaskiran. But can we prove it?'

Jaskiran wrinkled her nose in the way she did, a trait Rajesh had begun noticing, and he found it endearing. 'Nothing concrete yet,' Jaskiran replied. 'But Annie gave me this,' she said, pointing to the reams of paper laid out on the counter. 'It's the application Deepak was working on before he died. Annie suggested it was the reason for the final argument between Deepak and Rahul. The applicant is a company called New Horizons Pvt. Ltd. It's just a shell company, so I can't get any information on the real owners yet. But I'd bet it's connected to Rahul Yadav in some way. The company's registered address is in Cullak Pur, north of Delhi. I think we should pay them a visit.'

'Now?'

'No, it's getting late. We can go first thing in the morning. I just wanted to tell you everything because we're doing this together, right?' Jaskiran asked, seeking confirmation of their commitment to work together and put the morning's ugliness behind them.

'Right,' Rajesh answered reassuringly. 'Can I drop you home?' Rajesh was suddenly aware that he was holding his breath in anticipation of her response and how much he wanted her to say yes.

'Sure,' Jaskiran agreed as she picked up the papers on the counter and placed them in her bag. 'I almost forgot. When we were at Annie's, I noticed a photograph was taken from Deepak's study. Annie told me that it shows Rahul Yadav at their wedding. It corroborates their close relationship. She's sending me a copy from her family in Kerala.'

They walked out together, Rajesh feeling considerably better than when he had entered. It had not been such a bad day after all. His appeal to the magistrate would make Vivek's situation a little better. Jaskiran had a real lead, and there seemed to be no hard feelings between them.

However, his quiet satisfaction was disturbed when Jaskiran clenched his arm tightly. He turned to her and saw she had turned ghost-white, her expression one of fear.

'What's the matter?' he asked.

'Over there, it's the guy who attacked me the other day.' Rajesh followed her line of sight and saw three young men, perhaps no older than he, standing around his scooter across the road from them. One of them sat across the seat, talking to his two friends and spitting paan juice out onto the road. They now noticed the presence of the reporters standing all of thirty yards from them. They were dressed in dirty T-shirts and jeans, and all possessed lean, sinewy physiques. Everything about their demeanour told Rajesh that they were there for a confrontation.

'What do we do?' Jaskiran asked, desperately trying to mask the tremor in her voice.

Rajesh now saw a glint of metal emerge from the pockets of one of the men.

'Run,' Rajesh could barely get the words out as he started edging away.

'What?'

'Run!' Rajesh shouted, and the two of them set off as fast as they could.

Going back past the cafe, they turned the corner into a quiet side street. Here, the sparse streetlamps created pools of light amid chasms of darkness. Jaskiran could barely see where she was running and feared tripping on the uneven surface. They hurtled past a pack of sleeping dogs who were startled awake and began yapping at the fleeing reporters. Rajesh's athletic build made him a natural sprinter, and he was yards ahead of Jaskiran, who was doing everything she could to keep up. Rajesh looked back and saw the three thugs turn the corner after them. He caught Jaskiran's determined expression mixed with fear. Rajesh slowed down and grabbed Jaskiran by the hand, gripping it tightly.

Cutting through a narrow lane, they were soon approaching a busy road, but rather than slowing down, Rajesh kept up his breakneck speed. From the quiet of the residential street, they suddenly burst into three lanes of speeding traffic. Weaving through the unending stream of moving metal accompanied by the blare of horns and the shouts of angry drivers, it was all Jaskiran could do to keep her legs moving while she followed Rajesh's lead.

Just as they were approaching the other side of the road, Jaskiran suddenly heard the deafening screech of brakes as an oncoming autorickshaw shuddered toward her, the agonised face of the driver fast approaching. She lost her grip on Rajesh's hand and was rooted to the spot in fear. She threw up her hands in a futile gesture and waited for the impact, but it never came. Opening her eyes, she found her outstretched palms touching the warm glass of the autorickshaw, the driver clutching his heart in relief. Having avoided a collision and a costly meeting with the police, the driver's elation now turned to rage at Jaskiran, but before he could begin his cursing and ranting, Rajesh once again took Jaskiran by the arm and pulled her away.

'No time for a break, look!' He pointed back across the street where their pursuers were now emerging from the side street.

With that, Rajesh began again, running past the endless shops and stalls, sprightly avoiding the perusing shoppers as he did so. The near collision had given Jaskiran the adrenaline injection she needed to keep going, but she knew she wouldn't be able to keep up this pace for much longer. Turning off the busy road through a narrow alleyway between two stores, they made their way over uneven ground, feet splashing through filthy puddles of waste. They emerged into another residential street of gated blocks and high walls. Away from the blaring horns and calls of bystanders, there was only their heavy breathing and the pounding of their footsteps to keep them company. Jaskiran's feet were beginning to feel heavy, and her pace slowed. Looking back, Rajesh could see the chase had taken its toll on Jaskiran.

'Look.' Rajesh pointed at a large iron gate at the end of one block as he made his way towards it. 'We can lose them in there.' On reaching the gate, he cupped his hands, ready for Jaskiran. She placed a foot in his hands, and he lifted her up until she could reach the top of the gate and vault over.

Just as she disappeared from view, Rajesh heard a call behind him: 'There he is!' one of his pursuers called out.

Rajesh abandoned any idea of climbing the gate, believing Jaskiran would be safer if he led the thugs away. He still had plenty of energy and was confident that he could outrun them. Turning around to see all three of the thugs fast approaching, he turned into a dark narrow lane that ran adjacent to the compound. The lane was littered with rubbish and pieces of disused furniture. Manoeuvring himself as fast as he could, Rajesh ventured deeper into the darkness until, to his horror, a wall emerged out of the darkness before him. He came to a complete halt just in front of it, his legs throbbing, chest aching, the taste of blood at the back of his throat. He was trapped.

Doubling back, he searched for another way out. And there it was – the service entrance to the apartment complex. Making straight for the small metal door, he ran his hand over it searching for a handle, but there was none. Finding the gap between the frame and the door, he tried to prise it open, but it wouldn't budge. In desperation, he began banging on the door with his fists and then kicking it as hard as he could, but to no avail.

'Shit!' he banged on the door again, the metal echoing his desperation into the surrounding night.

He suddenly heard laughter behind him, and he turned to see the silhouetted shapes walking toward him.

'The fool has run into a dead end. He's caught himself.'

Rajesh faced the thugs, their profiles growing larger as they approached. Abandoned by the door was an upturned wooden table, three legs staunchly upright in the air. He knelt at the corner where the fourth leg should have been and found it splintered on the ground. Picking it up, he was relieved to feel its solid weight. *This might help*, he thought. He gripped the two-foot wooden leg in both hands and raised it above his shoulder like a cricket player readying himself to slog a ball for six. He knew his only escape was back the way he came. He would have to fight his way out.

Rajesh began to move towards the three thugs, who seemed momentarily surprised at his audacity. They stopped ahead of him, and the leader among them turned back to his friends. Even in the little light, Rajesh could see he was grinning. Suddenly his right hand disappeared behind his back, reappearing grasping a large knife. Its long, slender form and sharp edge sent a shudder down Rajesh's spine and made the hairs on the back of his neck stand on end. He noticed more shapes emerging from the shadows before him. Was that the hook of a crowbar? And that, the blunted end of a screwdriver?

He felt the strength sap away from his arms and the fight die within him. *Who are these guys?* he wondered. *Maybe we could just talk things over?*

Before he could find his voice, there was the sharp clang of metal on metal, like a bolted lock being pushed back. Rajesh turned to the door in the wall as it swung open, creaking loudly on its hinges. He was met by the sight of Jaskiran. There was a brief silence as his colleague took in the scene before her.

'Quickly, in here!' Jaskiran blurted out, and before anyone else could react, Rajesh threw the table leg at the knife-wielding thug as hard as he could. It flipped through the air and caught him flush against the side of the face. He let out a cry of pain and fell back in a crumpled heap on the floor. Rajesh dived past Jaskiran, who swung the door shut behind her a moment before the remaining thugs could reach them. They began to strike at the door while Jaskiran jammed the bolt lock back with an almighty bang.

Jaskiran helped Rajesh to his feet. 'You're crazy,' she said. 'You were really going to fight those guys?'

'Well,' Rajesh said catching his breath. 'I was hoping it wouldn't come to that.'

The pounding against the door had now ceased, and they could hear the retreating footsteps of the thugs.

'You think they'll try to climb the gate like you did?' Rajesh asked.

'It's possible, but we can find another way out,' Jaskiran replied as she led Rajesh down the narrow path to the furthest end of the compound. Once there, they found a tall plant pot they used to help them climb the wall, and they descended onto the rubbish-littered street on the other side. Rajesh wasted no time flagging down a passing autorickshaw and the two of them jumped in, with Rajesh directing the driver back to his scooter. Jaskiran collapsed back in her seat. With her body still, she could feel her heart bursting against her chest in a combination of fear, exhaustion and euphoric relief. After Rajesh had given his instructions to the driver to avoid the route they had just travelled, he sank back into his seat beside her. A few seconds passed as they both enjoyed the calming sense of relief and safety before they turned to look at one another in silence and then simultaneously burst into laughter.

40

AS JASKIRAN REACHED HOME, she entered the dark hallway and shut the door gently behind her, careful not to make too much noise. She wasn't sure she could face a grilling from her brother or parents about her whereabouts. She leaned back against the locked door, allowing herself to embrace the feeling of safety. After the initial euphoria of escaping their pursuers had passed, grave questions had begun to fill her head. *Who were those thugs?* she wondered. *Were they just trying to scare us off the story, or did they mean real harm? Were they the ones who killed Anjali?* The questions replayed in her head like a broken record. One thing she could be sure of was they were working for Rahul Yadav.

Suddenly, noises coming from down the hall pulled Jaskiran from her thoughts. She realised she wasn't the only one up. She could make out the high-pitched tone of her sister-in-law, Nisha, and her brother's brief, gruff responses coming from the living room. The light emanated into the hall, and the passing shadows told her Nisha was pacing the floor.

Not wanting to be seen by either of them, Jaskiran removed her shoes and stepped silently towards the stairs. Taking each step in time, she began ascending the stairs to her room when she stopped. Curiosity now getting the better of her, she stood still halfway up the staircase, her hand gripped the banister, as she focused on the voices coming from down the hall.

'Is this all you know how to do?' Nisha's distinct voice became clear to Jaskiran.

'I'm tired,' Gurvinder responded, his usual aggressive tone replaced by a defensive placation. 'I've been at the factory since six this morning. So what if I drink to cool off?'

'You're either at that blasted factory, or you sit here drinking like a man your father's age. You never want to go out anymore. We never go to see friends or even go out for dinner. You know, the things married couples are supposed to be doing.'

'What do you want from me?' came Gurvinder's response. 'I am responsible for the factory now. That's our future.'

'What future?' came Nisha's cutting reply. 'Don't you remember the tall promises that you made me before we got engaged? You working in finance, us moving to Mumbai. And look where we are! You work in a plastics factory and still live at home. You should be ashamed of the lies you told me so I'd agree to marry you.'

'How was I to know how things would be? And I'm not some gaandu on the assembly line either. I own the business now. I'm the boss, Nisha. Give me some respect,' Gurvinder replied, but Jaskiran could hear there was no fight in his voice.

'Respect!' Nisha spat back. 'I'd have more respect for someone who keeps their promises to their wife. You told me that we would have our own place. Five years later and here we are – still living in your parents' house. You know, all my friends have their own place with just their husbands. Shriti and Tej, they just bought a place in Vasant Kunj.'

'Why do you keep bringing this up? My parents treat you well.'

'That's not the point. I want my own house to run, not live under their rules. And your mother always makes comments whenever I go out or about her friends who have so many grandchildren. She thinks that she is being subtle.'

'What do you expect? She is from a different generation.'

'She should not get involved. I'm a married woman. What does she think I am doing? The one she should be worrying about is Jaskiran. Where is your sister now? Out late every night with no interest in getting married. That's perfectly fine with your mother, yet she has to be on my case daily.'

'Leave Jaskiran out of this.'

'Why? Why does she get a pass but I don't?'

'What pass? We are always telling her to get married. What, should we force her now? Is that the husband you want to be married to?'

Jaskiran was surprised to hear her brother defend her against his own wife. It wasn't something that she had ever heard before.

'Don't twist my words. She's out late, probably meeting guys who are all laughing at you – the big brother who can't even rein in his little sister before she destroys her reputation and it becomes impossible to find her a decent husband.'

Jaskiran felt a flash of anger, and she fought the sudden urge to pace down the hallway and confront Nisha.

'That's enough!' Gurvinder's outburst stifled her thoughts of retribution. 'You know that's not who she is. Look at this.' Jaskiran could hear the folding of paper. 'These articles she writes. She's working hard to be successful on her own.'

'Is that a dig at me? Because I don't work?'

'No, that's not what I meant.'

'Screw you! I don't work because you told me that you would provide me with everything. Another lie of yours.'

'What haven't I given you? You have everything you want. Do I ever stop you from doing as you please? What else can I give you?'

'How about a happy marriage, or do they not make those at the factory?'

Jaskiran held her breath, but there was silence from her brother.

'Typical. Nothing to say now,' Nisha continued. 'Fine then, I'm going to bed.'

Jaskiran could hear footsteps approaching the hallway, and she quickly tiptoed to the top of the stairs and crept into her room.

As she lay in bed, Jaskiran went over everything that she had overheard. She knew that her brother's marriage had its problems, but she never considered their relationship could be so fractured. Gurvinder had sounded so weary, yet even in the face of Nisha's wrath, he had found it in him to stick up for his sister. A feeling of tenderness swelled within Jaskiran for her brother. It was a feeling that she had not felt for a long time. It took her back to the days when they were kids. He would always protect her, making sure that the other kids in the neighbourhood didn't play too rough with her and shouldering the blame for her disobedience to their parents. It touched her that there was still some semblance of her loving brother beneath the hard, cynical man he had become.

Jaskiran thought of how Gurvinder would react if she told him about that night's events and the details of the story that she was investigating. He would probably forbid her to leave the house, and he would most likely get her parents' support too. But she knew now that it was her brother's clumsy way of protecting her. He did not mean to stifle her.

41

THE NEXT MORNING, JASKIRAN and Rajesh drove to the registered address of New Horizons Pvt. Ltd, the company named in the folder given to Jaskiran by Annie Rao. The distance was too far to cover comfortably on Rajesh's scooter, so Jaskiran had borrowed her mother's small WagonR for the journey.

'Nice car. Why have we been suffering on my scooter this whole time when we could have been riding in luxury?' Rajesh said while running his hand down the plastic dashboard.

'Because it's not mine, and it's hardly luxury. Hey, don't touch that.' She slapped Rajesh's hand away from the air conditioning dial. 'Maa gets very fussy when people adjust the AC. She likes it a particular way.'

'Okay, okay.' Rajesh raised his hands in supplication. 'What about the radio? Am I permitted to defile your mother's car by changing the radio station?'

'You may change the radio station,' Jaskiran replied, smirking.

After an hour of driving, the traffic began to subside as they left the busy interior of the city and approached its outskirts. They travelled in relative silence, both pretending to enjoy the Bollywood pop playing on the radio, the things unsaid hanging heavy in the air. It was Jaskiran who finally broke the embargo.

'So, are we going to address the elephant in the room?' Jaskiran ventured.

'What do you mean?' Rajesh replied, but Jaskiran could see that he knew what she meant from his expression.

'Those guys yesterday, they meant to hurt us, right? When I found you in the alley, I saw that the one who attacked me before was holding a knife.'

'I think that they just wanted to scare us,' said Rajesh. 'They wouldn't have actually done anything.' He was trying to play the incident off lightly because he didn't want to consider the possibility of his life having been in danger, not now that they were closer than ever to breaking the story.

Jaskiran glanced over at Rajesh while he avoided her gaze, looking out the window at the passing cacophony of Delhi life.

'I hope you're right,' she added solemnly.

They followed the winding, poorly marked roads for another hour before they arrived at Cullak Pur, an empty expanse of farmland banked against the Yamuna.

'Not exactly what I expected,' Rajesh said, scanning the passing surroundings. 'For a company applying for a loan of ten crore rupees, you'd think they'd be housed in a smart office block.'

'I know what you mean. There's nothing here.' Jaskiran stopped the car and checked the address. 'We should be pretty close, but there are no signs posted.'

'Let's ask someone,' Rajesh said, opening the door. He saw a young woman with an infant and stepped out to ask for directions. She pointed them to a small farmhouse in the middle of a nearby field. They left the main road and followed the dirt track towards the solitary building. Even from a distance, it was evident that the building was in a state of disrepair. Rajesh knocked on the front door but there was no response. He knocked again and waited before turning to Jaskiran and saying, 'Looks like no one's here.'

Jaskiran scanned the surrounding fields. The harvest was complete and the land was mostly bare, but in the distance she saw a man cutting wheat stems by hand. The fields ran down to the banks of the Yamuna, where the mud turned darker and became saturated with river water. She noticed a small jetty that looked ready to collapse into the murky waters. She pondered it for a moment before turning once again to Rajesh.

'Maybe he knows something,' Jaskiran said, pointing to the figure in the field who was as yet oblivious to their presence.

Rajesh and Jaskiran made their way over the scraggy, uneven ground to where the man was shearing and laying the harvested crop in a large plastic haulage bag. The man continued his work, seemingly unable to hear them approach, stopping to look around only when the reporters cast long shadows over the crop before him. There was a brief look of fear on his face when he saw them. He blinked in the sunlight and placed a hand across his brow to shield his eyes. The fearful expression disappeared when he concluded that the reporters were no threat.

'Sorry to disturb you, Uncleji,' Rajesh said warmly. 'We are looking for an address. Is this Dahesra Farm?'

The old man looked at them, his head tilted in a way to indicate he had only one good eye to see them. He had messy white hair and a goatee. His back stooped from a lifetime of working the fields. 'What is this about? Who are you?' he asked, assessing them both.

'We are just looking for a company, New Horizons. They are registered at this address,' Jaskiran replied with a disarming smile.

The old man was silent for a few more moments before he spoke again. 'This is Dahesra Farm, there is no one from Horizons here.'

Jaskiran quickly followed up, 'But you know them, yes, Horizons? They have been here?'

'Yes, they have been here. They bought my land from me. But I haven't seen anyone for a few weeks. I only came back to harvest the crops. Otherwise, they would just let them die in the field.'

'This used to be your farm?' Jaskiran continued.

'Yes, but they were offering good money, and what am I going to do with the farm now? My sons have all gone to the city for work. If I don't sell now, they will sell it when I die. At least I can rest knowing I secured a good price.'

Jaskiran looked around at the surrounding fields, perhaps six acres of undeveloped land. The exposed soil looked parched, but being so close to the river with no defences it likely flooded during the rains. Jaskiran wiped her sweating brow with the edge of the shawl she used to shield herself from the harsh sun.

'Did they say what they wanted to do with the land?' she asked, turning back to the old man.

He shook his head slowly. 'No, they wouldn't tell me,' he replied. 'I don't think they told the others either, or no one has mentioned it. Either way, I don't care. Let them have it.' He was already turning to continue with his work, seemingly bored of the conversation and satisfied it was no concern of his.

'Others?' Rajesh asked.

'Yes, yes,' the man said, almost annoyed. 'They are buying everyone's land. Look all around. It will soon all be theirs.' With that, he folded the handles of the large haulage bag together and lifted it onto his arched back, the straps straining against his forehead. The bag was stuffed with wheat and close to overflowing. The weight must have been a tremendous burden on the old man's frame, but he carried it with no protest. He ambled away through the bushes towards the road and out of sight.

Jaskiran and Rajesh looked at one another in silence before Rajesh asked what they were both thinking, 'Why is Rahul Yadav buying up land all the way out here? He fancies retiring and becoming a landowner? It doesn't make sense?'

'I know,' Jaskiran mused, her attention drawn to the river again. Her confusion concerning Rahul's motives gave way to a growing curiosity about the farm itself. 'I'm going for a walk.'

'Where to?' Rajesh asked, surveying the empty fields.

'To the river,' she replied, almost sure her hunch would be fruitless.

She followed a path in the dry dirt, unsure of what she was even looking for. Turning, she saw Rajesh had reluctantly begun following her. As they got closer to the river, the crops came to an end, and the land gently curved down towards the bank. The mud became clay-like underfoot, baked into shallow trenches. She stopped and counted, an electric charge running up her spine. 'Tyre tracks!' she called back to Rajesh.

When he had finally caught up, Rajesh looked down and saw the two parallel tread marks that followed the dirt track to the jetty.

'You see,' Jaskiran pointed. 'The tracks don't show up in the dry dirt, but here, where the water is saturated, the weight of a vehicle made the tracks.'

'Yes, I see, but what's your point?' Rajesh replied, seemingly unimpressed.

Faced with Rajesh's cold scepticism Jaskiran wasn't sure what it indicated, and she replied softly, 'Well, Anjali was taken away in a car, and her body was found in the river …' She pointed to the jetty.

Rajesh exhaled loudly. 'That's a stretch, even for me. There are so many other spots along the riverbank where they could have dropped her body. They could have even done it from a bridge. Why come all the way out here?'

'I don't know,' Jaskiran replied, walking onward towards the riverbank. Other than the clearing beside the jetty, the riverbank was bordered by shrubs and trees, and she began quickly searching through them. 'Perhaps because you bring her to a place you already know will be quiet. A place you know is private. Out of the way. And somewhere you can put a body knowing no one will find it in the same place.' She was getting breathless as she tossed aside branches to check underneath the trees and behind bushes.

'Right, but you can't just push a body into the water from here,' Rajesh retorted. 'You'd need to row out into the middle of the river. And this jetty doesn't even have a—'

'Boat!' Jaskiran cried, unveiling a small, upturned canoe hidden beneath a bed of bushes close to the water's edge. She smiled triumphantly at Rajesh, who smirked and nodded his approval.

'Damn, you're good.'

42

AYESHA BEGUM SIPPED ON her morning coffee as she sat by the marble-top dining table in her spotless, modern apartment and looked out over the haze-filled cityscape beyond the balcony doors. Another packed day of engagements and meetings lay ahead of her. Her first stop would be at a school for underprivileged girls. She could picture the scene already in her mind: the sea of smiling, hopeful faces as she told them lie after lie about how they too could become important women just like her if they studied hard and always did the right thing.

She scoffed and shook her head. She would be lucky if one reporter showed up for that, and it certainly wasn't going to be on any front page. What's more, that brat from the *Delhi Daily* had cut short their interview, and Ayesha was loath to go crawling back to them after being shown such disrespect. However, she now had information that would make waves across the city.

The deputy commissioner had revealed to her that he had been working for Rahul Yadav to cover up the murder of Anjali Mangal and pin the blame on her ex-boyfriend Vivek Trivedi. If she leaked this news to the press, it would be the biggest story of the year. The ensuing scandal would bring down Rahul Yadav, cutting off key finance for her rivals. She would reap the political capital that played to her strength as a voice for justice for women.

Deputy Commissioner Sagar would also be painted as a villain and his career would end too. However, that made no difference to Ayesha. The man had already divulged all he knew and was now useless to her. She wouldn't falter from her objective by worrying about collateral damage. What did give her pause, though, was that she had no verifiable proof.

If she leaked the news with no evidence, she would only give Yadav and Sagar the opportunity to cover their tracks and use their considerable influence to ensure that nothing came of it. By pointing the finger at Rahul Yadav, she would also have to keep claiming that Vivek was innocent despite the police supposedly having evidence that he had murdered a young woman. If Ayesha played it wrong, the fallout could potentially destroy her credibility with the public.

There was a buzz from the intercom that interrupted her thoughts. A member of her staff announced that her car had arrived. It was time to go. Ayesha took one last sip of coffee before rising. *It wouldn't do to act in haste*, she told herself as she headed for the door. She would have to bide her time and keep this to herself until the time was right.

43

IT WAS ALREADY LATE in the afternoon when Rajesh and Jaskiran returned from their trip to Cullak Pur. Despite Jaskiran's suspicions, it was an otherwise fruitless endeavour. Jaskiran was keen to spend what was left of the day trying to dig up more information on New Horizons from the office. Rajesh had other plans. Arriving at the Delhi Financial Corporation's office he was convinced he would not have to wait long before Rahul Yadav left for the day, concluding that a man of Rahul's age and wealth had no need to burn the midnight oil.

He parked his scooter across the road from the office building, where he had a clear view of both the main entrance and the employee car park.

In the parking area, three men sat on plastic garden chairs, playing cards using a fourth chair as a makeshift table. 'Excuse me, is Mr Yadav inside?' Rajesh asked as he approached the men.

They looked at him with just a hint of suspicion. 'Why are you asking us?' asked one of the men gruffly. 'Go inside and ask the girls at the reception.'

'I did, but they won't tell me. I want to speak to him about getting a loan.'

One of the other men began to laugh. 'Are you stupid?' he said, chuckling. 'It doesn't work like that. You have to fill out loads of forms, and then they decide. You can't just ask him to give you a loan. You think he just carries money around in his pocket?' The man looked at his companions and chuckled some more.

'A cousin of mine told me that Mr Yadav has the power to grant a loan with a click of his fingers,' Rajesh persisted. 'I just need five minutes with him. Please, do you know if he is inside?'

'Yes, he is inside,' the first man replied shortly, annoyed at Rajesh's presence.

'But you better hurry,' the third man spoke up. 'His driver will arrive to pick him up at 6 p.m. sharp. Mr Yadav always leaves at six.'

Rajesh thanked them and made as if he was heading toward the office entrance before doubling back unseen to his scooter.

At the stroke of six, a white Ambassador stopped at the office entrance. Barely a minute later, Rahul Yadav walked out of the building with a cursory nod to the driver, who held the car door open for him, and then he was out of sight. Rajesh hadn't known what to expect, but seeing Rahul for the first time, he was surprised by his diminutive frame. He looked old and somewhat frail. He hardly seemed capable of committing murder.

Rajesh began following the Ambassador. With no prior experience at tailing anyone, Rajesh found it a steep learning curve. Before they had even reached the end of the street, he was right at the Ambassador's rear bumper. The driver waved Rajesh ahead, but he stuttered to a stop, feigning engine trouble. He waited for Rahul's car to turn the corner before resuming the pursuit. After that, Rajesh ensured that he kept at least one vehicle between them, careful not to be spotted in the rear-view mirror. He was close enough to see the Ambassador turn through the gates of an imposing red and white two-storey house in Golf Links.

Rajesh stopped a little further down the street and noted a security guard by the gates. The guard sat on his stool smoking a beedi, oblivious that he was under surveillance himself. Rajesh suddenly had an idea. He quickly drove to a street corner stall selling beedis and paan at the next junction.

'Excuse me, Uncleji,' Rajesh said politely to the owner. 'Do you see the big red and white house over there?' The stall owner nodded. 'The security guard there enjoys a smoke, yes?'

'Yes, his name is Aadhan,' said the shopkeeper with a smile. 'He's a regular customer.'

'He's a friend of my father,' said Rajesh, returning the smile. 'I was going to surprise him at work. What brand does he usually buy?'

The stall owner thought for a moment with his hand hovering over his selection of wares. 'He likes these Sundari ones,' he finally said, picking up a pack in a colourful paper wrapper bearing the face of the company's founder warning smokers against imitations and an image of a tar-filled lung.

'Does he not smoke cigarettes?'

The man shook his head. 'I've told him he should. It's healthier, but with the excise duty, who can afford to pay these prices?'

'Give me one of your best cigarette brands,' said Rajesh.

Among his selection of Indian tobacco and cigarette brands, the stall owner also had some imported Marlboros that he kept hidden to ensure no quick-fingered thieves got away with them while he was distracted. He handed the packet to Rajesh, quickly taking the money in return and stuffing it down his pocket before anyone saw it. Rajesh thanked the stall owner and headed back towards the guard, unable to shake the feeling he should have haggled over the price. A tightness in his chest formed at the thought of the few notes left in his wallet until payday.

Approaching the security guard at Rahul Yadav's house, Rajesh called out in a familiar manner. 'Aadhan,' he said cheerfully. 'Nice to see you.'

The guard looked up to see a smiling stranger approach. 'Who are you?' he asked, the confusion clear on his face.

'My name is Rajesh. I wanted to speak to you.'

'Me?' Aadhan replied. He turned to check there was no one else around.

'No need to worry, I'm a friend. It's to do with your boss, Mr Yadav.'

On hearing his boss's name, the man shook his head and made a dismissive gesture with one hand. 'If you have questions for Mr Yadav, you should ask him directly,' he said. 'I just sit here in the evenings. I don't even speak to him.'

'Relax, Aadhan. I'm not trying to get you into trouble.' He pulled out the packet of Marlboros. 'Here, have a smoke,' he said, handing the man a cigarette, making sure he could see the packet it was taken from. 'I'm told that these are very good.'

Aadhan hesitated, but his desire to taste the premium cigarette got the better of him. He took the cigarette gratefully, still unsure of what to make of this young stranger. He put the cigarette to his lips, sparked a match, took a long drag and exhaled slowly, enjoying the moment. 'It is good,' he said. He smiled at Rajesh, a little more at ease. 'I have always wanted to try these.'

'There's more where that came from,' Rajesh said, indicating the open packet in his hand. 'I just want to know if you were here last Friday night.'

Aadhan nodded almost immediately. 'I haven't taken a day off in months.'

'Did Mr Yadav come back from work at the same time that he usually does?'

The guard replied, 'Yes, Mr Yadav is very punctual. He came back at the usual time.'

Rajesh drew in closer to the man. 'Did he leave again that night?' he asked quietly. 'Think carefully.'

In an exaggerated gesture that suggested he was considering the question, Aadhan looked away as if in deep thought. After what felt like an age, the guard slowly shook his head. 'No, he never left again that night.'

'You're sure?' Rajesh asked, trying to hide his disappointment.

Aadhan took another puff. 'Yes, I remember because I was watching the cricket that night.' He pointed toward the small TV set within the hut. 'Besides, Mr Yadav rarely goes out once he returns from work.'

Rajesh mouthed an obscenity in frustration and turned away. He had been sure that the guard would confirm his suspicions about Rahul being the one Anjali met the night she was murdered. But if Aadhan was speaking the truth, it couldn't have been him.

Rajesh turned back to the guard. 'What about big bust-ups?'

'What about them?'

'Have you heard Mr Yadav arguing with anyone recently?'

'No, I told you already,' Aadhan said, smiling. 'I don't talk to Mr Yadav. I just see him drive in and out. Now please?' He gestured for the cigarette packet.

Rajesh's frustration grew. The money he spent on them now seemed a waste. He took one from the packet and gave it to the guard, whose smile disappeared.

'Only one? But I answered your questions?' said Aadhan, feeling cheated.

Rajesh shrugged. 'Sorry, but I was hoping for more than that.'

Taking pity on the guard, Rajesh pulled another solitary cigarette from the packet and handed it over. Aadhan looked longingly at the packet. 'I can tell you other things,' he cried desperately as Rajesh turned to leave. 'The CM visited him once!'

Rajesh stopped and turned his head. 'When?' he asked, hopeful.

'About six months ago,' Aadhan grinned sheepishly.

'Nice try.' Rajesh almost swore and then continued walking away.

'Okay, some guys came here last night.'

'Who?' Rajesh called back without breaking stride.

'I don't know, but one of them was bleeding from a cut under his eye. The whole side of his face was swollen and bruised.'

Rajesh turned and walked back to Aadhan. 'Were there three of them?'

Realising he had Rajesh's attention, Aadhan continued, 'Yes, exactly. They came here late last night. The one that was bleeding was angry, shouting that he wanted to see Mr Yadav. Of course, I told him that they couldn't enter – it was too late an hour and sir would be asleep. I told them to leave or I would call the police.'

Rajesh was stunned into silence. There it was – the confirmation that the men who had pursued them yesterday had done so at the bidding of Rahul Yadav. It was becoming clear to him that Rahul must be involved in Anjali's death, and he was now doing whatever he could to keep Rajesh and Jaskiran from finding out more. Rajesh was so wrapped up in his own thoughts he barely noticed the guard gratefully slip the packet of cigarettes out of his hand.

44

JASKIRAN WAS AT HER desk when her phone buzzed with a message. After reading it, she grabbed her bag and stepped out of the office and onto the street below. Before she had finished scanning the street, Inspector Shah was by her side.

'Looking for me?' he said, smiling.

Jaskiran almost jumped. 'Shit, you scared me. Did they teach that at the academy? How to sneak up on suspects?' Composing herself, she began to lead him away toward the chaiwallah on the corner of the street.

'Ha!' Shah laughed sarcastically. 'You think they actually teach anything at the academy? The only education for being a policeman is walking the streets. No textbook can replace it,' he said confidently.

'So tell me, with all that walking the streets, what have you found out?'

The question knocked the confidence out of the inspector, and he avoided Jaskiran's gaze. 'Well, there have been a few inquiries, but no solid leads just yet.'

'Which is police code for you haven't got a thing, right?' Jaskiran was now smirking.

'Yes, actually, that was one thing they teach you at the academy – how to bullshit.' They both laughed together.

Jaskiran ordered two teas from the vendor, handing one of the clay pots to the inspector before continuing to walk towards a nearby market.

'Lucky for us both, I've made a lot more progress on my investigation than you.'

'Really?' Shah seemed surprised. 'You found someone new connected to Anjali?'

'Not new,' Jaskiran replied, scrutinising an array of vegetables on offer at one busy stall. 'Annie, Deepak Rao's wife, contacted me.'

'How did she find you?'

Jaskiran shrugged matter-of-factly. 'I left my card with her neighbour.'

Shah looked sheepish. 'My, my, Jaskiran, you're beginning to show me up. None of the neighbours wanted anything to do with me when I spoke with them.'

'Well, have you seen yourself?' she teased. 'You can be quite intimidating.'

Shah took it as a compliment. 'What did Annie tell you?'

Jaskiran stopped walking. 'She believes Rahul Yadav had her husband killed. They were close friends and had been running scams together for years before they fell out a few weeks ago. She also believes Anjali may have known something that got her killed too.'

'Yadav?' Shah's jaw tensed. 'I spoke to him the day we met. If what you're saying is true, he puts on a pretty good act. He seemed genuinely upset over Anjali, and he never mentioned anything to say he was close to Deepak. Does Annie have any proof?'

'In a way.' Jaskiran pulled a face that made her uncertainty clear. 'She gave me the details of a company that is defrauding the Delhi Financial Corporation out of ten crore rupees. The company is registered to some land they are purchasing out in Cullak Pur and used to be owned by an ancient farmer who is definitely being used. Annie and I believe Rahul Yadav is the likely real owner of this borrowing company. He wanted Deepak's help to get the application approved. Deepak refused to help, and for that, he was killed.'

'You believe Rahul is the real owner, you don't know?'

'No. The farmer had no idea. That's why I need you.'

'Me? What am I supposed to do?'

'I need you to do some digging. Is there no one at the Income Tax Department, Enforcement Directorate or even the CBI that you can turn to?'

'Jaskiran,' said Shah, scratching the back of his head, 'I hate to say this, but I'm just an inspector. I don't have that kind of authorisation. If I start approaching central government agencies, they'll want to know why. It will certainly get back to the deputy commissioner.'

Jaskiran shook her head in frustration. 'You wanted me to be open about what I find. I come to you with the only lead you have on the case, and you tell me you can't even make enquiries? Do you want to find out the truth or not?'

Shah thought for a moment before responding, 'Okay, I'll see what I can do, but no guarantees.'

'That's fine. I'll send you the details of what I have,' Jaskiran said before walking back to her office.

45

Coming home that evening, Rajesh was met by the sight of his siblings sitting atop his charpoy, their faces illuminated by the flashing lights of the TV. He sat between them, patting Amit's hair as he did so, causing the boy to shift and protest at the disruption.

'Hi to you too,' Rajesh said as he squeezed his brother's cheeks, which brought on further protestations. 'And you, Roopa. No homework today?'

His sister gave him the briefest of looks and shook her head before snuggling up against him as she continued to watch the latest talent show featuring aspiring young children who sang and danced for the audience's entertainment.

When his mother appeared out of the bedroom, Rajesh greeted her with a mute smile. He knew that she wasn't angry at him any longer, but what hurt him deeper was the disappointment that she must have felt. She had counted on him, and he had let her down. He couldn't help but look at her and feel ashamed.

For his mother's part, she had forgiven her son, understanding he was entitled to make mistakes. She could see that despite himself, Rajesh still carried the burden of losing his father. But it was not necessarily sorrow she saw in him; no, it was something else – more akin to doubt. At times she looked at her son, the grown man that he was, yet he wore the look of a boy. It was at these times she lamented that she could not fill that role. His father had always been the boy's guide, setting him in the right direction for his journey through life. She watched him now as he rose from the charpoy and headed for the door.

'Where are you going?' she asked.

'I just remembered that I have to take care of something. I won't be long.'

He closed the door behind him and made for the stairs to the ground-floor apartments, knocking on apartment number six.

After a few moments, with still no answer, Rajesh was about to knock again when Mr Khurana came to the door and sighed heavily before Rajesh even had a chance to greet him.

'Do you know what time it is? I was about to have my dinner.' He inhaled heavily through his large nose, causing it and his shaggy grey moustache to twitch. An elderly man, Mr Khurana lived with his wife and had become a stickler for routine in his retirement. In his haste to answer the door, he had thrown on a knitted cardigan over a sorry-looking grey vest that many moons ago had been a pristine white. His ensemble was completed with a pair of stained pyjama bottoms and hole-riddled socks.

'Does your son-in-law still work in a jewellery store?' Rajesh asked.

'Work? He manages the store. Earns big money,' Mr Khurana answered, affronted. Just then, Mr Khurana's grandson came into view behind him.

'Daada, you said I could play on your phone before dinner.'

'Yes, we will be eating now. I just have to deal with this interruption.' Mr Khurana gestured toward Rajesh.

'But please, I nearly finished the level I was playing.'

Exasperated, Mr Khurana took out his phone from his cardigan pockets and handed it to the boy, who took it gleefully.

'Always asking for that bloody thing,' the old man said, looking back at Rajesh. 'His parents will be here soon, and they'll expect him to have had his dinner. Come, come, what do you want?'

'Your son-in-law, he bought my mother's earrings. I need you to get them back.'

'Why? He paid her a fair price,' Mr Khurana said defensively to deter any notion of wrongdoing.

'I'm sure he did,' Rajesh replied, unconvinced. 'But I'll give him something to replace them.' Rajesh reached under his collar and, undoing the clasp, brought out a thin gold chain with a rectangular pendant with a Sanskrit Aum inscription. A gift from his parents, Rajesh kissed the symbol that had rested on his chest for as long as he could remember and held it out to Mr Khurana, who took it reluctantly.

'I need you to get him to buy it from me. It's twenty-two-carat gold. You should get a good price for it,' Rajesh said reassuringly as Khurana looked at it as if it had just soiled his hand.

'Maybe, if there were three times as much gold on it. It's as light as a feather.'

'But the pendant, the workmanship is first class,' Rajesh continued enthusiastically.

'Ha,' Khurana laughed scornfully. 'Jewellers sell thousands of these every day. It's worth no more than its weight in gold, and that is not substantial,' he said, letting his wrist rise and drop to punctuate his point. 'This will not cover the money my son-in-law already paid your mother for the earrings.'

Rajesh looked disheartened, forcing Khurana to come as close to taking pity on him as he knew how.

'I assume you are having money trouble?' He tutted. 'If you really want to raise some cash, I'll buy that scooter of yours. My nephew wants one for his birthday. I don't want to buy him an expensive one, and then he crashes it. Better get him a junk one he can learn on.'

Ignoring the barb, Rajesh thought the offer over for a moment before shaking his head. True, the scooter was little more than a rust bucket he had saved from the scrap heap, salvaging what parts he could. But its practical usefulness outweighed the sentimental attachment he had to the piece of jewellery.

'Maybe another time. But for now, just the chain. I'll pay your son-in-law back anything I owe,' Rajesh replied. Khurana paused a moment and gave Rajesh a disapproving look. He didn't like the bargain Rajesh had made, but he felt compelled to take it. 'Fine, have it your way,' Khurana sighed. 'Come by at the end of the week for the earrings. And bring some money,' he added by way of farewell before shutting the door. Rajesh walked back towards the stairs but stopped. Something in the interaction with Mr Khurana brought back his visit to Anjali's apartment. At first, he couldn't fathom the connection, and he stood in silence, pulling on the thread of an idea until it came to him. He needed to see Roshan.

46

Jaskiran could hear music and laughter coming from the other side of the high wall that marked the boundary of Ashok Chopra's three-storey home in Jor Bagh. The sweet smell of jasmine scented the air. The guard took her name, phoned the house and finally admitted her with a curt nod.

Making her way up the tiled drive, she passed broad-leaf palm trees, manicured lawns and tropical flowers. Festival lights overhead and coloured spotlights hidden within the flowerbeds lit the way to a white building the size of a small apartment block.

There were small groups of people dotted around the garden, which wrapped around the side of the house to the back, enjoying a smoke or the added privacy away from the other guests. The home seemed minimalistic from the outside, with the most distinguishing feature being the oversized front door, which was obsidian black and looked like an immovable object between two panels of glass positioned on either side.

As Jaskiran approached, the heavy door slowly swung open, and she was welcomed with the cheery expression of one of the staff. They offered a glass of champagne and led her from the double-storey entrance hall down a seemingly never-ending hallway. As they walked, Jaskiran stole snatching glances through every open doorway, revealing a series of elegantly styled rooms. The hallway eventually opened into a grand kitchen and entertainment area at the back of the house. Much like the outside, it was a combination of white and black surfaces, minimalist design and little clutter. Huge glass windows stretched across the back wall, revealing the garden beyond.

The room was filled with the great and good of Delhi's political and social scene. Both men and women were dressed in a mixture of formal Indian and Western attire. The men wore tailored suits and expensive shoes and the women designer dresses and trendy sarees. Jaskiran suddenly felt out of place in her striped skirt and blouse. She recognised several high-profile politicians from the central government and members of Delhi's high society among the guests.

Walking through the kitchen toward the garden beyond, she caught a few words from passing conversations. The seemingly innocuous remarks and Delhi gossip on the lips of many seemed innocent enough. Still, Jaskiran knew that such events were more than just a chance for wealthy people to party the night away with others in their social class. They were also occasions to sow the seeds of new business ventures and form alliances, both professional and personal. Here, powerful industrialists and financiers rubbed shoulders with artists and film producers looking for funding for their next projects; founders of non-profits and charities sought out powerful patrons; new affairs were initiated with illicit looks over cocktail glasses.

She walked through the kitchen towards the garden. From the patio, Jaskiran could see a number of tents erected around the central lawn, which was lit by string lights that crisscrossed overhead. Staff walked around refilling drinks and handing out canapés. A DJ in the corner bounced to the rhythms of Bollywood dance numbers that he was playing from his speakers. Incense sticks and burning sandalwood scented the air and kept the mosquitoes at bay.

'Jaskiran!' Ashok cried out from the foot of the stairs. He bounced up the steps and embraced her with a kiss on the cheek. 'I'm so happy you came.'

'Well, you did invite me,' Jaskiran said, embarrassed by their embrace. She noticed that a few of the other guests were snatching glances at the two of them.

'You look beautiful,' Ashok said merrily. Jaskiran was a little surprised and alarmed at this new assertive, forward persona.

'Thank you,' she said, trying to recover her confidence. 'You look very dashing too.' Ashok had the good grace to feign embarrassment. He wore a fitted Nehru jacket, which was unlike him but suited him so well. Jaskiran could see now that, had he chosen to, Ashok had the charisma and looks to be a Bollywood leading man.

'What do you think of the party?' asked Ashok.

'A very different crowd from any party I've been to before. You have quite the friends.'

'Please,' Ashok said, leaning in closer and whispering, 'Many here can't stand me, and the feeling is mutual. But we all need each other. So here we are.' He took a step back and raised his glass to his oblivious guests.

Jaskiran looked around at the assembled guests and wondered if she fell into the same category in Ashok's eyes. 'You have an amazing home,' she said, trying to take her mind off such thoughts.

'Thank you, I have been fortunate,' Ashok replied. 'I renovated the whole place before moving in. May I give you a tour later?'

'Sure,' Jaskiran replied.

Just then, an attendant walked up to Ashok and whispered something in his ear. He looked at his watch and agreed, taking a swig from his champagne flute.

'Here, come with me. It's time for my announcement.' He grabbed her hand and led her down the steps to the lawn.

'What announcement?' Jaskiran asked, trying not to spill her champagne as she kept up with Ashok.

'You'll see in one moment. Wait here.'

He left her on the manicured lawn by an enormous table covered in a silk shroud. 'Ladies and gentlemen, could I have your attention, please!'

The immediate chatter died down as nearby guests looked towards Ashok with hushed excitement. The silence travelled like a ripple outward as more guests turned their attention to Ashok. Soon, those in the house spilled out onto the patio to get a better view.

Facing his captive audience, Ashok addressed them all.

'As many of you know, the Delhi Development and Regeneration Bill – *my* bill – is now in its second reading, and with the votes we have in the assembly, it will be passed, unchanged, into law tomorrow.' Ashok paused as a cheer rose and applause spread around the lawns. He had the presence of mind to look humbled as he waited for it to die down before continuing.

'Thank you, thank you. It will be a monumental moment for Delhi because it will unleash the full power and potential of Delhi's government as we work as one with our partners in the private sector – represented by many of you here today – to deliver on our vision. A vision that I will share with you now.'

With that, he pulled the edge of the silk covering with a flourish to reveal a three-dimensional model city covering every inch of the display table's surface, complete with high-rise buildings, small model cars on wide roads, bridges over waterways and even little people dotted around green spaces and plazas. 'I present to you Delhi 2.0, a city built for the future.'

Sounds of awe and excitement passed through the crowd as they took in the sight of the idealised cityscape before them. More applause arose, and Jaskiran herself could feel the excitement run through her body. She felt privileged to be there at such an unveiling. 'What you see before you is phase one of the city's regeneration. It will be the first carbon-neutral district in the country. There will be new tram and train lines, and the roads will be designed with electric vehicles in mind. All polluting vehicles will be banned.' Jaskiran could see the visible nods of appreciation from the assembled guests and heard another round of applause.

'Just as the British did, this will be a planned city. But unlike them, it will be one accessible for ordinary men and women. There will be defined residential areas along with state-of-the-art schools, shopping malls and recreation grounds as well as science and industrial parks. My friends, this bill will unlock all of this.' He paused now before adding, 'And it won't hurt my political ambitions either.' He raised his glass as laughter and cheers burst from the adoring crowd. Jaskiran also joined in the final round of applause. She could hear the remarks now from nearby guests.

'Didn't I tell you that he was a shrewd operator?' a tall, greying elderly man said as he addressed his glamorous young wife. 'This will propel him to the top of the party. He'll be the new chief minister, mark my words.'

His wife seemed uninterested in politics. 'He's certainly very handsome. I'll give him that.' She nodded approvingly. 'Surprised he isn't married.'

'He enjoys playing the field, but before you get too excited, from what I understand, even you're too old for our Mr Chopra,' the husband said, smirking as his wife rolled her eyes.

She saw Ashok looking directly at her, beckoning her over. 'Jaskiran, come. I'd like to introduce you to a close friend of mine. He is the managing director of the Delhi Financial Corporation …'

The polite smile Jaskiran had prepared froze on her face when she realised who was in front of her.

'… Jaskiran Sohal, meet Rahul Yadav.'

47

THE APARTMENT COMPLEX WAS quiet this time of the evening. Rajesh had easily managed to bypass Iqbal, who had been dozing at his station, his wireless radio still playing Hindi tunes into the darkness.

Rajesh followed the path to the front of Roshan's apartment. He noticed a faint light coming from the window beside the door. Peering in, he found Roshan sitting on the floor in front of the TV, illuminated by the glow of the screen. Once he was sure that there was no one else in the room with him, Rajesh tapped on the window.

When Roshan looked up, Rajesh signalled for him to come outside. Roshan looked towards the apartment's interior, where his parents must have been. Then he quickly got up and quietly opened the door. He was barefoot and wearing his pyjamas. 'Hey, Roshan. What are you watching?' Rajesh asked, eager to put the boy at ease.

'Cartoons. Mummy says I can watch them before bed, so I don't get nightmares.'

Rajesh thought he knew why the boy had been suffering from nightmares and didn't delve any further. He exhaled and placed a reassuring hand on Roshan's shoulder. 'Listen, Roshan. I've come to ask you a question. But before I do, I want you to know that I'm your friend, and you must always tell your friends the truth.'

Roshan looked apprehensive. 'Am I in trouble?' he asked.

'Not if you tell me the truth,' Rajesh replied. 'Do you have Anjali's phone?'

Roshan began backing away, fear in his eyes.

'It's okay, Roshan,' Rajesh pleaded. 'It can be our secret. No one needs to know.'

'I didn't steal it,' Roshan began on the verge of tears. 'She gave it to me.'

'I know, I know.' Rajesh gently squeezed the boy's shoulder. 'Do you still have it with you?'

Roshan nodded.

'It's important that you give it to me now. It can help us find out,' Rajesh hesitated, 'who … took Anjali.'

Roshan seemed buoyed by the realisation that he could help find justice for his friend. He nodded again and wiped his eyes before quietly entering the apartment. Reappearing a few moments later, he held out his hand and slipped a thin black phone to Rajesh.

Rajesh's hands were shaking as he flipped the phone around and pressed the power button. The phone came to life and a moment later, the prompt for the security code appeared on the screen.

'It's locked,' said Rajesh. 'Do you know the PIN?'

'It's our apartment numbers together – 11 and 16.'

Unlocking the phone, Rajesh was unsure what to do next. His fingers were shaking above the screen. Finally, he opened the call log, bringing up Anjali's most recent incoming and outgoing calls. He gasped in shock and felt an icy chill run up his spine as he read the name at the top of the screen.

48

'NICE TO MEET YOU, Ms Sohal,' said Rahul Yadav. His thin lips almost disappeared as he forced them into a smile. He was older than she had imagined, skinny to the point of malnourishment. But Jaskiran surmised it was a look he had carried his whole life and had nothing to do with his current state of health. His eyes were dark and cold, but he looked at her with no semblance of recognition. He held a cane in one hand and extended his free hand for her to shake. Jaskiran took it and felt his cold, tight grip. Despite his appearance, he was strong. Jaskiran forced herself to smile politely but found that she couldn't get any words out.

'Rahul has been one of my greatest supporters for many years,' said Ashok. 'In fact, in many ways, the development bill was his idea.' Ashok beamed at Rahul, who seemed agitated by the praise and attention.

Jaskiran felt like she had been delivered a body blow. *How could Ashok have anything to do with this man?* She knew him to be corrupt, everything Ashok was supposed to be against. She looked over at the model of the future district, its shiny new towers and pristine gardens, scanning the topography for any landmarks she could identify.

'Is that the Yamuna?' she asked, walking over to the table to put some distance between herself and Rahul, who seemed less interested in her.

'Yes, that's right. We are going to repurpose whole tracts of land by the Yamuna. See here? These will be riverside residential buildings. I have no doubt that they will become some of the most exclusive apartments in the whole country.'

'Where will you build it?'

'This development is earmarked for North Delhi, Bakhtawarpur, Palla.'

'... Cullak Pur?' Jaskiran enquired, her eyes darting to Rahul, who seemed to flinch. His brow furrowed.

Ashok hesitated for a second as he noticed the exchange of glances and then nodded. 'Yes, that will be the most northern end here,' he said, pointing at what looked like large storage sheds. 'It'll be the industrial district.'

The pieces began to fall into place. Why Rahul Yadav was busy buying up farms and derelict land north of Delhi. Jaskiran felt the urgent need to put some space between her and Rahul. She needed time to think.

'Please excuse me a minute, I need to use the ladies' room,' she said, looking to Ashok, who seemed confused by her actions.

'Sure, back in the house. One of the attendants will show you the way.'

Jaskiran hurried up the steps towards the house. Just before she went in, she looked back and saw that Rahul was still watching her. His face twisted into a snarl as he turned and said something to Ashok. It was enough to make her blood run cold. She walked in a daze through the house, the conversations of the other guests now merging altogether and making no sense at all. The smiling faces, moving in slow motion, now seemed so sinister. Their laughter was somehow directed at her. Jaskiran could feel her breathing intensify as she began to panic. The lights seemed blinding and the air stifling.

Suddenly, she felt a vibration in her clutch bag. It was her phone. Clumsily meandering through the crowd, she struggled to retrieve it. Finally, when she thought she might scream, she pushed past another throng of guests and into the hallway.

'Hello!' she answered, flustered.

'Jaskiran—call—Anjali—' came the broken reply.

'Rajesh? I can barely hear you!' Jaskiran said, deciding to withdraw somewhere quieter.

Opening a door to what she thought was the bathroom, Jaskiran entered a large, dark room. There was a smell of engine oil in the air, and the shapes of two cars parked beside each other were visible only by the light coming from the hallway behind her. Jaskiran realised that she had inadvertently entered the garage.

'Jaskiran!' Rajesh's pleas were now clearer. 'I found Anjali's phone. She called Ashok Chopra the night she was taken. They were in a relationship. There are dozens of calls and messages between them.'

The words hit her like a hammer blow, and she felt as if the walls were coming down around her.

'It can't be …' was all she could muster.

'It doesn't make sense to me either, but I'm heading to the newsroom now; Sabeena is meeting me there. We have to hand the phone to the police as evidence, but before we do, there's time to write up the story. It could be enough to get Vivek out of jail. Can you meet me there?'

Dumbfounded, Jaskiran stood in the dark, finally answering, 'Yes, yes, I'm on my way.' She cut the call and began to retrace her steps when something stopped her. *Anjali called Ashok the night she died*, Jaskiran told herself. She looked back at the shadowy shapes within the garage. She felt along the wall and hit the switch for the lights. There was a short delay before the fluorescent bulbs flicked and buzzed into life, bathing the room in white light.

She could see an orderly tool bench along one wall, each piece of equipment neatly displayed in its place. She spotted the car she had ridden in the day of the rally at Ramlila Maidan. It sparkled under the lights and must have been freshly cleaned and polished by the driver. But the second car was hidden under a black cover, and she felt the need to take a closer look. Stepping onto the concrete floor, she knelt by the back of the car and picked up the cover. Raising it above her head, she exposed the number plate and chassis of a silver Mercedes C-Class cabriolet.

Jaskiran gasped and backed away, bringing her hands to her mouth. As she retreated, unable to take her eyes off the unmistakable badge, she collided with a stack of garden tools, sending them crashing to the floor. The abrupt explosion of noise shredded her nerves further, and she was beginning to panic. She felt trapped.

Moving back to the hallway, she closed the door before turning quickly toward the front door and colliding straight into Ashok. Taken completely by surprise, Jaskiran screamed in shock.

'Sorry, I didn't mean to make you jump.' Ashok held up his hands to placate her but to no avail.

'I have to go,' she panted as she pushed past him. There was now nothing between her and the front door, but Ashok reached out and grabbed her arm. She felt her body tense up as she turned and stared at him, anticipating what he would say next.

'Hey, what's gotten into you?' Ashok seemed concerned. Jaskiran struggled to free herself, but his grip was like a vice. There was no way Jaskiran was getting out of it without escalating the situation. Finally, she stopped struggling and tried to stay composed.

'I didn't see you there. You gave me a little fright, that's all,' she said.

'What were you doing in there?' Ashok asked.

Jaskiran looked at the garage door and hesitated as she tried to think of a way to explain.

'Oh, I was looking for the bathroom and opened the wrong door.' Giving Ashok no time to respond, she quickly added, 'Look, thanks for the invitation, but I really should be going. I have an early start tomorrow.' She tried again to ease her arm out of his grip, to no avail.

'Go? But you just got here. Have I done something?' His tone was now firm.

'Ashok, please. I have to go,' Jaskiran said softly.

There was silence for a few moments as Ashok looked down at Jaskiran, confusion wrought across his face. He maintained his grip as his head turned slightly towards the garage door. As he contemplated an idea that was forming, a call rang out from the kitchen. 'Ashok! Come over here and meet Mrs Agarwal. She's a great admirer of yours. She insists you meet her daughter.' Jaskiran peered around Ashok's frame to see a middle-aged woman waving back at them from the kitchen.

'It looks like you're wanted.' The relief was palpable in Jaskiran's voice.

She felt Ashok's grip slowly loosen until she could finally release her arm.

Saying nothing else, she stepped back before turning and hurrying to the front door and the fresh-scented air outside. Ashok stood silently as he watched her go. When the front door closed and he was left alone in the hallway, the deathly stare slowly melted away as he turned to the woman and smiled weakly, holding up a finger to indicate that he needed a moment. He opened the garage door and stepped inside.

He saw that the cover of his Mercedes had been moved. He stared at the car before looking into the middle distance, remembering what Rahul had just told him about Jaskiran.

'Cullak Pur,' he muttered to himself.

He stood quietly under the lights, unmoving. His breathing increased in speed and volume until he couldn't hold it any longer.

'Fuck,' he whispered.

49

SLAMMING THE CAR DOOR shut, Jaskiran's hands shook as she tried and failed to find the ignition with the keys. Feeling like she might scream, she closed her eyes and took a deep breath. Releasing the air slowly, she looked at her hands once again. Satisfied she was in control, she tried again, this time finding the ignition on her first try. She fired up the engine and pushed the pedal hard to the floor, sending the wheels spinning before they finally got traction and sped her away.

As she drove, she dialled Rajesh's number and held the phone to her ear. He answered immediately. 'Jaskiran! Are you safe?' Rajesh sounded concerned.

'Yes, I'm fine. Listen, Rajesh. It's Ashok. He's Anjali's killer. She called him that night because he was coming to pick her up.'

'Can you be sure?' Rajesh sounded stunned.

'Yes,' Jaskiran replied. 'I found a silver Mercedes in his garage. The one Roshan saw them leave in and the one captured on the CCTV at the toy store.'

'But why would he want to kill her?'

There was silence as the question stumped Jaskiran. They had found the evidence, but what possible motive could Ashok have for murdering poor Anjali? A few minutes ago, Jaskiran had no idea the two had ever met.

'Jaskiran, you still there?' asked Rajesh.

'Yes, yes, I'm here,' came Jaskiran's agitated reply, feeling as if a shroud was covering the truth before her eyes.

'Good, I'm at the newsroom now. I can start writing this up, but where does this leave us with Rahul Yadav?'

'Of course!' cried Jaskiran as the pieces fell into place. 'Rahul was there tonight at the party. He and Ashok are working together.'

'How do you know?' Rajesh asked.

'The development bill! Once it passes into law, the land Rahul purchased in Cullak Pur is earmarked for redevelopment. The Delhi government will have to purchase the land at a greatly marked-up price,' stated Jaskiran.

'And we know Rahul murdered Deepak because he wouldn't allow company funds to be used for purchasing the land. What if Anjali knew about the fraud? And instead of going to Rahul, she went to her boyfriend, Ashok, and he killed her,' Rajesh ventured.

'So it was just to hide their crooked deals. For money.' Jaskiran was shocked at the senselessness of it.

'This is it, Jaskiran. We have all we need.'

'I'll be there soon,' Jaskiran replied before putting down the phone.

She thought about Ashok and how foolish she felt for believing everything he had said about making Delhi a better place and the city safer for women. *How many other women had fallen for those lines?* thought Jaskiran. *I'm just as gullible as any of them.* It all seemed like such a sham now, just the type of thing a politician would say. *What does it say about me that I had wanted to believe him?*

With all these questions bearing down on her, she felt her anger swell once again.

She shouldn't be berating herself. It wasn't her fault she wanted to see the good in Ashok, to believe someone wanted to help others less fortunate than himself.

She turned her anger on Ashok, the supposed new face of Indian politics, unlike any of the others. Ha! He was a cliche. He had been exposed as corrupt and a murderer, two credentials that didn't even set him apart from other Indian politicians.

In his rise through Delhi politics and a life of wealth and privilege, how many lives had he left ruined in his wake? How many families destroyed? And while they were left to pick up the pieces, he got away with it. She thought now of his carefree attitude that evening at the celebratory party for his bill. Its success would allow him to score a huge victory in his political ambitions and catapult his name onto the lips of every Indian for years to come. And it would make him filthy rich in the process. No wonder he was in a good mood.

Jaskiran pulled off the main street and into the narrow lane that led to the car park behind the *Delhi Daily* office building. She came to a stop in an empty bay, but before getting out, she checked her mirrors. Something made her feel uneasy. Convinced that no one was there, she stepped out of the car. The parking lot was quiet. The solitary streetlamp at the entrance was broken, making it difficult to navigate across the potholed surface. The sound of a glass bottle smashing to the ground somewhere behind her froze her to the spot.

'Hello?' she said, turning to face the darkness, but no reply came.

Jaskiran stood in silence, listening for any movement. Finally, the fear that had gripped her waned and, remembering to breathe, she turned back toward the main street. She walked as fast as she dared over the uneven terrain when she suddenly heard another noise coming from behind her. She froze once again and listened. There it was, this time louder than before. It was getting closer. Jaskiran began moving again, but the sound followed her. It was clear now that it was the sound of footsteps rushing toward her over the gravel. They could only have been a few feet from her, and as she turned once again, she tried to scream, but something struck her hard on the head. The last thing she felt was intense pain and the sensation of falling.

50

WITHOUT JASKIRAN THERE TO help, Rajesh had the difficult task of laying the case against Rahul Yadav and Ashok Chopra on his own. Sitting down at his desk in the empty newsroom, every keystroke reverberated across the room, heavy with the weight of the story taking shape on the screen. He had to explain everything he and Jaskiran had discovered in their investigation over the past week: murder, corruption, fake companies, secret meetings, false arrests, botched police work and witness accounts that combined into a convincing argument that the antagonists were guilty of murdering Anjali Mangal, Deepak Rao and many other offences. That two young reporters had taken the story as far as they could, and it was time for the public to demand that the police take action.

Fortunately for Rajesh, Sabeena was seated directly over his shoulder, there to make sure that they told a good story without straying over the line into defamation. She had to think of the paper, after all.

After another half an hour of revisions, edits and threats from Sabeena to wake up the paper's lawyers if Rajesh didn't remove a libellous line, the article was complete. Rajesh finally sat back and exhaled.

'Good work, Rajesh,' Sabeena said, laying a hand on his shoulder.

'Thanks,' Rajesh replied, savouring the moment. It was the first time Sabeena had ever complimented his work.

'I just wish Jaskiran was here too. She deserved to have written it more than me.'

Sabeena held out her phone, squinting at the screen. 'Yes, I know, I can't get through to her. I'm not sure if it's me or . . . can you try her?'

Rajesh did as he was told, dialling her number; her phone went straight to voicemail.

'No, nothing. It must be switched off.'

A feeling of unease began to take hold of him. He looked at his watch again. *She should definitely have been here by now*, he thought.

'Well, we can't wait any longer. Send the files,' Sabeena said, bringing Rajesh's thoughts back to the task at hand. He nodded in agreement and, with a few clicks, sent the pages to the printers before slumping back in his chair, stifling a yawn.

'Go home, Rajesh. I'll take care of the rest,' Sabeena said, gesturing for him to vacate his seat while she stood and moved her chair back to Jaskiran's desk before noticing something lying across her keyboard. 'What's this?' Sabeena asked, holding out a small, flat parcel. She flipped the brown cardboard over. 'It's postmarked from Kerala.'

Rajesh thought for a moment before making the connection. 'It's from Annie Rao. She said she would have her family send us a copy of the photograph taken from her home when it was raided.'

He took the parcel from Sabeena and opened it. Inside was a faded photograph taken at a wedding. It showed the bride and groom flanked by some of the guests.

'This must be Annie and Deepak's wedding,' Rajesh said as he began to scan the faces of the guests.

'Why did she send us this?' Sabeena asked. 'What's the significance?'

'There!' Rajesh said, pointing at the small, unassuming figure standing close to the front of the crowd. 'That's Rahul Yadav. He must have taken the photograph to hide his close connection to Deepak and Annie.' He handed the photo to Sabeena for her to see while he packed his notebook into his messenger bag.

Sabeena continued to look at the photo, her face visibly contorted as she struggled to understand the rationale. 'But why take it? Everyone knew they worked together. Taking the photo wouldn't hide that,' Sabeena was thinking out loud.

Rajesh was heading out of the room when he stopped, unable to find a suitable answer.

'You're right,' he said. He walked purposefully back to the photo and took another look. There was Deepak and Annie, Deepak smiling while Annie appeared suitably modest as was the expectation in those days, her head slightly bowed and eyes looking to the floor. Both bride and groom were flanked by their respective parents. He looked again at Rahul, who had a position in the front row beside Deepak's parents, a sign of his importance. Rahul wore an impassive expression. No discernible joy or happiness could be found in those dark eyes.

It was then that Rajesh saw him. 'Oh my God,' Rajesh exhaled. His legs felt weak, and he pressed his arms against the desk for support.

'What is it?' Sabeena asked from across the room.

Rajesh looked up, terror in his eyes.

51

JASKIRAN AWOKE IN DARKNESS. It was a few moments before she felt the stabbing pain at the back of her head. She raised her hand to touch the wound and winced as the pain intensified. She could feel her fingers were sticky with blood. Resting her head on the reverberating floor, she soon realised she was in the trunk of a car. She could hear the engine revving and the car's suspension straining as it bounced over an uneven road. The air was musty and heavy with the smell of diesel.

She clawed in the dark against the confines of the space, looking for a latch to open the trunk from the inside. She couldn't find one. Next, she contorted her body to feel around the trunk floor for anything she could use to force the door open or as a weapon, but her search was fruitless. Giving up, she exhaled from the effort and breathed heavily. She felt utterly helpless and tears began to roll down her cheeks. She sobbed silently for a while before her desperation grew, and she kicked out at the trunk, first once, then again and again. She slammed her hands against the trunk roof repeatedly before finally beginning to scream for help, losing all sense of herself as a primal desire to escape took over. Her lungs ached with the effort she was exerting, but she continued for as long as she could before the pain in her head became too much to bear, and she began to feel nauseous.

She rested her head back onto the trunk floor, closed her eyes and hoped the feeling would pass. With the gentle rolling of the car, it wasn't long before she began to feel drowsy and soon she felt as if she was falling through the floor of the trunk, down into the ground. Looking up, she could see her body's dark outline while she continued descending down a dark well. The pain in her head subsided as she slipped out of consciousness again.

52

WHEN JASKIRAN AWOKE, IT was as if from a nightmare. She was sweating and suddenly aware through the absence of the gentle rolling of suspension and the hum of the engine that they had stopped. She had no idea how long she had been trapped there or how far they had travelled. Her head no longer throbbed as before, but she didn't know how she would feel on her feet.

For a few moments, everything was silent, until she felt the suspension shift slightly and heard a gentle thud as the car door closed. There was the sound of heavy footsteps on dirt and the sound of a metallic latch and hinges creaking. A few moments later, she heard the footsteps again, louder as they approached the car. Whoever it was now sat in the driver's seat, started the engine and began to steer the vehicle off the road and over more uneven terrain.

After a few minutes, the vehicle came to a stop once again. Jaskiran heard someone get out of the vehicle, but this time their footsteps came towards the trunk. Jaskiran heard a key being inserted and then the trunk lid rose. She saw a figure silhouetted against the moon. As her eyes adjusted, Jaskiran gasped in horror. It was Inspector Imran Shah.

The betrayal hit Jaskiran like a punch to the gut, and she opened her mouth to speak but no words formed. For a moment, he did nothing, seemingly savouring Jaskiran's shocked reaction and the fact that he had deceived her so completely. Having his fill, he grabbed her roughly by the waist and dragged her out. Jaskiran surveyed her surroundings. They were in a field by a river. She could see a farmhouse not far from where Shah had parked the car. She recognised it now as the farm in Cullak Pur.

Shah dragged her behind him as he walked towards the farmhouse. 'Why are you doing this? Please stop,' she pleaded and tried to resist him. Digging her heels into the soft dirt, she attempted to pull him back, but he was too strong. With a grimace, he yanked her in front of him and shoved her forward. She tripped on a mound and landed hard in the dirt, scraping her hands as she tried to cushion her fall. Before she could move, he grabbed her by the hair and pulled her up. She screamed in pain, but he took little notice, shoving her forward again.

Once inside the farmhouse, Shah led Jaskiran by the arm through one of the open doorways and into a large rectangular room, its white walls stained with the decay of time.

'Take a seat,' Shah said as he shoved Jaskiran toward a wooden chair. The force propelled Jaskiran to trip over the chair and tumble to the ground. She managed to roll over and quickly backed herself into the corner. Shah turned and went to the table on the far side of the room by a window and a large steel door that led out to the fields beyond.

The room was dark, lit by a solitary oil lamp on the table.

She saw a figure of a man sitting in the shadows, his sinewy fingers wrapping around the head of a walking stick.

'You?' she gasped at the sight of Rahul Yadav, who seemed to be studying her silently. She looked at both men in turn, and things began to make more sense.

'It wasn't Ashok. It was you,' Jaskiran said to them both. 'You killed Anjali.'

Shah actually smiled. 'You finally worked it out.'

'When I saw the river just now, I saw it as Anjali would have seen it. Ashok picked her up that night, but he didn't kill her.'

'Because he is a coward like the rest of his kind. They talk tough, but in the end, they're too scared to get their hands dirty.' Shah's expression turned to a scowl. The spittle was visible at the corners of his mouth.

'But why would Ashok want her dead?' Jaskiran asked.

'Because she found out things she shouldn't have,' Rahul interjected, leaning forward in his seat so she could see him better in the dim light.

'She discovered the fraudulent applications,' Jaskiran stated.

'Yes,' Rahul confirmed. 'Applications that had been signed by Deepak to grant funds for the purchase of land at Cullak Pur and other sites across Delhi. But the applications had a timestamp created by our computer systems that cannot be tampered with. She saw the dates were after Deepak's death. Like you, she began digging into matters that didn't concern her.'

'She discovered you were using company funds to purchase land through shell companies,' Jaskiran affirmed. 'And she went to Ashok for help.'

'She didn't realise that he was involved from the start and had staked too much of his political career on the development bill's success to let anything stand in its way, not even her. But instead of dealing with the problem himself, he came to me for help. And so I had him bring her here,' Rahul gestured to the window and the remote farm outside. 'Where Shah was waiting.'

'And the two of you are partners in this?' Jaskiran gestured at the unlikely pairing.

Shah scoffed in derision, which was followed by a stern look from Rahul, prompting Shah to retreat silently back to the far wall.

'Inspector Shah has worked for me since he was a boy back in Gwalior. His family was destitute. He would go door to door across the wealthy parts of town pleading for work, with little success. What work he found was barely enough to feed the family beyond a day or two. Nobody would hire him, but I saw his potential,' Rahul said, holding a finger in the air. 'I gave him a job. I found him work tending to my house. Eventually, he became my driver. I could see he was willing to do whatever it took to succeed. So years later, I brought him to Delhi, where he helped me with other matters,' Rahul said gravely, leaving Jaskiran in no doubt about what he meant. 'Finally, it became clear to me that having Shah in the uniform of the Delhi police force would offer additional advantages. So I made sure he was admitted and quickly promoted to the rank of inspector. His family is destitute no more. He provides everything they could ever need. His children will want for nothing.'

At the mention of his children, Jaskiran looked at Shah, but he avoided making eye contact, lowering his gaze momentarily before pulling a packet of cigarettes from his pocket. He lit one before waving the match out and throwing it across the room. He took a long drag, the cigarette glowing between his fingers.

'So why bring me here now and tell me all this? To gloat?' Jaskiran asked, looking back at Rahul.

'Not just that. I was curious about you. You have a comfortable life. You could go on living it and not want for anything. I know that your family is wealthy. No doubt you would have married into a good family. But what do you do? You go around sticking your nose into other people's business. And why? What do you gain?' He stopped now and looked at her, the silence dragging out while he waited for a response.

'Maybe I don't like the thought of men like you doing evil things and thinking you could get away with it,' Jaskiran finally answered, her voice low.

The response seemed to confuse Rahul, and after a few moments, he shook his head in resignation. 'You poor girl,' he muttered almost in disappointment.

He looked back at Shah, who understood what he had to do. He dashed the cigarette to the floor and put it out with his heel.

'I see,' Jaskiran said, looking at Rahul. 'The real reason you came. You wanted to make sure no more mistakes were made. Anjali was supposed to look like suicide, correct?' Jaskiran's voice began to rise. 'You think you can do that to me? That people won't get suspicious?'

Shah approached closer, a strange detachment in his expression, a coldness that made it clear he had made up his mind about what needed to be done.

Jaskiran was beginning to panic. 'Please stop,' she pleaded again, edging away. She moved the chair between her and Shah in a futile gesture. 'It's over. You must know you can't get away with this?'

'What do you mean, it's over?' Rahul inquired, halting Shah's approach.

Jaskiran was momentarily lost for words, the sad fact being she hadn't expected a response.

'It's ... it's ... over,' Jaskiran said, finding both her voice and growing confidence. 'The story is coming out tomorrow morning. There's no stopping it now. We have enough to tie Ashok to Anjali and the land scam. The bill will never pass now. The land is worthless. You gain nothing from killing me.'

Rahul's jaws seemed to clench, and his grip on the walking stick tightened as he lifted himself off his chair.

'And what do you expect me to do with someone who tries to sabotage my life's work? You try to tear me down for doing what everyone else is trying to do to get ahead.'

'Committing murder?' Jaskiran replied resolutely.

'Doing what's necessary!' Rahul grew incensed. He raised his cane to strike Jaskiran but suddenly froze at the sight of flashing lights on the wall behind her. He looked back over his shoulder and could see through the window the red and blue lights in the distance. The wail of multiple sirens grew louder as the police vehicles approached closer.

Inspector Shah and Rahul moved toward the window to get a better look.

'What is this? Were you followed?' Rahul shouted, indignant that his plans had been disturbed.

'No, I was careful,' Shah said, looking out of the window. 'Behenchod,' Shah spat the words as he watched the bouncing headlights navigate the uneven terrain toward the farmhouse. Seeing both her captors distracted, Jaskiran knew this was her one and only chance for escape. She darted for the open door and out into the courtyard. Rahul heard her flee and grabbed Shah by the shoulder.

'Take care of her. I can't be seen here.' He moved to the steel door, unlocking the latch and swinging it open.

'And what about me?' came Shah's reply.

'Once you finish her off, say you found her like that. I will pull the strings for you. You'll be fine.'

'And if I'm not. Then?' Shah asked, unmoving.

'We planned for such an event. Your family will be taken care of.' Rahul feared to linger any longer, and he left Shah in the doorway as he fled toward the treeline as fast as he could. Shah exhaled loudly at the approaching lights before slamming the door shut.

Jaskiran raced across the courtyard to the large steel door. She grabbed the handle, twisted it and pulled, forcing it to rattle loudly on its hinges. She tried again with more force, causing the whole door to reverberate, but it was no good; it remained locked. She noticed the bolt locks in place at the top and bottom of the door, securing it to its frame.

'Oh my God,' Jaskiran said as she suppressed the urge to scream in frustration. She reached up and pulled the rod out of the latch. It came free with a mighty crash as the rod connected to the metal bracket. Jaskiran was sure Shah and Rahul would be on her any moment. In a panic, she quickly swung down and pulled free the remaining rod, it too clanged loudly against the metallic frame. In one swift motion, she grabbed the door handle and pulled with all her might, but it shook just as it had before. Jaskiran failed to comprehend, she pulled at the handle again, but the door stubbornly refused to open.

'You need this,' Shah's voice was almost amused.

Jaskiran turned to face him as he held up a key.

Jaskiran's nerves were shredded, and she realised there was no getting away from him; if she wanted to survive, she would need to fight. As he moved in closer, she swung her right leg across, landing it against the inside of his right knee. She heard a crack, and Shah's formidable frame crumpled to the ground, his face contorted in agony. 'You bitch!' he screamed as Jaskiran ran past him to the staircase that led to the upper level. She launched herself at the stairs, taking them two at a time as Shah staggered back to his feet and came after her again.

At the top of the stairs were four doors leading off the hallway, and Jaskiran hurried to the nearest one, bursting into a small bedroom. A bed and a small, tattered almirah were pushed against one wall. A broken mirror had been left where it fell. She slammed the door shut behind her and was grateful to find a small bolt lock that she pushed into place. It wouldn't stop a man as big as Shah, but it might slow him down. She could hear him coming up the steps.

Jaskiran went to the bed and, grabbing it by the metal frame, began to drag it towards the door. It was heavier than it looked, or perhaps her energy had been sapped by the ordeal, and she strained as the bed screeched across the floor. She heard Shah outside the door as he turned the handle, but the lock kept the door in place. He slammed his weight against the door, and still, the lock held.

Standing against the door, Jaskiran had pulled the bed as close as she could. She began to move to the other side of the bed to push it the remaining few inches to barricade the door completely when the door crashed open in a shower of splintered wood, sending Jaskiran sprawling to the floor.

With her head still spinning, she looked up from where she lay at the sight of Shah struggling to fit through the gap as the door jammed against the bed. Jaskiran looked at the window and, seeing they were not barred, forced herself to her feet. Struggling to the window, she pulled the handle and pushed it open. The fresh breeze felt like freedom. She could see three police cars coming to a stop outside the farmhouse, their headlights shining on her.

She lifted herself up onto the windowsill but was suddenly pulled back with immense force and sent crashing to the floor. She screamed as Shah stood over her again, his eyes devilishly red. His jaw set to a maniacal grin.

'You thought it was going to be that easy?'

He fell on top of her, his hands searching for a grip around her neck as she struggled and began clawing at his face. He roared in fury and slapped her hands away before finally pinning her down and wrapping his calloused hands around her neck once again. This time the pressure was immediate and intense, and Jaskiran's airways were closed completely. Her eyes were wide in mute panic, and her face began to turn red as she tried desperately to push his hands away. She tried in vain to pry his fingers from their iron grip, but his weight on her legs made it impossible to kick him off.

The edges of her vision began to blur, and all she could see was the demon atop her, who watched as he choked the life out of her. She averted her eyes, not wanting the last thing she ever saw to be her murderer. Beside her, she saw the shattered mirror, its shards reflecting her violent death. She stretched out an arm, her fingertips caressing the cold, sharp glass. She pawed at it some more until she could finally grip it in her palm. Using the final vestiges of strength she had left, she swung the shard of glass up until it made contact with Shah's neck.

Immediately, Shah's grip slackened enough for her to wheeze a breath into her starved lungs. As she removed the jagged piece of mirror from his neck and let it drop, a fountain of bright red blood began to pulse from the wound. Shah's hands went to grip his own neck and preserve the life force he was trying to extinguish in Jaskiran. He shifted off Jaskiran, who was still struggling to breathe, and fell back against the wall. He sat there watching Jaskiran with a shocked and frightened expression. His breathing was loud, and he coughed and sputtered as he choked on his own blood.

Jaskiran forced herself to sit up against the wall, her airways still compressed and bruised. Looking across at Shah, every fibre of her being wanted to strike him again, to take out all her fury until there was nothing left of him, but she didn't. She just sat there and watched as he took his last breaths. He looked afraid. His eyes gazed almost longingly at Jaskiran for help as the blood completely soaked his shirt. His hands, losing strength to stem the flow, began to waver, and he let them rest on his lap. He looked down at them, covered in his own blood. She could still hear the air spluttering in his throat, but the intervals between breaths were getting longer. The inhalation became more laboured. He never looked back at her.

She sat watching him. He was now motionless except for the trickle of blood that still flowed from his neck. She could hear, too, a door crashing down in the distance and the echo of heavy boots. Her vision began to blur again, and the room slowly rotated as she fell to her side and into darkness.

53

FLEEING THE FARMHOUSE, Rahul Yadav was soon traversing through fields of long grass and thickets as swiftly as his legs could carry him. Ignoring the pain in his hip, he persevered over the uneven ground, gripping the end of his cane ever tighter with every painful step. Thorny shrubs scratched at his hands and face, but he was in too much of a panic to notice.

With the pain taking its toll, he stumbled crossing a small gully and fell to the ground, losing his cane to the black water. Crawling out and now covered in dirt, with his trousers soaked to the knees, he pushed ahead exhausted.

A few minutes later, he tripped again as his foot became caught in the undergrowth, sending him crashing into the dirt as his glasses fell from his face. A searing pain shot up through his hip, causing him to cry out in agony. Eventually, the pain subsided just enough for him to breathe again, and he spat the dirt from his mouth. The scratches crisscrossing his face stung from the sweat now pouring into the wounds. He breathed heavily before attempting to crawl to his feet, but the movement triggered the pain once again. He lay back in the dirt, howling in anguish.

After a few moments, Rahul heard a sound approaching from the darkness. With no other option, he tried to drag himself into the undergrowth to stay out of sight. His fingernails dug into the dirt, every heave a colossal effort, but the footsteps kept getting closer. Giving up, Rahul turned to face his pursuer.

Out of the darkness, he saw a large figure appear.

'Rahul Saab,' said a casual voice. 'What are you doing all the way out here?'

'Arvind, Arvind! Thank God it's you!' Rahul was relieved. 'Get me out of here quickly.'

There was a moment of silence before Sagar replied, 'That's deputy commissioner, saab.'

Rahul looked up and could see that the senior cop wore an expression of disdain as he stared down at Rahul, prone and helpless in the dirt.

'Listen, deputy commissioner,' Rahul said, now reassessing the situation. 'I'll make you rich. You were right. I have other deals in the pipeline. This is not the end.'

'I'm afraid this is for you,' said Sagar, now unholstering his sidearm.

'Arvind … deputy commissioner, don't be insane. You can't kill me! You don't understand. I can make you rich!' Rahul began pleading.

'You know, I never liked you, Rahul,' said Sagar, casually aiming the gun at his stricken target. 'I am not against a man wanting to get ahead in life. It is part of the human condition. We are all guilty of it, even someone like me. But here in Delhi, to live our lives as we do, to elevate ourselves through illicit means requires great skill and takes years to master. We must play the game carefully in order to preserve balance. Every move we make must maintain order. If we don't, there will be anarchy. We would regress into a land of savages. That is why maintaining order is so important. And why I despise men like you. Because men like you don't respect the game we play here. You don't even want to learn the rules.'

'I have always been discreet about my affairs. This is the only time things have gotten out of hand,' Rahul pleaded defiantly.

'Discreet? A young woman was found strangled in the river that runs through the middle of the city. That is your idea of discreet? And you then wanted me to murder an innocent boy in police custody to cover up your crimes. Can you not see the road to destruction you were leading us all to? Do you think that because you gave me a few rupees, I would do your bidding? You really think I have no morals?'

Even in his stricken position, Rahul couldn't bear being spoken to in such a manner by someone he considered a subordinate. His fury got the better of him.

'Do not preach to me!' came Rahul's defiant call. 'You fool yourself all you want, but we both know there are no rules for people like us. We come from the dirt, and the only way we pull ourselves up is by doing whatever we have to do. That is the only rule. Order is a prison to stop us from reaching the top. You forget this, and it will be your undoing. One day, I hope soon, you will be in my position – lying at someone's mercy. I just wonder who it will be to pull the trigger on your fat, miserable—'

A loud pop cut Rahul off as the deputy commissioner pulled the trigger on his sidearm. Rahul's expression was one of surprise, and then he grimaced in pain. His chest felt like it was on fire. Breathing became difficult, as if there were an immense weight sitting atop him. Rahul sucked in air to breathe, never getting enough.

The deputy commissioner stepped forward and fired three more shots into Rahul's body. Rahul slumped back, exhaling his last breath. The deputy commissioner retrieved a handkerchief from his pocket and used it to extract another handgun from his belt before placing the gun in Rahul's motionless hand. He then stood back and admired his handiwork.

54

Rajesh sat by Jaskiran's side in the private hospital room. The heart monitor beeped faintly as she lay in bed unconscious, breathing through an oxygen mask. Her neck had turned a deep purple from the extensive bruising. Rajesh felt a tremendous amount of guilt for not reaching the farmhouse sooner. He knew that it was almost a miracle that Jaskiran had survived against a seasoned killer like Inspector Shah. He felt in awe of her strength and ability to survive against the odds. He reached out for her hand before hesitating. Finally making up his mind, he placed his hand over hers and squeezed her fingers gently. Jaskiran's eyelids trembled, but she did not wake.

It was Rajesh who had led the police to the farm and had been one of the first to find her passed out in the upstairs bedroom, barely breathing but alive. Much of the blood staining her clothes belonged to Shah, who sat motionless against the opposing wall. On the journey to the hospital, she had flitted in and out of consciousness, mumbling incoherently. He whispered to her that she was safe, that he was with her and wouldn't leave her side. She never replied, but Rajesh told himself that she had heard him and felt at ease.

When they arrived at the hospital in Alipur, the doctor examined the cut to her head and indicated Jaskiran likely had a concussion, but they expected her to make a full recovery. They advised she spend the night in the hospital under observation. Rajesh looked at the clock. It was past 5 a.m. He knew that the day's issue would already be hitting the news stands across the city. Their story would be the topic of discussion over breakfast tables, in train carriages and between street hawkers and their customers. It would undoubtedly be picked up by the TV news channels too.

Rajesh heard a throat being cleared behind him. He turned and saw Jaskiran's brother standing forlorn at the door. His eyes were bloodshot as he looked at his little sister. Rajesh immediately moved his hand from Jaskiran's and stood up, but Gurvinder held up a weary hand to tell him everything was fine.

'You must be Rajesh,' he said. 'I need to thank you.' Gurvinder stepped closer and extended his hand, which Rajesh shook. 'The police told me that you helped them find her.'

'I came too late. It was all her.' Rajesh turned to Jaskiran. 'She did it all by herself.'

Gurvinder moved closer to the bed and gently touched Jaskiran's hand. Rajesh knew that he should leave and give the two of them some privacy but was unable to take his eyes off Jaskiran. Her hulking brother wiped the tears from his eyes as he spoke softly to his sister, 'The police are with Maa and Papa,' he said, reaching out with his fingers and letting them fall gently on Jaskiran's. 'They should be here soon. Papa is anxious, but I told him not to be. I told him you were stronger than any of us could imagine. Stronger than me, for sure.'

Gurvinder turned to Rajesh. 'You know, I always envied her,' he said. 'She had the strength to follow her own path, you know? I only listened to what Maa and Papa wanted me to do. What I studied, who I married … I even took over Papa's business because he wanted me to. I did all this because I was afraid to go my own way. But not her.'

Rajesh nodded, understanding that Gurvinder was probably expressing something that had lain heavy on his chest for a long time.

'I've messed things up, Jaskiran,' continued Gurvinder, now addressing his unconscious sister. 'With you, with Nisha, with the business … because I've always been scared to do what is difficult. But that's going to change. There's no way I can be afraid when you show me every day how to be strong.'

Jaskiran began to stir. Rajesh and Gurvinder looked at her as she opened her eyes. She blinked and turned her head slowly to face Gurvinder and squeezed his hand.

55

ASHOK READ THE TEXT as it scrolled across the screen with a deep sense of dread: 'Breaking news: Explosive new evidence emerges on the murdered Anjali Mangal, more to follow.'

The camera cut back to the studio, where the newsreader began reading from the teleprompter.

'Explosive news has rocked Delhi and India this morning,' she began. 'Reports from the *Delhi Daily* implicate prominent Delhi politician Ashok Chopra in the disappearance and murder of Delhi Financial Corporation employee Anjali Mangal. These are sensational accusations and are supported by the discovery of Ms Mangal's mobile, which shows calls and texts made to Ashok Chopra on the night she died.

'It is suspected the murder is connected to a potential land scam Ashok Chopra was involved in with Rahul Yadav, the Delhi Financial Corporation's executive director and Anjali Mangal's boss. In the exclusive report by the *Delhi Daily*, the pair are accused of fraudulently funnelling money from the corporation to a private business in order to purchase land that will skyrocket in worth if Mr Chopra's landmark development bill passes into law later today.'

During the early morning hours, Ashok had received a flurry of calls from friends and political allies to alert him about the breaking story and, more importantly, to find out if any of it was true. In a state of shock, Ashok had denied and deflected as best he could but, for once, had failed to sound convincing. Given the evidence emerging against him and the implications, he knew the game was up. Already his advisors had stopped taking his calls. No doubt they were looking for new employment. His friends and allies would now distance themselves from him too. Many would even begin speaking out against him to save their own skin. He knew he was alone.

One of the channels flashed a photo of Rahul and Jaskiran. 'We are also receiving reports that Rahul Yadav was killed in a shootout with the police. At the scene, officers found journalist Jaskiran Sohal, who broke the story of Yadav and Chopra's alleged criminal activity. Ms Sohal had been assaulted. She was taken to hospital but her injuries are not life-threatening. The quick response of the police is what saved Ms Sohal from meeting the same fate as Anjali Mangal. We can now go live to Deputy Commissioner Arvind Sagar, who led the operation and managed to subdue Rahul Yadav.'

Ashok couldn't bear to hear any more. His actions had almost led to Jaskiran being killed too. *How did it come to this?* he thought as he walked in a daze into his garden. The hazy sunrise visible through the trees. The sight of a new dawn would usually fill Ashok with optimism for the day ahead, but now it filled him with a sense of impending doom. The night was a far more fitting blanket for his ill deeds than the light of day.

He circled around the model cityscape, studying every inch of the planned city that he knew would now never be built. Not anymore. Leaning in, Ashok picked up the small figure of a man in a suit placed by a row of shiny, new office buildings. He looked at the faceless man, deep in thought, and that's when he heard the police jeeps approaching. Their sirens growing louder until he heard the vehicles screech to a halt outside his house. He sighed and placed the man back on the table before heading toward the house.

56

IT HAD BEEN TWO days since the events at Cullak Pur and as the city of Delhi passed by her window, Ayesha Begum was deep in thought. While it had worked in her favour that Rahul had met his end and would no longer be able to throw money at her political rivals, Ayesha still felt aggrieved that she had not been the one to expose his crimes to the world. The deputy commissioner had robbed her of the moment that would have seen her catapulted to a central role in the upcoming elections.

She looked over to Sagar now as he sat across from her in the back seat of his car. He had been taking a seemingly endless number of calls. Ayesha thought that his considerable frame seemed to have swelled even larger since their last meeting, engorged with feelings of self-importance and pride. He would never know how close he had come to being cast as the villain along with Rahul.

But to her consternation and surprise, Sagar had now made himself indispensable to her ambitions. Ayesha would have to continue to keep him close, which meant tolerating his lecherous looks and clumsy attempts at seduction for some time to come. She sighed and took solace in the fact that Ashok Chopra now languished in a cell, his party in disarray.

'Forgive me,' Arvind smiled and placed a comforting hand on Ayesha's knee, misinterpreting her uneasiness for boredom. 'I must be the most famous man in India today.

I've never known anything like it. But now I'm all yours. What did you want to see me about?'

Ayesha placed a soft hand on Arvind's and gently removed it from her knee. 'Arvind, you are certainly popular,' she said. 'But with that comes a lot more scrutiny. We must show a little more discretion in how we conduct ourselves. The one thing the public likes doing more than building up idols is tearing them down. It wouldn't do for them to find out that their hero was also a philanderer and a cheat.' She smiled at him. Beneath her warm words and gentle touch, he sensed the undercurrent of a threat.

'You have a profile now,' Ayesha continued. 'That's a good start. But I can show you how to turn it into something bigger.' Sagar perked up at the idea of a mutually advantageous deal, the foundation on which he had built his career.

He returned her smile and asked, 'Tell me, dear, what do you have in mind?'

Ayesha moved in closer. 'My party will organise rallies in your support,' she said. 'We will mobilise women's groups and throw everything we have behind you.'

Sagar looked confused. 'But why?' he asked. 'It's not like I'm standing for election!'

'No, you don't understand.' Ayesha shook her head. 'With my help and the millions of women the party can mobilise, we will build you up as the only man the women of this city can trust to clean up its streets. We will demand that you be announced as the next commissioner of police.'

'Commissioner?' Sagar muttered in surprise. He turned to look out the window at the passing traffic as the idea sank in. Even after all the praise and fame he received following the events in Cullak Pur, he had never once envisioned that it would lead to the top job in the Delhi police force. 'Do you think it would work?' he eventually asked.

Ayesha could see that he was enthralled by the power she dangled in front of him. He had given her the response she had hoped for. 'We are discovering the female voice,' she began. 'When guided and used en masse, it is a powerful force in politics. I know how to wield that power, Arvind. I can use it to bring down my enemies but also elevate my friends. If it is what you want, I will see it done.'

Sagar looked at her once again, but this time it was not lust that Ayesha saw in his eyes but recognition. 'What will you need from me to make this happen?' he asked earnestly.

'We will have to craft your public profile carefully,' she replied. 'You are the number one story today but will be old news tomorrow. We will have to keep the press fed with more tales of your heroics going forward to keep you popular with the masses.'

It was Arvind's turn to look pleased with himself. 'I may be a political novice,' he smirked, 'but it seems I learn fast. I already have some ideas on how to work with the press.'

57

AFTER SPENDING A COUPLE of nights in the hospital under observation, Jaskiran's doctors were happy to finally discharge her, advising plenty of rest in the care of her family. However, Jaskiran couldn't rest, the story was on everybody's lips, and there was no escaping it. Her story had people hailing her as a warrior for social change. Student unions and activists across the country were pushing for more protests against the corruption she had exposed. Reading the comments on social media, Jaskiran felt as if she was being carried on a wave with no control. Occasionally, however, she would read a comment from a mother or father calling Jaskiran a true modern-day superhero and a role model for their daughters. She enjoyed reading these comments, and they eased her anxiety over what would happen next, knowing she had already been through the worst.

The TV news media, having missed the initial scoop to their print rivals, now ran the story twenty-four hours a day, highlighting every detail as if it were another groundbreaking development. They hosted hourly debates, with half a dozen faces beamed on screen from around the country, heralding Jaskiran's courage and journalistic grit as well as Deputy Commissioner Sagar's bravery in administering ultimate justice to Rahul Yadav. Rajesh had already brought her up to speed with the fate of both Ashok Chopra and Rahul Yadav. She remembered being strangely detached and emotionless on hearing the news, as if nothing would ever surprise her again. Ashok Chopra's rivals denounced him as a murderer and scam artist. They extracted as much political capital as they could from the story and attacked his party as a pack of criminals and dacoits.

Sabeena had called and told her that the story had gone international and that she had received requests for interviews with Jaskiran from as far as New York and London. She made it clear that Jaskiran had an incredible opportunity, and it was necessary, in such circumstances, to strike while the iron was hot. She also mentioned that with Jaskiran keeping a low profile since the story broke, Deputy Commissioner Sagar was taking more screen time, using the story to catapult his standing within the country and the police force. Realising that she needed to be seen and tell her side of the story, Jaskiran made the decision, against her family's wishes, to return to the office.

On arriving at the newsroom, Jaskiran received a standing ovation from her colleagues. She wasn't sure what to do and stood awkwardly in the foyer until Rajesh came and grabbed her by the hand. 'Shouldn't you be resting?' Rajesh asked with a look of concern.

'And let you get all the plaudits for our work?' Jaskiran asked jokingly. Rajesh tried to laugh, but Jaskiran had hit upon a sour note. The truth was that very few people seemed to care that Rajesh had shared the byline with Jaskiran. Due to her ordeal, it was Jaskiran's name on the lips of everyone across the country.

'New style?' Rajesh deflected by tugging playfully at the scarf Jaskiran had wrapped around her neck to hide the bruising.

'Yes, just for a little while anyway,' Jaskiran replied, before her expression became more serious. 'Look, Rajesh. I wanted to tell you how grateful I am. If it wasn't for you calling the police and telling them where to find me. I—'

'Hey,' Rajesh cut in, holding Jaskiran by the shoulders. 'Jaskiran, it was you,' he said, smiling reassuringly. 'The picture from Annie. You were the one who asked for a copy. If I hadn't seen it, I would never have known.' A silence fell between them, finally punctuated by Sabeena.

'Jaskiran! Back so soon, you crazy thing.' Sabeena was almost in tears as she embraced Jaskiran closely. 'This is great. We'll run a follow-up for the morning issue. By tomorrow we'll have you on every network channel giving interviews.'

'But first,' Sabeena continued before Jaskiran could even respond, 'somebody wants to talk to you.' Sabeena nodded toward Vinod's office, where Jaskiran could see the managing editor sitting behind his desk speaking to another man across from him. Jaskiran couldn't see the other man's face, but she could see he wore the khaki-coloured uniform of the Delhi Police and had a large frame that seemed to spill over the confines of his chair.

'Who is that?' Jaskiran enquired, puzzled.

'It's Deputy Commissioner Sagar,' Rajesh said, recognising him from the press briefing. 'What's he doing here? Does he think we don't know he was involved just because he killed Rahul Yadav?' Rajesh continued, agitated.

'He wants to talk, that's all. Get the record straight. Come on,' Sabeena said, leading the way. Jaskiran was apprehensive and shot Rajesh a glance to indicate her hesitancy and confusion. In return, Rajesh placed his hand on her arm as the pair walked together toward Vinod's office, where Sabeena held open the door. Omitting Jaskiran, Sabeena placed a hand in front of Rajesh, forcing him to stop.

'He's asked to speak to Jaskiran only.'

'But ...' Rajesh was stumped, searching for the words. 'It was my story too.'

'No one denies that, Rajesh. But he's asked for an audience with Jaskiran. It's not like you two are joined at the hip.'

Sabeena's words knocked the air from Rajesh. *Sajid was right*, he thought bitterly as Sabeena closed the door in his face. She may not have meant for it to happen, but Jaskiran had taken his story. And not just any story – perhaps the biggest one he would ever land in his career. His disappointment and confusion gave way to anger, and he stormed out.

From inside the office, Jaskiran could see the pain in Rajesh's eyes as Sabeena closed the door. Before she could object, Vinod's voice boomed out behind her. 'What an occasion,' he declared. 'I have the two most famous people in Delhi right now here in my humble little office. Jaskiran, I'm sure you'll be happy to finally meet Deputy Commissioner Sagar.'

Jaskiran froze as Sagar turned his head slowly to look at her. He seemed to take her all in before raising his frame to tower above her.

'You've become quite the star. Not only do I see your face all day on TV, but also my own family can't stop talking about you. It's a pleasure to finally meet you,' he said warmly as he held out a hand.

Jaskiran looked at his hand, unmoving, before she felt a prod in her back from Sabeena. She reluctantly extended her hand, which Sagar gently shook.

'Well, I'm glad that you two have finally had a chance to meet,' said Vinod quickly. 'Now, I'm sure that the deputy commissioner is busy, and Jaskiran too has work that she must attend to—'

'No, no, it's fine,' interrupted Sagar. 'I have just a small matter to discuss with Ms Sohal, and then I'll let you all get on with your day.' Sagar pointed Jaskiran towards the chair next to his before sitting back down himself.

Jaskiran glanced at Vinod, who nodded helplessly. She had no choice but to sit down as asked.

'Now, I won't treat you like a fool, and I expect the same in return,' said Sagar, turning to Jaskiran. The warmth in his voice had been replaced by cold precision. 'I know that you wrongfully suspected me of doing Rahul Yadav's bidding by arresting Vivek Trivedi.'

Jaskiran shifted uncomfortably in her chair but said nothing.

'But that couldn't be further from the truth,' Sagar continued. 'In fact, I wanted to personally tell you that just this morning, I signed Vivek Trivedi's release papers. Since we discovered Inspector Shah's involvement with Rahul Yadav, it became clear that Vivek was used as a scapegoat. From our initial investigation, we have concluded that Inspector Shah worked alone to frame Vivek. He was the interrogating officer, after all.' He looked at the three faces around the room to confirm his point.

'I take it you don't dispute these findings or have any evidence that says otherwise?' the deputy commissioner continued, now looking solely at Jaskiran, who shook her head solemnly.

'That's good,' said Sagar, now sounding cheerier. 'I would hate for more evidence connected to this matter to be published in your paper without my knowledge. It's important to restore the public's trust in the Delhi Police, wouldn't you agree?'

'Absolutely, sir,' Vinod said quickly. 'If we come across anything, we will surely bring it to your attention for comment before we go to press.'

'In that case,' the deputy commissioner replied affably, 'I will leave you to carry on. I'm sure plenty is going on in Delhi to keep you busy.' He smiled at all three in turn before getting up from his chair and heading for the door.

'Were you the one who killed Rahul Yadav?' Jaskiran suddenly asked, also standing. Sagar's hulking frame came to a stop by the door. He turned and faced her. 'That's right,' he replied, his expression now serious. 'I chased him into the woods, but he must have known that he was being followed because he laid an ambush and fired at me. Thankfully, he missed. That's when I drew my gun and returned fire.'

'That's odd,' Jaskiran said. 'When I spoke to him at the farmhouse, I didn't see a gun.'

Sagar studied Jaskiran for a moment as he considered his response. He then looked at Vinod, who stood taut with his brow glistening with sweat. The officer allowed himself a soft chuckle before saying, 'You take care, Ms Sohal. I have a feeling that we will meet again.'

58

IT WAS STILL MORNING, but the temperature was already oppressive. The air was thick with moisture. Rajesh looked up at the grey, shifting clouds. *The monsoon would arrive any day now*, he thought. Looking at the faces of the passing pedestrians, he thought about how breaking the story had changed the lives of so many people, not least Jaskiran's. Yet, despite everything he had helped expose, his world was exactly as it was before. The same worries and pressures weighed him down. Jaskiran would surely be reinstated to the crime rotation, leaving him out in the cold. He still had no idea how he would support his family and pay off his debts. Karishma too was disappointed that Rajesh wasn't getting a share of the limelight, robbing her of the all-important bragging rights amongst her friends.

'There he is,' said a voice behind him. 'The forgotten man.'

Rajesh turned to see the deputy commissioner coming down the stairs. He felt a surge of rage burn within him at the deputy commissioner's words, but he refused to react. Instead, clenching his fists, he looked back toward the street. Sagar came and stood beside him. He extracted a cigarette from a packet, offering one to Rajesh, who shook his head in refusal, before lighting it. He drew on the tip and let out a long, satisfactory exhale of smoke that dissipated into the air before him.

'Your friend has a great story,' he began. 'A young, attractive journalist kidnapped in the line of duty fights for her life, slays her captor and exposes powerful men as murderers and frauds. It's the talk of the whole world. She's a new star, an icon for millions of women.'

Rajesh knew that he should have felt proud of Jaskiran. However, it was frustration that ate away at him. He sighed. 'You're trying to provoke me,' he said. 'Why?'

Sagar chuckled. 'I am trying to help you,' he said. 'Your friend is a star. And bright lights wash out everything else close to them. You have to find your own space to be seen.'

'What are you saying?'

'Leave this place,' Sagar said, the smoke from the cigarette wavering as he moved his hand to indicate the building around them. 'You should be a TV reporter. That's where the future is in your business. I could make it happen,' he added, taking another drag from the cigarette while he watched Rajesh closely.

'Why would you help me?'

'I could always use friends in the media,' replied Sagar. 'The higher the profile, the better.' He stubbed out the cigarette against the wall and flicked it away before taking an envelope from his back pocket.

'I think you need this,' he said, extending it towards Rajesh.

Rajesh looked at the stuffed brown envelope. He knew what it contained and what it would mean if he took it. After a moment, Rajesh reached out tentatively and accepted the envelope, unable to look at Sagar as he did so.

The deputy commissioner patted Rajesh on the shoulder before heading towards a luxury SUV parked nearby. When the driver opened the door for Sagar, Rajesh caught sight of an attractive woman sitting in the back. She looked familiar, but Rajesh couldn't place her. The door closed, and soon the SUV revved into gear and drove off.

Rajesh looked at the envelope again. Then, checking to be sure no one was watching, he opened it slowly. As he had expected, inside was a bundle of cash. He closed the envelope and slipped it into his trouser pocket. He stood in the shade of the atrium for a few moments longer, looking out at the tumult of Delhi life passing by on the street beyond, before sighing heavily and making his way back up the steps to the newsroom above.

Acknowledgements

I OWE A GREAT DEBT to my agent, Priyanka Kedia. Thank you for championing the book and for your support throughout this long journey. Thank you also to Anuj Bahri and the rest of the team at Red Ink Literary Agency.

I am incredibly grateful to my wonderful editor, Mekhala Moorthy, and the team at Bloomsbury, who helped polish the manuscript into the story it is today. Thank you for believing in this book and for your outstanding guidance throughout the publishing process.

Lastly, I wish to offer an apology: first to my wife, for all those vacant expressions over the dinner table while I wrestled with the plot, and to my two boys, Jeevan and Arjun, for all the days I couldn't play for long because I still had pages to write. Your love and understanding allowed me to finish writing this book.

About the Author

Balraj Juttla was born in the United Kingdom and grew up fascinated by his family's history and relationship with India. Four decades later, the infatuation that gripped him as a child still holds firm.

Balraj graduated with a Bachelor of Arts in English Literature and Creative Writing in 2008 and is the editor of *PRIME*, the international journal of aesthetic and anti-ageing medicine.

He currently lives in Sydney, Australia, with his wife and two boys.